ALL DUKE AND BOTHERED

DUKES AND SECRETS
BOOK ONE

MARIAH STONE

Stone Publishing

This is a work of fiction. Names, characters, places, and incidents either are the products of the author's imagination or are used fictitiously. Any resemblance to actual persons, living or dead, businesses, companies, events, or locales is entirely coincidental.

Cover design by Qamber Designs and Media

Editing by Beth Attwood

Proofreading by Laura La Tulipa

GET A FREE MARIAH STONE BOOK!

Join Mariah's mailing list to be the first to know of new releases, free books, special prices, and other author giveaways.

freehistoricalromancebooks.com

ALSO BY MARIAH STONE

MARIAH'S TIME TRAVEL ROMANCE SERIES

- Called by a Highlander
- Called by a Viking
- Called by a Pirate
- Fated

MARIAH'S REGENCY ROMANCE SERIES

- Dukes and Secrets
- Seven Dukes of Sin

VIEW ALL OF MARIAH'S BOOKS IN READING ORDER

Scan the QR code for all ebooks, paperbacks, and audiobooks.

1

London, 1813

"The first Almack's ball of the Season," declared Miss Penelope Beckett's father as they entered the grand ballroom together. "Aren't you glad your old papa managed to get you the voucher?"

Penelope clutched her skirts, her hands sweaty inside her elbow-length gloves. "Indeed, Papa," she said, striving to keep her tone even. "The most exclusive ball in London."

The expansive room bustled with a crowd of hundreds of elegantly dressed ladies and gentlemen. Ladies' feathered hair accessories swayed as they moved, while the light from countless candles and two-tiered crystal chandeliers shimmered on the dark glass panes of six round-arched windows. Pale blue swagged draperies framed the windows beneath elegant, scrolled pelmet heads.

The long walls featured pale blue bays separated by pink marble columns adorned with scroll-like spiral ornaments.

Some bays displayed Roman-style sculptures of striking half-naked men. Penelope longed for a pen and paper to sketch them. Others featured rococo mirrors, creating the illusion of an even grander space. Friezes, festoons, and paterae—shallow dishes used in ancient Rome—decorated sections of the walls.

The twelve Almack's balls held each Season were not only the most exclusive, but also the most significant events in an unmarried lady's quest for a husband. However, Penelope had a different goal in mind.

She fidgeted with her earlobe, attempting to calm her nerves. After three unsuccessful Seasons, she had undoubtedly been cast aside as a spinster, unfashionable and unwanted. A different path lay before her. The Duchess of Ashton, London's most ardent patroness of female artists, would be present. An introduction to the duchess might afford Penelope the opportunity to showcase her art and perhaps embark on her career as an artist. Who needed a husband for that?

Beside her stood her cousin, Miss Alexandria Beckett, who observed everything with the same wide-eyed fascination as Penelope. Alexandria was a beautiful young woman with sweet, well-defined features, her hair styled in small curls. She looked striking in her pale lilac ball gown.

"Yes, I am glad to be here, Papa," Penelope said as they walked deeper into the ballroom. Her father remained oblivious to the true reason for her enthusiasm. Her eyes scanned the guests, searching for a lady in her fifties with salt-and-pepper hair and dark eyes, whom she had occasionally glimpsed at other social gatherings, but to whom she had never been formally introduced.

A band played an English country dance tune from the musicians' gallery above. The room was full of humming conversation and the mingled scents of wine, perfume, and perspiration.

"Though, how did you manage to obtain the voucher?" Penelope added. "And why now, when I've been out for three Seasons already?"

Despite her being considered a spinster, he must still be thinking of marrying her off.

Her father, a short, paunchy man in his fifties, pursed his lips, causing wrinkles to form on his cheeks. He had lost some of his handsomeness since her mother's passing. Perhaps it was due to his reddened, puffy face, a consequence of excessive port and brandy consumption, as well as his sleepless nights spent away from home. His pale blue eyes with yellowish whites narrowed at her. His powdered wig, a fashion from the previous century, quivered as it always did when he became angry.

"Aren't you grateful that I managed to get you in at all?" he said. "I daresay it took quite a few favors. But I did it."

Penelope's chest tightened. How she wished Mama were still alive. Papa had always been a better man with her around. Since Mama's passing, it seemed as though Papa barely acknowledged Penelope's existence. He had forbidden her from pursuing art some time ago, insisting that a woman's duty was to raise children, nothing more. However, his frequent absences allowed her to continue painting and drawing against his wishes.

"Where's your dance card?" he asked. "I see the Viscount of Bridgemere approaching."

A sinking feeling settled in Penelope's stomach. *Not this again*, she pleaded silently. If Papa had gone to such lengths to bring her to Almack's, he must be truly determined to find her a match. Yet, chances were that her future husband, like most men of the time, would share Papa's opinion and forbid her from seriously pursuing art.

A tall man with a round belly and narrow shoulders

greeted them. As a well-bred lady, Penelope flashed a bright smile—one she often wore at these balls, leaving her face feeling wooden by the end of the evening. She was her mother's daughter, after all, and she wouldn't embarrass her papa or tarnish the family name.

"Bridgemere," said Papa, his face adopting a broad smile that Penelope hardly ever saw. "Allow me to introduce my daughter, Miss Penelope Beckett, and my niece, Miss Alexandria Beckett."

Bridgemere looked her over from head to toe with his large, wide-set eyes and nodded. The strange glossiness of his eyes made her want to shudder. "Miss Beckett, Miss Beckett," he acknowledged Alex with a slight nod. "Delighted to make your acquaintance." He turned to Papa. "Lord Beckett, your daughter is, as they say, a true beauty."

Penelope shot Alex a brief, puzzled glance, and her cousin widened her eyes in response. *As they say?* Hadn't Penelope been dismissed by the ton as an unfashionable, unsuccessful bride?

Confused but wanting to be polite, she broadened her smile until the corners of her mouth ached. "How do you find the ball, Viscount Bridgemere?" she asked.

"I daresay I've had the privilege of attending better ones," he replied, his gaze drifting elsewhere. "The bread slices are too thin and the butter too thick for my liking. And dry cake always gives me heartburn."

His voice was slow and monotonous, and Penelope's jaw tightened as she suppressed a yawn. She glanced at Alex again, who subtly raised her eyebrows and hid a smile.

"Quite," agreed Penelope. "I do hope you feel better." Struggling to find a topic of conversation, she suggested, "Perhaps some weak tea might help."

"Perhaps," he said, looking her over once more as she

maintained her bright smile. "My, my, you have the most charming smile, Miss Beckett. May I have the honor of the next dance?"

Penelope opened her mouth, hoping to quickly think of a reason to refuse him, but moments passed, and she found none. "Of course, I would be delighted."

After that, they mostly stood in silence. Viscount Bridgemere, for some reason, seemed unwilling to leave her side. More men approached her, encouraged by Papa. Within ten minutes, she had three dances filled. As she looked through the ballroom for some excuse to leave his side, she froze.

Only ten feet away, the Duchess of Ashton talked to the Duchess of Grandhampton, a wonderfully pleasant lady. She was the grandmother of Spencer, the deceased Duke of Grandhampton, one of the best friends she had had in the ton.

Spencer...the thought of the wonderfully kind man was a heavy sadness weighing in her chest. The news of his death had reached her last September, and she couldn't believe her ears. She missed her conversations with the duke. They had similar tastes in art, and he encouraged her greatly to pursue her goal. He was the only one she had confided in about her ambition, and he'd supported her. It had seemed as if they could talk about anything. He'd told her how admirable her independent views were, that a woman didn't need to get married, and that he thought a woman should enjoy the same privileges as a man.

Of course, she knew he'd never been interested in her beyond that. He was a known rake, and the women he'd pursued were much more experienced than she. But Papa didn't like her talking to and spending time with him. He had lied at least twice when the duke had come calling on her, telling him she wasn't at home.

The duke had introduced his grandmama to her, and if

only she had a chance to free herself from the circle of men that now surrounded her like flies, she could take those ten steps and greet her. The Duchess of Grandhampton would surely introduce her to the Duchess of Ashton.

She was forced to dance the three dances she had promised. As she danced, she noticed that almost every man stared at her—old and young. Talking to each other. Eyes glistening with something. Staring at her chest, at her legs moving under her ball gown as she danced.

What had happened? During the previous two Seasons, she had done her best to avoid any romantic connections because she was afraid a husband would forbid her from painting like her papa did. How could she have turned from one of the most insignificant young ladies on the marriage mart to the very center of attention?

Finally, her last dance ended. Thanking her partner, she applauded the band of musicians while scanning the guests for any sight of the Duchess of Grandhampton.

Alex came to join her. "How was it?" she asked softly, leaning close.

Before Penelope could answer, the applause died and every person in the ballroom stilled, staring towards the doors.

The crowd separated in front of a man like the sea before Moses, and a shiver went through Penelope. He was tall, and so handsome it was hard to look at him. Hair as dark as Spencer's, cut in a fashionable, windblown style with short sideburns. He had chiseled features, a square jaw, and a straight nose. Under a high forehead, strong brows swept low over beautiful deep-set onyx eyes with long, curly eyelashes that any lady would die for. His mouth was straight and wide, with full lips and a prominent chin.

The hostesses, Lady Jersey, Lady Castlereagh, and Countess Lieven, the patronesses of Almack's, rushed towards him.

"The new Duke of Grandhampton," whispered Alex as she and Penelope watched the three ladies greet and bustle about the duke. "The richest man in England. The biggest rake."

Not as terrible as his older brother was. Spencer had told her about his brother Preston. And she'd seen him at balls. Seaton was a highly respected name, a noble line dating back to the War of the Roses. Arrogant and gorgeous, all three brothers had notorious reputations. Although everyone wanted their daughter to marry into a duke's family, these men were considered more likely to ruin daughters than marry them.

And yet, at the back of their minds, every matchmaking mama no doubt dreamed of her daughter taming one of the rakes and becoming the wife of a duke.

"I know," said Penelope, her heart drumming in her ears so loudly she could hardly hear her own voice.

He barely acknowledged the women around him, looking over the crowd and making his way through the people.

When his eyes landed on Penelope, her heart trembled in her chest like a rabbit before a cobra. She'd always found him mysterious, brooding, and intimidating. It seemed he held a deep dislike for her. Whenever their gazes met, she felt as though the flames of his hatred were burning her to cinders. Though she could not understand why he despised her so.

As the duke approached her, Papa appeared next to her as though out of thin air. People threw odd glances at the duke and at Penelope, making unease crawl down her spine.

"Lord Beckett," said the duke when he stood in front of her papa.

"Your Grace," said Papa in a strange crackling voice. His foot tapped nervously against the floor, one knee shaking. He seemed to avoid looking straight into the duke's eyes. Penelope could understand why. "I didn't expect to see you today."

The duke was at least a head taller than her, looming over her like a dark tower. "Hm" was the duke's reply, and then his black eyes found her again.

There it was—the strange, cold fury at the depths of his eyes. She felt like she needed to run away from him but stood transfixed. The vast, glistening, sparkling ballroom suddenly seemed like a shrinking cage around her, and it became difficult to breathe.

"Would you not introduce me to the two young ladies, Lord Beckett?" he said, still trapping her with his gaze.

Papa's jaw flexed as he gritted his teeth.

"My daughter, Miss Penelope Beckett. My niece, Miss Alexandria Beckett. Duke of Grandhampton." Papa took her by the elbow and tugged. "Forgive me, Duke, I have to introduce my daughter to—"

But the duke interrupted. "May I have the honor of your next dance, Miss Beckett?"

Penelope swallowed. Every instinct screamed for her to run. But if she said no to him, she'd have to say no to everyone else. And she'd offend him. She couldn't offend Spencer's brother.

Sadness over Spencer's absence was like the stab of a needle deep in her heart.

It would be fine. She'd just get through the dance, and then it would be over. Then she'd return to her mission: to try to talk to the Duchess of Ashton.

And so, once again, she put her social smile back on. "I should be delighted."

He nodded and finally tore his gaze away from her. "Ah, Grandmama," he said, and for the first time since he'd come inside, his gaze warmed. "You're here."

"I am," said the Duchess of Grandhampton, coming to stand by their side. Her silvery-gray hair was done in an old-fashioned, high updo with many curls. She was dressed in a violet sack-back gown and supported herself with a walking stick. She had the gracefully aging face of a woman who had been beautiful when she was young. "Miss Beckett, you look lovely tonight. Ah, this is my old friend, the Duchess of Ashton."

Penelope's head swam as she stared into the kind, sad, chocolate-brown eyes of the duchess. She was stunning in her fashionable scarlet gown with a high waist and puffed sleeves, which complemented her flawless complexion.

"Pleasure to make your acquaintance, Duchess," Penelope breathed out. "This is my father, Lord Beckett, and my cousin, Miss Alexandria Beckett."

This was her chance. Finally, she was meeting the woman who might change her life.

"The pleasure is all mine, Miss Beckett." The duchess nodded. "It is wonderful to meet all of you. Is this your first time at Almack's?"

"It is."

"And how are you enjoying it so far?"

"It is very splendid." She beamed at the duchess. "I couldn't help but admire the statues. I wish I could draw them."

"Are you an artist?" asked the duchess with curiosity.

"No, she is most certainly not," said Papa. "My daughter will not be involved in such nonsense. Like all women, she'll be a wife and a mother one day."

Curiosity died in the duchess's eyes, and she frowned. Penelope's face burned as though scalded. Heavens, she wished the floor would crack open and swallow her like a sea beast. With just three sentences, Papa may have ruined her rare chance to make an important connection in the art world.

"Then why did you say you wanted to draw them, Miss Beckett?" asked the duchess.

Penelope opened her mouth to say something, but Papa interrupted her.

"To please you, of course, Your Grace," replied Papa. "My Penelope only cares for the happiness and comfort of others. Just like her deceased mama. As a woman should be."

Penelope felt the hot glare of the duke on her skin.

Now would be a great moment for the ground to swallow her. *Now, please, God!*

Before she could say anything to defend herself or save her reputation before the duchess, the next dance was called.

"Shall we?" asked the duke.

2

Pushing aside her instinct to refuse him and save her reputation as an artist, she smiled politely to both duchesses, Alex, and her papa.

"Excuse me," she said.

Under Papa's heavy glare, she followed the duke. Her knees trembled as she threaded her way through the crowd, assailed by the perfume of roses, sandalwood, and lilacs. Her own cheeks were still ablaze, her hands and back were moist, and she pleaded with herself to calm down.

They both took their places in the lines of ladies and gentlemen, facing each other. He looked at her with a glare that could freeze a snowman.

The orchestra struck the first notes of an English country dance, and she and the duke moved. Every time his hand touched hers, a shiver ran through her skin despite the glove. They danced silently for a while. She shook off the unease that he seemed to have bestowed upon her from the moment he came in. Why should she let him intimidate her? He was just a man. Just another obstacle in her path towards making a favorable connection with the Duchess of Ashton. After the dance, she would try to talk to the duchess alone and salvage the situation.

"It seems the entire ballroom is enthralled with you tonight, Miss Beckett," he said finally as he grasped her hand to take the next four steps together.

Despite her resolve to not be affected by him, heat crept from her face onto her neck and upper chest. "I'm sure you're mistaken."

"I'm never mistaken."

She chuckled. "That can't be true. No one is without fault."

"I have faults. Being mistaken isn't one of them."

Her chest rose and fell quicker with an unwelcome anger. He was a very arrogant man. But never mind that. Perhaps he knew something about tonight that she didn't.

"And what, pray tell, is the reason for their interest, then?" she asked.

"I know for a fact that all the men who are interested in you tonight want a flirt with a decent enough face who would please them no matter what they said or did."

The rudeness of his words hit her like a slap. She stumbled, skipped a step, and hurried to resume the dance. How could a duke—a gentleman—be so boorish?

"Excuse me?" she asked through a parched throat.

"You heard me. Even your papa confirmed that."

Anger roared through her. Her breath accelerated as she and the duke walked in a circle as part of the dance, holding hands. Worst was that was exactly what she thought of herself. She knew she had a decent face, thanks to her mama, who had been a beauty.

But she was also raised to be obedient, to be pleasing, to smile, and to hold an entertaining conversation.

And so, she was obedient and pleasing to her father, holding off her dreams, never openly confronting him about him forbidding her to paint, never mentioning her unconventional goal to be a true artist.

But a flirt...no. He was definitely wrong there. She never flirted with a man aside from showing a polite interest. She did nothing that would give anyone a false hope.

"How dare you?" she demanded. "You do not know me at all."

"But I do," he said, his voice full of malice. "I watched you with my brother. You smiling at him at every moment. You smile at every man here, encouraging them, do you not?"

She was boiling now from the inside out. She kept stumbling and taking the wrong steps, barely able to breathe. "Encouraging what?"

"You know what. Everyone knows your father is penniless and you need a rich husband to save him. You hunt for fortunes."

Papa was penniless? She knew things were bad, but penniless? Looking for a rich husband—no. She had never thought to improve their situation through a marriage. And no matter how much Papa ignored her, he would never want her to marry a rich man knowing she'd be unhappy her whole life.

She ached to abandon the dance and just run. But Papa had managed to get the vouchers for the ball with great difficulty, and if she left, that would be a complete social disgrace. And not just on her, but also on Papa and on Alex.

"That was all you wanted from Spencer, was it not?" continued the duke.

Her chest was about to burst. Prickly tears burned the backs of her eyes. She could not cause a scene in the middle of Almack's! She could not!

"I did no such thing. Your brother, God save his soul, and I were nothing more than friends."

The duke shook his head, his beautiful chin protruding angrily. "Lies and more lies. You knew you were so much more than that to him. All you wanted was his money."

She needed to remember to breathe, she reminded herself. If she didn't want to burst into tears, she needed to breathe. She just had to get through this dance, and then she would not be required to talk to him ever again.

"I always knew dukes were prejudiced, arrogant, and self-centered," she hissed, "and you are the best example."

A lazy one-sided smile spread on his lips. "Finally. Telling the truth, Miss Beckett."

"If you think so ill of me, why did you ask me to dance?"

"I wanted to confirm whether or not my impression of you was true."

"And you're basing your conclusion on the few words that we've just exchanged with each other?"

The music ended, and she pulled away, but he held her gloved hand in his, his touch scalding her. He cocked his eyebrow and lowered his face closer to hers. "I knew the real you long before we were introduced."

"Well, Duke, you won't have to bear my company any longer. I do not want to be in yours ever again."

She tore her hand from his and hurried from the ballroom. She marched by Alex.

"Penelope—" Alex called after her, but she didn't stop. There was a door opposite the cloakroom and she rushed inside. A large tea room, empty and quiet now. Moonlight fell through the arched windows onto the sofas and round tables and the grand piano in the corner. The noise and the laughter coming from the ballroom were muffled here, but anger surged through Penelope.

She slumped onto a sofa and breathed heavily, the need to burst into tears burning her chest. But she wouldn't cry because of him.

She couldn't believe her ears. Where did he even get all those notions about her? Yes, Papa's financials hadn't been good in the last few years. Yes, she had male friends. Yes, she did her best to be pleasant and polite, but weren't smiling and offering a kind word part of that? None of that meant she was a fortune hunter.

The door behind her opened, and a tall, dark shadow walked in.

It was him. The duke. She jumped to her feet, breathing hard. She needed to flee. Not only was she being compromised by being alone with him, but she couldn't let him see her in such distress. She wouldn't give him the satisfaction.

She marched towards him to exit the room through the open door. "Excuse me," she said without looking at him as she tried to pass him.

But he stepped in front of the door and blocked her way.

The feeling of being trapped coiled around her like a snake. She looked up into his face. His dark eyes were on her lips. They were so close, her breasts were touching his waistcoat. She could smell the clean scent of herbal soap, and his cologne—a sharp scent of bay leaves, pepper, and something citrusy.

Her body swayed towards him. Her bones melted under his dark and seeking gaze. She should demand for him to let her pass—why didn't she?

A fiery longing passed through her veins. He was dark and dangerous and made the hair on her skin stand up.

"You're not behaving like a gentleman," she said.

A wicked smile stretched his lips. "That is because, dear Miss Beckett, I'm not going to be one."

One arm wrapped around her waist, and he whirled her

around and backed her against the wall. It was hard and cold against her back even through the dress.

His eyes glimmered with mischief, and then he lowered his head and kissed her.

His lips should have been hard and cold, like him. Instead, they were plush, and soft, and hot.

For a moment, she couldn't move, frozen in place, unable to comprehend what was happening. The man who had spoken so badly of her, like no one had before in her life, was kissing her!

Then something grew in her. A desire for more of that delicious scent, that taste, and that soft, warm touch.

She parted her lips, craving more, and his tongue dipped into her mouth, gently swiping at her own, bringing fire and need rising from somewhere deep in her stomach. She should push him away and run.

She must stop him! If someone saw them, she'd be ruined.

Instead, she melted against him. The slides of his tongue sent jolts of white-hot longing through her. She wanted more. She pressed herself against him, and his embrace was an iron-hard rod.

Just as a strange, needy sound escaped her throat, his weight against her was gone, and she was cold.

He stood two steps away from her, looking at her from under his gorgeous, dark eyebrows, his chest heaving just like hers. He wiped his mouth with the back of his hand like he had just had a good, long drink.

"Whyever did you do that?" she asked, dazed.

"I wanted to prove you're nothing but a flirt. And you're clearly not as innocent as you claim to be. Like I said, I am never mistaken, Miss Beckett."

She hugged herself tightly, her cheeks flushing as embarrassment washed over her.

His beautiful mouth stretched in a wicked grin. "You said you didn't want to be in my company ever again, Miss Beckett? I am sorry to disappoint you. This is just the beginning."

And with that, he strode from the room.

3

Later the same night, at four o'clock in the morning, Preston drank brandy in the main salon of the gentlemen's club Tyche. But even though he kept his eyes on the golden liquid rolling in his glass, his thoughts were back at Almack's, back in the dark room where he'd kissed Penelope Beckett and could barely make himself stop.

How good she had felt in his arms. Her dark blond hair silky under his fingers, and her blue-gray eyes growing darker with fury and then passion when he'd had her so deliciously cornered, pressed against him. Her mouth, so soft and plush and divine, the innocence she'd tried to fake with unsure movements of her lips and tongue. And good Lord, that divine taste of her, and the scent of vanilla and apple in his nostrils that had made his head spin as though he'd gone up in a hot-air balloon.

Impossible. He couldn't feel anything like that for her, not with what he had in mind.

Tonight, the room was full. The ball at Almack's wouldn't

officially end for another hour, but no doubt, it lacked gentlemen, as around a hundred of them were here.

The salon was loud. Every chair, every sofa was occupied, and many gentlemen still had to stand. Candles flickered as men talked. The air was thick with the scents of snuff tobacco, alcohol, and cologne. Servants passed through the room carrying trays laden with glasses of brandy, champagne, and wine.

The walls were all dark mahogany wood. Rich red pelmet heads of giltwood over each window supported swagged draperies of the same color. Crystal chandeliers hung from the ceiling, their candles casting flickering reflections on the oil paintings of hunting scenes, great generals, and interpretations of Greek myths. Around the room, statues of the Greek goddess Tyche in different poses—most bare-chested—spoke to the name of the establishment.

Tyche was a gaming hell for noblemen only. Just like the Greek goddess of fortune, chance, providence, and fate, this place made fortunes and ruined lives. Investments were whispered about, discussed, and made before anything went public. Deals, including dirty ones, were sealed with a handshake.

And every member could be sure that nothing would leave these walls. By buying a membership to the club, a gentleman bought silence. If someone didn't have enough money or assets to settle a debt, he was welcome to bid other important things... his daughter's virginity, a night with his wife, or even an offer to pleasure another man. Humiliating things were done here, and the nobles loved it and kept coming back for more.

It was here that Lord Neville Beckett, a minor baron, had started gambling heavily a few years ago, and had very quickly gotten into debt.

Then more debt.

And more debt.

He kept borrowing from Solomon Eastbourne, the owner of Tyche, as if there wouldn't be repercussions.

And it was here, in August of last year, that Lord Neville had asked Eastbourne to recommend a man who would rough up Spencer to keep him away from Penelope. Clearly, Neville wanted to marry her off to a rich husband, and a rake such as Spencer would only damage her reputation.

Only, the roughing up had gone wrong. And instead of giving him a black eye so that he wouldn't show his face in polite society for a while, they'd killed him.

The thought twisted Preston's stomach with another wave of grief and sorrow for his older brother. Spencer, who'd been a bigger man than Preston ever would be. The man who had sat in Parliament and fought for the rights of women, children, and animals. The successful duke who'd run their duchy so that it brought in a sizable income. The brother who Preston had fought with every day of his life, and now missed as if he'd had a limb cut off.

Preston's gaze found Lord Beckett, who entered the salon by Solomon Eastbourne's side. They went to stand at the farthest wall, to face every gentleman in the room. Neville, with his ridiculous powdered wig, looked nervous. Preston had noticed the man's knee jiggling back at Almack's, and now it practically had a life of its own. His jaw muscles worked under his reddish, meaty, and puffy skin. The previously broad shoulders had slumped, and his round stomach protruded like a large sack.

Solomon Eastbourne was a man in his forties with a thin figure and a face like a hawk. Small, sharp, dark eyes watched everyone and everything without blinking. He always wore silvery tailcoats and dark breeches, and the combination made a stark and unforgettable contrast.

No one forgot Solomon Eastbourne if they met him once. The man was highly respected and even more feared. Lord Beckett having a debt of ten thousand pounds to this man could mean a fate worse than death.

And that was exactly what Preston was after.

"Gentlemen!" called Eastbourne, and even though he wasn't loud, the room went silent at once. "Thank you. As you know, today we have an auction. For sale is Lord Beckett's daughter's hand in marriage. The proceeds will go to pay off Lord Beckett's debt to this establishment."

A satisfied rumble spread through the room as men stood up impatient, eager. At the ball earlier, they'd been able to try out the goods for sale. They could dance with her. Talk to her. Look at her.

And Miss Penelope Beckett was a pretty young woman, Preston had to give her that much. No doubt Spencer and all other men were charmed by her—her smile could light up a room. And she gave her smiles away so easily. Because she was a flirt.

"Starting bid is one hundred pounds," said Eastbourne.

The bids would have to go much higher if Beckett ever hoped to repay his debt. One thousand pounds was a good yearly income for an average peer. One hundred thousand pounds was an income that dukes and the richest industrialists had.

To get ten thousand, Beckett would need a wealthy bidder. And Preston was determined that the man responsible for his brother's death would never ever be able to honor his debt.

"Two hundred!" cried an old gentleman at the front.

"Three!" came another call.

"One thousand!" yelled someone else.

Preston sipped his brandy. Prices escalated quickly. Not all the gentlemen had come to bid. Some of them just wanted to see the spectacle. Many present had simply come to be part of things and to see who would be the lucky winner of Miss Beckett's hand in marriage. The auction had been whispered about in the club for two weeks now, and anticipation had grown.

The bids were now at the level where only a few men in the whole country could afford them. A few men, including Preston himself. But his bid wouldn't be a monetary one.

"Eight thousand five hundred!" said the Earl of Leighborough in his screechy voice.

A murmur went through the crowd.

He was a man of seventy. He had outlived three wives already and clearly had a great sexual appetite as he'd fathered ten children between them. At this hour, a man of the duke's age needed to be in bed, but there was impatience and greed in his milky eyes.

"Eight thousand five hundred," confirmed Eastbourne, calmly looking the gentlemen over with his sharp gaze. "Will anyone give me nine?"

No one replied, looking around.

"To hell with it! Nine!" cried the Viscount of Bridgemere.

Bridgemere was a younger man, well known for his lewdness. No one expected him to ever marry as he spent not a single night outside of a brothel. Chances were the man was rotten with French pox. Preston's jaw clenched even tighter. Miss Beckett deserved what was coming to her. She was guilty in Spencer's death, too. Had she not led him on, had she been honest with his brother that she never had any feelings for him, Spencer would have backed off. Lord Neville wouldn't have sent men to rough him up.

He would still live.

And yet, Preston hated the thought of her being with

the Earl of Leighborough or the Viscount of Bridgemere or any of the other men in the room.

"Nine thousand," said Eastbourne, the echo of a smile appearing on his face for the first time. "My, my. A little more, and you might get out of here with a profit, Lord Beckett. Will anyone give me all ten? Or will Miss Beckett's hand be won by the viscount?"

The men looked around, and the earl raised his hand again, but before he could say anything, Preston stood up, removed a letter from his red leather document folder, and raised the paper high up into the air.

"I have something else to bid," he said calmly.

He felt a hundred pairs of eyes land on him, but there was only one man whose reaction interested him. Lord Beckett. The man's eyes widened as he looked at the folded paper in Preston's hand.

Eastbourne's hawk eyes narrowed at him. "What is this?"

"The sworn testimony of someone who bore witness to a certain deal Lord Beckett did with Mister B."

Beckett paled.

Satisfaction spilled warmly through Preston's chest. Everyone knew Mister B was Thorne Blackmore, a man notorious for taking care of dark deeds no man of honor would consider. The testimony was that of a servant from Tyche who had heard Beckett looking for Thorne Blackmore to deal with Spencer.

Beckett broke into a sprint and, pushing gentlemen aside, elbowed his way through the crowd. When he stopped before Preston, he was breathing hard, his yellowish eyes bulging, a thin drop of saliva trembling on his bottom lip with every breath. How Preston despised this man. How he hated him. His brother's killer. The man who had forever hung the boulder of guilt around Preston's neck, the boulder he would not be able to lift as long as he lived.

Because nothing would get Spencer back.

Beckett's eyes were locked on the paper Preston still held high and out of his reach.

"Who is it from?" Beckett demanded. "What's in it? I demand that you show it to me."

"No. I will protect my witness."

The shorter man swallowed and nodded. "Right. May I talk to you in private, then, Duke?"

"No, you may not. I want your commitment *now*. For my silence, you will give me your daughter's hand in marriage."

Beckett closed his eyes for several deep and fast breaths. Preston rejoiced in the torment of this man. Let him suffer. His revenge would be sweet.

"Why are you doing it?" Beckett asked, desperation in his face as he looked at Preston again.

"Because then you can't marry her off to one of the gentlemen in this room and get your money. And you know why you don't deserve it. You know why you deserve to be ruined." Preston was going to take away Beckett's last chance to pay off his debt to Eastbourne. The marriage contract would be drawn so that Penelope's father would never get a penny from him. Not one acre of land. Nothing.

If Preston started a criminal case against Beckett, he could claim it was murder. And murder, even for noblemen, was a hanging offense. The baron didn't have the money to hire an attorney to defend himself at court. Preston had all the money in the world to hire the best attorneys in England and prove Beckett's crime.

The testimony was just the first piece of evidence. Preston's team would be able to find more.

Because Beckett was guilty.

As though in confirmation of that, the baron hung his head low in submission.

"Yes," he said. "The Duke of Grandhampton's bid wins."

The room erupted in cries of outrage. As Preston returned the letter to the red leather folder, Eastbourne came through the crowd with an uncharacteristically angry expression. Icy-cold malice spread through Preston's body as he watched Beckett desperately trying to explain to his creditor that they wouldn't be getting their money today.

Good, he thought. *And then, Spencer, brother, I will avenge you. Even if my own soul will burn in hell for all eternity, yours will be avenged on this earth.*

Miss Penelope Beckett's fate was sealed, and she didn't even know it.

4

"ARE you hoping to meet someone particular in the park?" Alex asked Penelope as they descended the stairs.

It was early afternoon the day after the Almack's ball, and Penelope and Alex were going for a walk in Hyde Park with Lady Brownhill, a neighbor, as chaperone.

Penelope chuckled. "Of course not."

"Then why are we leaving during morning calls? You should have many visitors after your success last night."

Morning calls, despite the confusing name, were held in the afternoon. The day after a ball, it was customary for interested gentlemen to pay a visit to the lady they intended to pursue.

But receiving such attention was the exact opposite of what Penelope wished.

Her mind leapt to the Duke of Grandhampton, causing an onrush of heat and dread. The kiss...the blasted kiss that had melted her very bones...from a man who hated her—and whom she hated! A man she hadn't been able to stop thinking about since they returned from the ball.

"I would like a stroll," Penelope said, avoiding Alex's gaze. "That's all."

The stairs screeched under her feet as she continued, the wood dry and old. The banister moved a little under her hand. But there was no money to fix either of them. As Alex and she reached the foyer, her eyes landed on her mother's watercolor of Hyde Park in spring—Mama's favorite place in London. Her eyes watered as she remembered how Mama had painted it, picking the colors and explaining her choices to Penelope. Though the yellow paint of the wood-paneled wall where it hung was chipped and cracked, the colors of the painting were still vivid and bright, with fresh green grass and purple wisteria hanging from a white pergola in the midst of awakening nature. Sweet pain always split her heart in two at the memory.

"But so many gentlemen paid their attention to you," said Alex as she tied the ribbons of her bonnet. The pale blue suited Alex's complexion so well. "I'm sure you'll receive a number of visitors."

"But that's exactly the reason why I don't want to be at home. I don't want any gentlemen to believe I'm interested."

As Penelope walked to the entrance door, she nodded to their butler, Tyson, who was a tall, young man from Yorkshire with thin pale hair and long bleached eyelashes. He had little experience, and therefore Papa had been able to hire him very cheaply. Tyson opened the door for her and Alex, his gaze briefly darting to Penelope's cousin. Penelope had a suspicion Tyson was quite smitten with Alex—there was always an almost puppylike admiration in his eyes. No wonder. Alex was quite a beauty.

Penelope had just stepped into the fresh April air, closing the hooks of her spencer, when a shadow momentarily obscured the light, and she hit a hard, warm wall. Two strong arms held her by her shoulders.

"I beg your pardon—" she started, but when she looked up the words died on her lips.

It was *him*. The Duke of Grandhampton, all tall and so handsome her stomach squeezed, his dark eyes on her. That was how they had been yesterday—but even closer. With his arms around her and his scent in her nostrils, and his lips on hers. Her first kiss...

Why did it have to be from *this* man?

Her cheeks heated as she remembered a dream she'd had about him last night. There was this longing, and more...more kissing...more rubbing...less clothes. She didn't know what she wanted, only that she needed to touch him, skin to skin... everywhere! She'd awoken in the early hours of the morning shivering, but not from cold.

"Are you going out?" the duke asked as he let her go and stepped back onto the porch. Alex followed Penelope out and stood by her side.

"Good day, Your Grace," she said.

He nodded briefly to her. "How do you do?"

Then his attention returned to Penelope, scorching her. Her eyes dropped to his lips, that broad, handsome mouth that was on hers last night, teasing, demanding, stroking...

Her heart slammed against her rib cage, her chest rising and falling fast. *Oh, calm down, you ninny.*

"Stay, Miss Beckett. Or you'll miss an important change in your life."

With that, he passed by Penelope, the scents of bay leaf and pepper and sweet herbs mingling in his wake.

An important change in her life? Something dark and heavy and cold sank in her stomach. She did not like the sound of that at all!

Through the open door, she watched the duke enter her home and announce his name to Tyson, who nodded and went to her father's study. While the duke waited in the dark hallway, he turned and met her gaze, a look of triumph on his face.

"What could he mean?" Penelope murmured to Alex.

"I don't know," said Alex. "Shall we stay or would you like to go to Hyde Park still? Lady Brownhill will be waiting."

Penelope swallowed as Tyson returned, said something to the duke, and both left in the direction of Papa's study. Penelope's feet felt like they were filled with sand.

She pulled the ribbons of her bonnet. "I do not have a good feeling, Alex," she said as she returned to the foyer and hung the bonnet on a hook on the wall.

"Oh, Pen!" Alex followed her, and together they walked to the door to her father's study.

Penelope stood, clenching and unclenching her fists, staring at the heavy mahogany door. What did the duke want with her papa that would change her future? The thought of the duke being involved in her life in any way chilled her whole body, head to toe.

"Don't worry, darling," said Alex, laying a soothing hand on her shoulder. But her voice didn't have the confidence she must have wanted to show. "It must be something good. But even if it isn't, your papa will protect you."

Penelope looked at her and forced a smile. Alex was ever so optimistic, so kind. She saw only the best in people. Penelope supposed she tried to, as well. But something about the duke made her hands tremble.

"You're right. Papa won't let the duke harm me."

"Harm you?" Alex asked in alarm. "Why would the duke harm you?"

"Did I say harm? I only meant I do not know the duke's intentions. And he clearly doesn't find me agreeable..."

But last night, he had kissed her. He'd claimed she was a flirt. Perhaps he'd come to ruin her completely.

"Don't worry, Pen." Alex took Penelope's hand, and the two stood staring at the door while dread replaced her blood drop by drop.

What felt like hours later, the door opened, and Papa marched out with a somber expression. He stopped abruptly when he saw Penelope and Alex standing there. There were dark circles under his eyes; he must have not slept at all last night. His jaw was set in a mournful expression, his mouth firmly shut. He wore the same plain tight-fitting coat with curving tails he'd had on at the ball. Tight knee-length breeches and stockings covered his legs, and a tall stiff linen neckband circled his neck instead of the cravat fashionable today. His powdered wig looked rather crooked over his flushed and sweaty forehead.

Sometimes, several days would pass without Penelope seeing Papa at home as he seemed to spend many nights in gentlemen's clubs and slept almost all day long. He often had dinner at the club as well, and Penelope had dinner by herself at home. During those lonely times, her only solace was her art.

Her passion felt like a dirty secret she had to hide. And she knew that if she wanted to pursue it seriously, she'd need to accept the loneliness that came with going against what was considered appropriate for a woman. She'd never have a husband—most men didn't approve of a woman who wanted a career as an artist—or, therefore, a family.

But she had the firm belief that despite his frequent absences and disapproval, Papa still loved her and would still protect her when it came to the important things. She knew he had her best interest at heart because he was her papa. With Mama gone, all they had was each other.

"Ah, Penelope," Papa said, eyeing her with a blank expression. "Come in. You may come in, too, Alexandria."

When Penelope and Alex entered Papa's study, the duke was standing against the mahogany bookshelves fit for hundreds of volumes, though all were empty. Dull, gray daylight fell on the dark desk, which held nothing but a pen, an ink jar, and a single piece of paper that looked like a contract of some sort. A half-full bottle of brandy and a single glass stood on the sideboard next to an empty vase. How long had it been since Papa had done any business related to their estate here—or any business besides drinking? Between the dark shelves, on the dull, mint-green paneled wall, was a darker rectangle left from a painting that no longer hung there.

Mama's painting of their country seat, Beckett Manor, where Penelope had grown up, where they had had rare happy days as a family...

Grandhampton seemed to occupy half of the study with his presence. He stood tall, broad-shouldered, and proud, one side of his face lit by the light coming through the window, the other in the shadow. He was dressed so immaculately—his black coat had a high, sharp collar and a pristine, handsomely tied cravat that highlighted his olive skin tone and chiseled features.

How could someone so cold and cruel and intimidating be so strikingly beautiful?

His onyx eyes were on her, the same strange, cold fury in their depths that had a drop of cold sweat roll down her spine.

Papa closed the door behind Penelope with a thud that made her shudder.

Grandhampton looked her over, his dark eyes glinting, making her feel small and vulnerable, as though she stood naked before him, despite the layers of her chemise, corset, dress, and spencer.

"I do like the look of the future duchess I just bought," he said. "I'll have to see you for the rest of my life, after all..."

Shock hit Penelope, and she gasped soundlessly. Alex's head turned sharply towards her.

With a crooked smile, the duke said, "Are you ready to pay for your sins?"

"What can he mean?" she asked, turning to Papa.

Papa went to the sideboard and poured brandy into a glass. When he'd downed the contents, he said, "You're betrothed to the duke."

No. No. No. He couldn't possibly mean that. He couldn't possibly betray her like that.

The floor careened under her feet. The dread she'd felt ever since she was introduced to Grandhampton turned into a dark storm. A thrashing gale that was sweeping destruction across her life.

She had thought, deep down, Papa still cared about her. That he was still grieving Mama and she needed to leave him alone to do that.

But marrying her off without even talking to her first? Marrying her off to this horrible, horrible man who would belittle her and humiliate her for the rest of her life?

If Mama were alive, she'd never have allowed this.

"Why are you doing this, Papa?" she asked. "Is it because he told you?"

"Told me what?"

Before she could reply, the duke cocked one eyebrow. "I kissed your daughter last night, sir. And no, Miss Beckett, I did not tell him."

Papa's eyebrows drew together, his upper lip crawling up to expose a snarl.

"You're compromised?" Papa growled. "Penelope, how could you? I had arranged the whole— Ah, it does not matter now."

How could *she*? She didn't kiss the duke—he kissed her! But that was not what was important now. And what did it matter if the duke wanted to marry her anyway—though for the life of her, she did not understand why he wanted to marry someone he despised so much.

She marched across the study and stood in front of Papa. "Then why?" she demanded.

"You need to teach your daughter some manners," said Grandhampton. "How about, 'It's an honor, Your Grace.' You're going to be the Duchess of Grandhampton, Miss Beckett. One of the richest women in England. Isn't this what you wanted all along?"

She shook her head in bewilderment. "You're terribly mistaken. I never—"

He strode to the desk and lifted the single paper lying there. Under his low, long eyebrows his eyes looked dark and bottomless. "Your father and I signed the marriage settlement. I already have the special license. We're to be wed in three days. The bishop was a good friend of Spencer's," he added somberly.

Three days? Such a short wait was unheard of.

"Of course," she said bitterly, "the whole of England would run to do the great Duke of Grandhampton's bidding, wouldn't it?"

Silence fell on the room as the duke and she stared at each other. How she hated him then. Poisonous, corroding anger gurgled in her veins. How dare he first insult her, then take her life away from her! All her dreams, all her hopes, all her plans to be independent—all that for absolutely nothing.

And, once again, she was alone, so alone. Against Papa, against the duke, against the whole world.

But instead of barking or snarling at her as he had done before, the duke said calmly, "It's a deal that will save your father's reputation and possibly his life. Your father signed it. He agrees. But you have the final word, Miss Beckett. I cannot force you to say yes. You must choose it yourself."

Her mouth opened as she stared at Papa, who pointedly looked at the floor as though he was on the verge of tears. The duke walked to the door and opened it, but before he left, he turned and met Penelope's gaze.

"You have until tomorrow. I will come in the morning to have your decision."

And then he was gone.

5

"How could you, Papa?" Penelope demanded.

With the duke gone, her helpless rage grew and expanded like a fire in dry branches.

"Perhaps it's best I leave you," said Alex politely, throwing a final glance full of empathy and support to Penelope before she walked out of the room.

When the door closed behind her, Papa turned to Penelope, his mouth twisting bitterly.

"It's all your fault!" he cried as he marched through the room, waving his arms. "You let him kiss you? You entangle yourself in the company of rakes? Why do you have to be such a flirt that men assume you're an easy target?"

His words were like a slap. How could Papa think that of her? The duke was bad enough, but her own father? And accuse her of entangling herself with rakes—did he mean Spencer? All she ever did was try to be friendly and kind, nothing more.

"This is quite unfair, Papa!" she said, fighting away the tears.

Papa sighed and stopped walking. He stood by the fireplace, laid one arm on the molding, and looked at the cold grate. She expected him to apologize, to agree with her that he wasn't being fair.

"There's something you don't know," he said. "I owe a great debt. I started selling things, but it's not enough. Even if we sell everything—the whole estate—it won't be sufficient to cover it."

Penelope's hand flew to her mouth. "Is it the gambling?"

"It does not matter. Your whole purpose was to find an excellent match." He looked at her over his shoulder. "Unfortunately, you were not born a man, so my title will not be transferred to you. But at least, you can help your father out and marry the duke."

So saving her father's reputation and his life, which the duke had spoken of, that must be about the debt. Worry for her papa twisted her heart. She went to stand by his side, no longer angry but concerned. He hadn't looked well for a long time. The burden of his unpaid debts must be what had been eating him alive. She'd noticed the lack of funds for new dresses, the diminishing staff in their home, the plainer and simpler food. None of that mattered to her. What she cared about was her papa.

"Will he pay your debts?" she asked.

"No." He straightened and faced her. "But your marriage will buy me time to fix things."

"I don't understand. Isn't that why you're marrying me to him? So that he gives you money?"

His face darkened, and he walked away from her to look down at the marriage settlement on the desk. "No, he isn't giving me money. But that shouldn't concern you. All you need to do is come to the wedding ceremony in three days and say yes. And by saying yes, you will save your old papa."

Save her old papa…and he wouldn't even tell her how! Save him by locking herself into a lifetime of misery with a horrible man—all because of his gambling debts.

"Will you at least tell me what it is that he is going to do for you in exchange for marrying me?" she demanded. "Perhaps, if I know what it is, we can put our heads together and find another way…"

"There is no other way!" yelled Papa so loud, the glass in the windows shook.

Penelope shuddered from his outrage. She'd never heard him shout.

"Well, then I have to refuse," she said. "That man hates me, and I cannot stand to spend one more minute in the same room with him. You cannot force me to endure a lifetime with someone who I despise. Especially not when I can—"

Not when she could paint and sell her art and earn an income and help her papa in that way. But he interrupted her.

"You cannot refuse. You're my daughter, and you will do what I say. In three days, you will stand before a vicar and say yes."

She backed from the room, desperate. "No, Papa. You cannot make me."

"Selfish girl!" he roared. "I gave everything up for your mother and you. For once in your life, do as you are told!"

Perhaps she was being a little selfish. Perhaps she wanted to pursue her own goals. With the Duchess of Ashton's patronage, she could be introduced to the artists she admired. The famous female Italian artist, Enrica de Luca, was in London now. Penelope could learn art properly, not just by trying and correcting it herself, but by having someone great guide her.

Her mother had taught her the basics; it was something that had brought them many hours of shared joy. And her mother had always said Penelope had a rare gift. But before her mother had died from fever, Penelope had still thought she would marry and have children.

Then, after her mother's death and her father's absence, Penelope had started reading more about art and artists to connect to her deceased mother, and she'd dealt with her painful emotions through her art. And eventually she'd realized that was what she wanted to do with her life. That she had no choice but to paint and no desire greater than to share her work with others.

Even if it meant loneliness.

"No!" she said firmly.

The only suitor she'd ever had was the Duke of Woodley. He was an older man, respectable enough and very rich. But one day, he had stopped calling on her and avoided her when he saw her at balls. Then a month later, he was engaged and soon after had married. She'd always wondered what could have changed his mind about her.

Since then, she'd never heard anything from her father about potential matches, and he usually cut all suitors off. She'd always thought Papa simply didn't care. And now to be ambushed like this...

Her father's upper lip curled. "It is *done*."

No. She wouldn't be simply passed from one disinterested man to another like a piece of property.

"It's not done until I say yes," she said and left his study.

As she ran up the stairs into her bedroom, her mind raced, looking for a solution, for a way out. She had been introduced to the Duchess of Ashton now. She could request an audience, explain her situation, and ask for help. She could run away and keep working on her paintings and sell them with the help of the duchess. She wouldn't be trapped in a loveless marriage with a man who was the devil himself.

It was a pretty morning the next day, with birds chirping from beyond her bedroom window, which looked out over the back garden. The sun had risen about an hour ago at six o'clock. The soft, pinkish sunrays played through the branches of the trees with fresh new leaves as bright and as delicate as lace.

Penelope closed her hand luggage, which lay on her bed and contained her watercolor paper, paints, brushes, and her drawing paper and pencils, as well as everything she had managed to paint so far. Another held a few items of clothing and her essentials.

She looked around her room. Her mother had not been alive to accompany her for her coming out season. She'd only lived on Vine Street, on the outskirts of Mayfair, during the past three years since she'd been out.

There were few memories of Mama in this house. All Penelope had known here was loneliness and rejection. So why did she feel such heavy sadness to be leaving? To be leaving everything she knew behind, even cutting her ties with Papa and leaving him to face whatever the duke was threatening him with?

Why was she sad to start the new life she'd always dreamed of?

To escape the duke's clutches and the marriage she had never wanted?

A soft knock at the door made her jump to her feet. Alex slipped into her room quietly, already dressed in her spencer and a bonnet. Her dark eyes were wide, her hair not done properly because the maid wasn't yet up. But she was still pretty in her natural beauty.

"Are you ready?" she said, breathing heavily. "I got the carriage. It's waiting for you at the corner."

Penelope inhaled sharply and looked around. "I think so. I have only these two pieces of luggage."

Alex nodded. "We'll manage them between us."

Suddenly, she rushed to Penelope and held her by both hands. "Oh, Penelope, are you sure this is the right way? Running away like this?"

Alex blurred through Penelope's tears, but she nodded fiercely, her chest clenching. "I am. I'm not going to be bullied into marrying him. Into a life of unhappiness when I could be a real artist, when, with time, connections, and hard work, I could support myself and Papa if only he would let me."

Alex's eyes glistened with tears, too. She grasped Penelope in a quick hug. "Oh, cousin! Hug my mama for me, please. I'll see you soon."

"I'm sorry I'm leaving you to deal with Papa's rage," whispered Penelope, wiping her tears with one hand. "Please tell Papa I'm sorry. But I can't be forced to marry like that. Not to that awful man."

They broke away, and each grabbed a piece of luggage and hurried downstairs. They passed quietly through the front door. Tyson was still busy with the morning chores, so he was nowhere to be seen. Penelope and Alex descended the front stairs and rushed through the tiny front yard. The terrace houses of Vine Street stretched to either side of her and Papa's house, their porticos pristine.

Vine Street was quiet, with no horses or passersby. A footman swept the stairs three houses down the street. The air was wet and warm and sweet with the scent of fresh, sticky leaves on the verge of opening. Across the street, another row of three-story terrace houses stretched with Kiln Lane cutting through the middle. The top floor of the houses was always shorter, with smaller windows, indicating those were the servants' quarters.

Penelope's and Alex's heels knocked quickly against the sidewalk as they hurried towards the carriage. It stood just at the corner of the street, half hidden behind a bush. The coachman attached her small hand luggage at the rear.

"Where to?" he asked.

"The Swan with Two Necks," Penelope said.

The coachman nodded. It was the departing place of the morning mail coach, which had a few places for passengers. "If we hurry, we should make it."

Penelope hugged Alex for the last time and got into the carriage. She should be at her uncle and aunt's home by tomorrow. From there, she'd think about what to do. She just had to get away from Papa and from Grandhampton.

But before she could knock on the front wall, indicating the coachman should drive off, there was a sound of hooves and wheels against the dirt-packed road. She looked out of the window. A rich carriage, all shiny black wood with a gilded crest of Grandhampton—two lions with their paws outstretched and vines all around them—pulled up in front of her house. In a moment, the door opened, and the Duke of Grandhampton jumped down, straightening his black overcoat as he walked. Wind ruffled the locks of his black hair.

His shoulders were slumped, his neck down. Then he straightened, his shoulders and back so stiff they could be a wall, and marched towards her house like he owned it.

Like he owned her.

No doubt, he had come to ask for her decision. But so early? Even the most polite of the society didn't break their fast until around 10 a.m.

Alex, who was still waiting to see her off by the carriage, turned to run towards him. Penelope got out of the carriage and hid behind the corner of the bush, watching as Alex greeted him and they exchanged some words.

Penelope's heart beat fast.

This was her escape. All she needed to do was get back into the carriage, knock on that wall, and let the coachman know she was ready to go. But what would the duke do to her father? She had declared her independence so freely, so bravely before.

But she still didn't know what exactly the repercussions would be for her father.

His reputation and his life, the duke had said.

She had a hard time believing it, but could she really have her father's honor and his life on her conscience?

Alexandria talked to the duke, all sheepish and nervous. The duke asked her something, and trembling, Penelope strained to hear what she said.

"...she will not be coming back," she heard Alex's words.

The duke stilled, as immobile as a statue. Then a figure rushed out of the front door of her house. Her father, only half dressed. This was an unspeakably early—or late—hour for him. He was missing his coat and didn't even have his wig on.

"Duke...what is going on?" Papa demanded.

"Your daughter is gone," said the duke. "It seems her answer is no."

Alex clutched her chest. Penelope held her breath. She shouldn't witness this at all. She should just get back into the carriage and command the coachman to drive.

Instead, as though mesmerized, she watched her father drop his head and lower his shoulders and stretch his hands out to the duke. Like a baby, he sobbed, clutching at the duke's hands.

No. Not her father who could, in her mind, slay a dragon for her if he must. Her heart split in half.

She'd never seen her father beg like that.

It was either her father's ruination or her lifelong unhappiness.

She was so close. She had packed her things. She had hired a carriage. She could make it to the mail coach, and run away, and do what she loved...

But her papa...her poor, old papa. He had no one else. He needed her. Perhaps she wouldn't be an artist and would imprison herself in a marriage full of resentment, but at least her conscience would be clear, and she would help her father avoid his destruction. She was his only child. She couldn't bear to abandon her father.

Not even at the price of her own happiness.

With her very core chilling, she walked towards the duke, Alex, and her father, her small heels clicking against the sidewalk.

All three looked up at her in astonishment. Her chest tore apart with grief for the life she'd never have.

But she shoved her tears and her sorrow deep down her throat so that no one could see them. She needed to be brave and to be strong for her papa.

"You wanted my decision, Duke," she said, looking straight into his hard, dark eyes. "You win. I will marry you."

Without another glance, she walked towards the carriage to retrieve her luggage, fear and sadness thundering inside of her.

Her life was over.

6

Two days later, they rode into the courtyard of Chalworth Place, traditionally the London seat of the Duke of Grandhampton. Penelope got out of the carriage after Papa and Alex.

She stepped onto the cobblestones, shivering from the inside. The day was warm for spring, but she hadn't been able to stop shaking all morning. Chalworth Place surrounded her from all four sides, looming over her like the Tower of London. Situated in the middle of Mayfair, the three-story mansion looked ancient, built with old brown bricks and gothic archways of blackening, crumbling stonework.

Dark, paned windows gaped at her. Between them, grotesques of dragon and lion heads and baby angels were carved on the stone corbels. She could see a sunlit London street through the arched gateway under which their carriage had driven. A pale pink apple tree bloomed among the bright green bushes, young leaves sparkling in sunlight. It seemed overnight London had transformed from naked and bare to fresh and green and lush, filling the air with the scent of new leaves and tender blossoms.

Birdsong filled the streets. People smiled brighter, a new spring in their step, looking forward to dressing in lighter clothes and shoes, to going for more walks, and to the start of the Season.

New hope. That was what London smelled like now.

But there was no hope for Penelope. On the contrary, she had left all that hopeful beauty behind the black archway. Before her was the mansion in which her life would forever be over.

Her father stared vacantly at the grand doors and walked towards them without waiting for her. She thought he might give her an arm to support her, say a word of encouragement, or simply thank her for doing this for him. But all he offered her was a view of his hunched shoulders under his powdered wig.

Darling Alex gave her a sympathetic smile as she took Penelope's hand and put it through her bent elbow. Together, they walked after Papa.

The butler opened the door, and they passed through. Inside, thick, fluted stone pillars carved with fleur-de-lis flanked the entrance hall and shot upward into a high, vaulted ceiling. When sunlight fell through them, two windows, one on either side of the door, which had appeared black to her from the outside, became ablaze with blue, yellow, red, and purple patterns of stained glass. One depicted a hunt and the other a medieval battle. Penelope's breath caught as she watched the play of colors reflected on the white stone of the entrance hall.

Stepping on a red carpet, they walked into a large hall with a grand staircase that led to the first and second floors. On the wall behind the stairs, a large coat of arms hung between two rows of stained glass windows.

Dark wooden panels on the walls had painted motifs of

medieval lords and ladies, peasants, hunts, and battles that looked like they belonged in a monk's book.

Chinese vases and a marble bust stood on an intricately carved, dark sideboard surrounded by beautifully carved, gilded chairs.

Centuries-old portraits of prominent men and women, their faces almost white against a black background, stared at her from the walls of the hall. The artwork was masterful, and despite herself, she ached to stop and study every detail.

Those must be previous generations of Dukes and Duchesses of Grandhampton. She was marrying the twelfth Duke of Grandhampton. And yet, she wanted none of this grandeur, none of these riches.

Though her father was a baron, his station and holdings were far below the duke's. This was a different world. And she knew that nothing would ever be the same for her.

When they entered the ballroom, she saw that her future husband, as well as several of his family members, stood on the far side of the room, next to a vicar. Unlike the previous rooms, this one was bright, with clear-paned windows casting light on the pale gray walls. Pillars supported mahogany beams that were arranged in a grid of rectangles against the coffered ceiling.

Her short heels clicked hollowly against the wooden floor. Her chest felt empty. The whole house, despite the artwork and architecture, and no doubt, centuries of history, felt desolate. Staged.

It seemed empty and cold, and it smelled dusty, despite, she was sure, a large contingent of maids. It didn't feel like home.

As the duke's dark gaze fell on her, her stomach dropped. She felt naked in her eggshell-colored gown. The skirt of it was heavy and tangled between her legs as she walked.

Tears blurred her vision. Helpless tears of anger. She couldn't even see who the guests were as she passed by them.

The vicar droned on and on, Penelope not really hearing him until he asked the question that would change her life. The duke, standing by her side, wore a black tailcoat and black pantaloons. His very presence next to her burned her skin through her clothes.

"I do," he said, his voice like a rumble in her bones.

"I do," she echoed, not recognizing her own voice.

And then he was putting the ring on her finger with his big, scalding, masculine hands. When her turn came, she shoved the ring on his finger with all the force she had and met his amused gaze.

The quill in her hand felt cold and hard as she signed the church register. Her signature looked shaky. Her husband's—sharp edges and lines.

Just like him.

And then the transaction was finished; they were married.

The guests came to congratulate them.

The Dowager Duchess of Grandhampton smiled compassionately at her.

"Congratulations, my dear," she said, "and welcome to the family. I'm delighted to have a new granddaughter."

Then came a man who resembled Spencer and Preston but had auburn hair and a softer, more pleasant expression than Penelope's new husband. His name was Richard—her new brother-in-law.

"Congratulations, brother," he said, shaking her husband's hand. "Many happy years." He moved to Penelope and nodded to her, his blue eyes warm. "If he gives you trouble, call on me."

Penelope gave a polite smile. Surely, he couldn't mean it. "I appreciate it, Lord Richard. Thank you."

He moved on, and a tall young woman with thick auburn hair and intense blue eyes approached.

"Please call me Calliope," she said with a kind smile. "I'm ever so pleased to finally have a sister."

Ah, that was her new sister-in-law. Penelope's heart warmed. Her husband's entire family, including the deceased Spencer, were kinder to her than the man she had married.

Then came Sebastian, Duke of Loxchester, with his wife, Emma. He was a striking man with dark blond hair who warmly congratulated her. The Duchess of Loxchester was a pretty woman with dark brown hair and a smile that lit up the room.

"Please, call me Emma," the duchess said. "My husband and yours are best friends, and I'd very much like it if you and I could be great friends, too. Please, call on me whenever. For tea, a walk in the Vauxhall Gardens or if you need anything, anything at all."

"Thank you," said Penelope, smiling for the first time in days. "I'd like that very much!"

Papa and Alex were the final two guests. Alex congratulated the duke and Penelope heartily. But Papa only dryly shook the duke's hand and hemmed to her, a bitter smile never leaving his face.

"Well, my darling," he said, looking around the room, "rejoice at the riches. At least you will not have my fate of being a poor, broken man."

Penelope felt her husband's heavy gaze on her. The butler invited everyone into the dining room for the wedding breakfast, and Papa and the others went ahead. Penelope looked up at the duke and met his dark gaze head-on. "See what you're doing to my papa, Grandhampton? I will not exaggerate by saying you're the worst person I've ever met."

Leaving him speechless, she marched down the large,

elegant ballroom. Gold flashed by her in gilt chandeliers and candle sconces, chairs with gilt-carved legs, and the frames of paintings and ornaments.

A golden cage in which she would spend the rest of her life.

The dining room was so large, it could seat a hundred guests at a single long table. It stood in the center of the room, mahogany so dark it was almost ink black. Intricate gilt candleholders stood along the table in the midst of white floral arrangements of Helleborus, ranunculus, and anemones.

Nine seats were prepared at the table.

The buffet table standing by the paned windows held a beautiful and rich selection of foods—sliced ham, bacon, cold cuts of roast beef, honey-roasted duck breast, smoked salmon, fried cod, omelets, fresh rolls, five kinds of jam, and a large plate with fruit, including apples, oranges, peaches, and cherries. The apples must have been overwintered, but where in the world had they found oranges, cherries, and peaches in April? She supposed they were imported from the south. Nothing was too expensive for the Duke of Grandhampton.

The wedding cake stood on the dining table in the middle of all the flowers, a long rectangle with white icing covered with powdered sugar. Four footmen and the butler stood at attention along the walls in red and gold livery.

As her eyes continued to wander around the room, they landed on a painting that held her breath completely still.

It was William Turner's *The Shipwreck*, which she and Spencer had seen at a poetry soirée. He'd sneaked her out of the sitting room during a reading and led her to the library. He'd lit a gas lamp, and Penelope remembered the sense of danger and inappropriateness of being with Spencer alone, and yet, she had trusted him.

They'd stood side by side, gazing at the painting. The angry sea was black and the sky stormy against the tattered sail and broken hull of a large ship. In the foreground, in three sloops, desperate seamen fought the elements amid the white and green foam of unforgiving waves.

She remembered Spencer asking, "What do you see here, Miss Beckett?"

She had been so overawed by the skill of the painter, she didn't quite understand the strangeness of his voice. All she saw were the perfect strokes, the contrast of white paint against the dark, the captivating composition that held the gaze and didn't let go.

"I see a master," she'd said. "One I hope one day to be worthy of."

"Oh," he'd said, his voice puzzled, intrigued.

"What do you see?" she'd asked.

"I see death."

What could this painting be doing here? And why would Spencer buy something that signified death for him? It had been one of the last events of the London Season the previous year, several weeks before she learned that Spencer had died.

And now she was here. Married to his brother.

As the guests filled their plates, the dowager and Richard came to talk to Penelope.

"I'm glad my Preston found someone like you," said the old lady. "Aren't you, Richard?"

"Yes, I am, too," Richard said, and small wrinkles formed in the corners of his eyes as he smiled. He followed his brother with his gaze as Preston entered the room as somber as a storm.

"He was so shaken by Spencer's death," said the dowager. "But now he won't be alone. He'll have you to love him."

Penelope suppressed a snicker. Love him? It would be impossible for her to love a man like that.

"Ah, do not give me that look," said the old lady softly. "I know you don't love him yet. He's still very hurt. But you don't know him like we all do. Please, give it time. You will see the true man he is under all those grim looks and that hard exterior. I know you will, even if you don't see it yet. And I wish you two every happiness."

Richard nodded and chuckled. "Don't let my brother scare you. I know he can be intimidating, but deep down he's as fluffy and warm as a kitten. He's the most loyal person you'll ever meet. He'd gladly die for the people he loves."

Penelope frowned, studying the straight back of the duke as he helped himself to an omelet.

"It's hard to believe you're talking about the same man," she said.

"I know, dear," said the dowager. "Give it time. And if you ever need my help or an ear to listen, my doors are always open."

Penelope nodded and smiled at her, grateful. She was sure she'd need to call upon the duchess more than once.

7

Bloody hell but she was lovely, standing at the window halfway turned to him and staring into the courtyard at the departing guests.

Alone with her in the dining room, Preston eyed the heaving bosom of his new wife, her small breasts rising and falling in quick, shallow breaths, restricted by the bust of her dress.

He should not look at her breasts, damn it. He also shouldn't notice how beautifully translucent her warm blue-gray eyes were in the sunlight coming through the windows. How the sun played in her silky hair the color of old gold with shades of bronze and silver sparkling in.

Why did she have to be so pretty, hell and the devil?

And what now?

She was Preston's. The last, most precious possession of the man responsible for Spencer's death. But getting his revenge by marrying Lady Penelope hadn't turned back time and saved Spencer. And he had forever tied himself to the daughter of his enemy.

Earlier, Preston had noticed her studying the paintings on the walls, the busts, and other decorations. Was she estimating the wealth she'd married into?

That wouldn't surprise him. She could now enjoy the opulent life she'd desired. This young woman, with her batting eyelashes and those strawberry-shaped lips that begged to be kissed, had led his brother on like no other. He hadn't heard their conversations. But he knew enough about her type. He'd seen ladies pull those tricks. Making herself attractive, innocent, and honorable enough, and getting under Spencer's skin to keep him coming back for more.

She was as responsible for his brother's death as her father was. As Preston himself was...

The thought tasted bitter on his tongue.

And therefore, there was just one thing he needed to do. He stood up from the breakfast table and went to stand next to her to watch the guests depart. Through the old glass, he saw the blurry figures of Grandmama, Calliope, and Richard get into one carriage. Miss Alexandria Beckett and Lord Beckett climbed into the other. Sebastian and Emma's carriage had already departed.

For a moment, he wondered if Penelope felt lonely now that her family had left and she was alone with him. He surely did, every day of his life.

How could one feel lonely in such a joyful and friendly family as his? With parents who'd loved each other and their children. With a grandmama who'd spoiled them rotten.

And yet, he was the only one of his siblings who hadn't spent his whole childhood at the Grandhampton country seat. He had disappointed his mama and papa so much with his rebellious, reckless behavior, with his silly rivalry with Spencer, they'd felt like they had to punish him, or he'd never change.

So, instead of being taught by a tutor at Grandhampton Court, he had spent most of his childhood at a boarding school near Eilean Donan in the Scottish Highlands. It was cold. It was dark. It was miserable.

But the worst was to know he was so bad, so unworthy, that he was the only one of his siblings who'd been cast away. He'd been surrounded by people but always felt alone.

Even for a spare, he was a poor one. And especially now that he had to spend so much time in this temple of the Dukes and Duchesses of Grandhampton. Every day he felt how distinctly Spencer belonged here while he did not.

If Penelope felt anything remotely similar to that isolation, he felt sorry for her.

And yet the next moment, he shook the thought off. Even if she may feel lonely, she had brought this on herself. Her emotions should be none of his concern.

"You're a duchess now," he said, his voice sounding as if he'd eaten gravel. "I expect you to perform your duties. Do you understand what they entail?"

She nodded and raised her head proudly. "I know what's expected. I'm the daughter of a baron. My mother taught me well."

Her voice broke as she said that last part, as though there was a pain behind those words. Right. Her mother wasn't present today.

Regret not to have seen his own mama and papa, as well as Spencer, stabbed him. Mama had died six years ago from fever and pneumonia, as many people had that year. Papa had worshipped his wife. He had been all about duty, and Mama, the daughter of a Spanish marchioness with blood ties to the Spanish branch of the Habsburg dynasty, had brought life and joy into his world. When she died, Papa's own health started to decline quickly, as though he gave up on life. Papa had died a year later from an apoplexy. One day, he was alive. The next, he fell down in a palsy. He was gone the next night.

Preston suppressed a wave of sadness. Was that how his wife had felt, too, when she'd lost her own mama?

No. Preston shouldn't care. He shouldn't pay attention to the little pains and hurts in her voice or if she found the whole situation—or him—agreeable.

And yet, he had to ask. "Your mother passed, didn't she?"

She nodded. "Six years ago."

"Just like my own," he said, his voice quiet and hoarse.

"I'm sorry to hear that," she said, all animosity gone. "What happened?"

"It was the epidemic of fever that swept the country," he said, his memories full of that one last, horrible night when Papa and his three siblings and he had all sat by her bed, for once united before the greatest fear of their combined lives. "Spencer and Richard were sick afterward, too, but they survived."

His wife's eyes were wide and wet. "That was what my mama died from, too. I was taken with the same illness, and I wasn't with her when she passed."

Their eyes locked, and for a moment, they were just two people united by the same grief.

Then he frowned as he recalled learning that it was six years ago Penelope's father had started gambling heavily. A pang of regret shot through his nerves. He knew how grief could drive a man to act rashly. Look at what he himself had just done.

He'd just locked them both into marriage for the rest of their lives.

She was supposed to be Spencer's. The thought slammed into him like a stormy wave. And she was partly responsible for his death.

He should keep both of those thoughts in mind.

"If your mama taught you well, I don't need to tell you that the life of a duchess means throwing lavish balls, dinner parties, and house parties as well as supporting charitable organizations and sponsoring musicians. You're expected to have the best, most tasteful gowns, shoes, jewels, gloves, hats. You will be busy keeping up your appearance, and that may lead to a great deal of stress as you strive to uphold the ideal. The highest rank in society doesn't just mean riches and a glamorous lifestyle." He gestured around the hall. "It also means higher expectations. And be prepared for scrutiny and criticism from the bitter and the jealous."

She shook her head. "I didn't ask for this."

That struck him as odd. Although there were challenges, a fortune hunter surely would rejoice at the abundance of funds available to shop and treat herself to the latest fashions at a modiste's, and to buy herself jewelry. And she now had not just wealth but status. As a duchess, she was as close as royalty as one could be in Britain. She could finally let go of her mask of innocence...

"That, Your Grace, we have in common. I did not ask to be a duke, either. Spencer was supposed to fill this role."

Their eyes locked, Spencer's name like a rope between them, connecting them. Was it sadness that he saw in her face?

No matter. He turned away from her. He should just lay it all out for her and be finished with this conversation before he started to give in to this strange desire to know more about her.

"There are certain rules you must obey," he said, looking at the blurry images of the carriages moving out of the courtyard.

"Excuse me?"

He stared at her. It was better like this, watching the frown of her pretty eyebrows, the flare of her gentle nostrils, the tension in her full upper lip about to curl up in an angry snarl.

"You're my wife," he said. "There are rules that you must obey."

She raised one eyebrow, staring at him in perfect composure. The only sign of her distress was her chest rising and falling quickly again.

When she said nothing, he slowly walked to the table, feeling her eyes following him.

"Rule number one," he said. "As a duchess, you'll need a budget for new gowns as well as all other feminine things. You shall have as much money as you might wish."

"Is that your rule? Buy myself dresses and gowns and things?" She crossed her arms over her chest, making her breasts plump up.

"No," he said, struggling to keep his eyes away from them. "The rule is that you must not give a penny to your father."

Her hands dropped to her hips. "Are you being serious? He's in trouble!"

"I know. And that's exactly the point. I do *not* want you to help him. As my wife, you must obey me."

She glared at him. "Or what?"

Bloody hell, why did she need to look so pretty in her anger, all flushed cheeks and red lips, her eyes brilliant and glaring?

The sight of her, so pretty...and so *his*...stirred something in his blood.

He approached her slowly, backing her up against the tall paned window. "Or you will be punished. Obey me, and I will provide for you and satisfy your every need," he said as he imagined relieving her of her gown, freeing the laces of her corset and dragging it down her body. Tearing up the damn chemise she no doubt had underneath.

"Every need," he said as he forced his gaze to meet hers. Her eyes darkened. From blue gray, they were now the color of a stormy sea. Good. Color rushed to her cheeks and her neck. Even better. He could smell her, vanilla and sweet orange and apple...and something of her own scent that he found the most irresistible of all.

"But disobey me," he said, running his knuckles down the side of her face, "and I will be forced to punish you."

Her lips parted in a tiny, silent gasp. An image came to mind, Penelope spread over his knee, her delicious bottom there for him to do as he pleased...smack it till it was rosy and she was squirming from pleasure...squeeze it...bite it... His cock hardened and twitched.

"And rule number two, Duchess," he said, brushing his knuckles against her cheek. Good God, how did she have such silky skin? "If you dare run away again, I will ruin your father. I do not mean just financially. He will lose his title, his honor, and, possibly, his life. Though, of course, not by my hand."

Grief for Spencer and guilt over his death covered him in a dark, bitter wave.

He rushed on, not wanting to get swept under. "As for my final rule, you have one week. I will not visit you tonight. I am not in a habit of taking advantage of women in distress. But after one week, I will expect you to perform your wifely duty. You will give me an heir and a spare."

With dark satisfaction, he watched her eyes widen, her cheeks flush with color, and her lips part.

Oh, those lips... The memory of their kiss had driven him mad every night since. He ached once again to fall into her soft, lush, velvety kiss.

He cleared his throat, tearing his gaze away from her mouth, and met her glaring eyes.

"Are you surprised? Surely, you must have expected that. We are husband and wife."

"No... I just... I..."

She didn't continue, and he could swear he saw embarrassment all over her face. Embarrassment when he had been so sure she was a flirt...and more experienced than a young lady should be?

He threw away any doubts about his previous opinion of her. If he let her charm him and soften him up, he'd be completely off his plan. He couldn't have any feelings for his wife. He just couldn't.

He swallowed hard and walked to the door.

"You have one week to get used to the idea," he said over his shoulder without looking at her. "Be ready."

8

"I'm leaving tomorrow with the morning mail coach," said Alex as she set her teacup down onto its saucer.

This was Penelope's second day as the Duchess of Grandhampton, the second day of her living in Chalworth Place, her new home. Only, it didn't feel like home, and even less so with such an announcement from Alex.

"Do you have to so soon?" asked Penelope.

Something trembled and shook in her chest. Alone. She'd be so, so alone here. With a cruel, unfeeling husband, whom she hadn't seen since their wedding, and in this ancient, cold mansion that, despite housing many things, felt empty.

Alex cocked her head slightly and smiled. "Your papa can't chaperone me everywhere. And you're married, so you can't, either."

"But I can!" Penelope protested. "That is exactly what I can do—help you get more introductions, get you into the balls... ensure you enjoy your first London Season!"

Alex reached out across the corner of the tea table. "Oh, darling," she said, her dark eyes glistening with empathy. "I'd love to, but I can't. I only came to London to see you, but now you're going to be busy, and I'll only be a nuisance when you should be spending time with your new husband and adjusting to your new life."

"But—"

But she'd be so alone without Alex. Her papa was unwelcome by her husband, and Alex was the only other relative Penelope had in London. She didn't really have any true friends, no one who knew her as well as Alex did...as well as Spencer had. No one she could talk to about her dreams and what was in her heart.

Penelope's heart was heavy with fear and sadness, but she refused to let those feelings consume her. Despite the crushing disappointment of her shattered dreams and the anger she felt towards the man who had caused them, she was determined to forge ahead and make the most of her new life.

"You're right, darling Alex," said Penelope, forcing an encouraging smile onto her face, though Alex grew blurry through the tears filling her eyes. "You should return home. Your mama and papa must miss you."

"They do," said Alex. "And all these glittering ballrooms and dashing gentlemen and secrets and intrigues of London aren't for me anyway. I'm a country lady. I miss walking in the fields and exploring the woods, and my garden."

Penelope nodded, understanding despite her own sadness. "Give my very best to my aunt and my uncle, please."

"I shall. And please, visit soon, would you?"

"Not before I summon you because I'll be so sad and missing your company."

"I will come as soon as you call," said Alex.

Penelope didn't say that she wished she'd spare them the time and just come to stay at this house with her now. It would have made her feel so much braver if she had a friend nearby.

But she couldn't be so selfish and ask Alex when it was clearly not what she wanted.

And so, when Alex finished her tea, they said their goodbyes. The last words from Alex were, "Please, please do not stop painting. You have a true talent, and I wish to see your paintings hanging in the best establishments and homes in the country."

And with that, she was gone, and Penelope was left utterly alone in the big, dark house that felt like a tomb.

That night, an insistent knock at Penelope's bedroom door made her jump. Her hand jerked, leaving a dark green blot over the line of trees she had been painting so carefully with watercolor. Exactly in the wrong place, where she wanted to have the biggest contrast of bright sunlight and the shadows of a pine forest. Drat!

She glanced at the clock. Almost half past nine; Grandhampton must be having his dinner. She knew he must expect her to join him, but she had claimed to be unwell. Spending an entire meal alone in his company was too much to bear.

The knock repeated, louder and even more urgent. Penelope put down her brush, jumped up from the chair and the easel, and turned around, wiping her paint-smudged hands over her gown and immediately regretting it. She'd never have done it had her heart not been slamming so loudly and so quickly. She looked down to see blue streaks on her cream gown. She had a perfectly suitable muslin cloth lying on the gorgeously carved mahogany desk for just this purpose.

The door opened, and he barged in, his nostrils flaring. She stepped back in a silly attempt to cover her painting and supplies, like the few times her father had come to her room like this.

The duke scanned her and the painting supplies, then

blinked. "You do paint," he murmured, his gaze lingering on the painting behind her.

She swallowed. Would he scold her like her papa? Find another reason to judge her? Forbid her from painting and throw everything away?

"Of course I do," she said, her sweaty hands clutching at the skirt of her dress.

"It's just your father said...at Almack's..."

She scoffed. "Indeed. He said I was not an artist and did not do any such nonsense. He has forbidden me to paint for years. He is convinced a woman's role is only to be a wife and a mother. As, no doubt, are you."

He scowled at her. "I do not share this old-fashioned opinion. My mama raised us to value a woman's independent mind, and I sorely disagree with your father."

Penelope blinked at him. Could he be the same man? How could the man who'd forced her to marry him believe a woman deserved any independence of thought or action?

"So...you don't mind me painting?" she asked.

"No," he said, and his gaze returned to her watercolor. "I don't mind you painting. In fact...I'm not such a great art connoisseur as my brother was, but I can see you have some skill. I only mind about three things, and I told you them yesterday."

Relief and delight mixed in her chest in one incredible cocktail. Was she even hearing him right? She had assumed he would forbid her everything that brought joy to her, including her art, but it seemed she was mistaken. Not only that, but he'd also just complimented her. And for the one thing that truly mattered to her.

"Right..." she said, somewhat dumbstruck. "Your three rules."

"My three rules," he echoed back slowly, his eyes lingering

on her as though seeing her for the first time. Then he shook off his thoughtful expression and scowled again. "Mrs. Brown said you're unwell. It's the second night that you're in poor health and can't have dinner with me. I have come to inquire after you."

Penelope swallowed hard. This was almost like her dream from last night. On the wall to her right, a dark mahogany door connected her and the duke's bedrooms—it was much smaller than the grand door to her bedroom through which he'd just come. In her dream, he'd barged in just like this, and she'd gone completely still in her bed, staring at his tall figure, just a shade lighter than the blackness behind him. Then he strode to her slowly, keeping her in the prison of his unyielding gaze. But she couldn't move. She knew he'd come to take her, even if he'd said he would give her a week. And like the king of shadows, he slid onto the bed next to her and kissed her, his lips gentle and yet firm, his mouth taking hers possessively. He wrapped his arms around her, drawing her to him, every inch of their bodies melded together...

Her treacherous nipples hardened at the memory of the dream, and an odd ache at the bottom of her belly made her skin cover in sweat. She needed to shake off this odd bewitchment, so she walked over the plush rug with intricate red patterns to the large fireplace with stone molding. She stretched her hands to the black grate with burning coals crackling inside, although she was already so hot, she felt like fire itself.

She kept her gaze locked on the shiny black surface of the grate, on the glowing coals visible through the holes. "I'm rather tired."

The duke's steps sounded closer, muffled against the carpet. Then he stood next to her. She didn't need to see him. His presence was like an orb of warmth of its own—she could feel it on her skin. "You do not look tired," he said. "And I see that you are well enough to paint. Which gives me hope. Join me for supper."

She turned to him then. Good heavens, they were alone. It was so dangerous to be alone with him. They either argued, or he kissed her...

Whatever she did, she shouldn't look back at the large four-poster bed with the scarlet hangings and matching bed cover. Especially given her dream. She shouldn't let herself be drawn to him in that way. She should keep herself together or he would surely consume her.

"Not tonight, I'm afraid," she said.

His gaze darkened. "I gave you time to get used to me when by law and by right you had to become mine. Having supper together is getting used to each other, but you're still defying me—"

The thought of spending time with him, even if it was eating in the dining room with several footmen present, made her stomach churn.

"Can you blame me?" she cried. "You're my jailor!"

A dark smirk crossed his face. "Your jailor? Oh, you have no idea."

Need he be so handsome in his black tailcoat and his black breeches, the dancing fire of the candles standing on the mantel reflecting from his dark eyes and hair and giving his olive skin a beautiful glow.

But however handsome he looked, however he had disarmed her just now with his permission to paint, with his compliment on her skill, she must remember he was the devil himself.

She straightened her neck and her shoulders. "You are determined to ruin my father for reasons you hide from me. You are telling me how to live my life."

"Am I?" he asked, his nostrils flaring.

"You are. But, Duke, no matter what you think to yourself... You. Do. Not. Own. Me. I will never belong to you."

Their eyes locked, and she was sinking in the black depths of his irises. She breathed heavily, glaring at him. He glared right back. It felt like the heat of the grate ignited the air between them.

"It is you who are mistaken, Duchess," he said in a low, dangerous voice. "I was patient with you. But you need to be taught a lesson. You are mine now."

He crossed the two steps between them, and his arms wrapped around her, locking her into the prison of his embrace. His lips sealed over hers, hot and delicious and wicked. She softened for a moment—but she knew she wasn't his, wife or not.

She needed to show to herself she was stronger than this aching need, this warm melting.

She pushed against his chest, expecting a struggle.

But to her shock, his arms left her, and she was suddenly quite free.

He stared at her, blinking, his eyebrows drawn together, the expression in his wide eyes murderous.

"Very well, madam," he said. "If that's how you want to play it. I will never force anything a woman isn't willing to give. Therefore, I will find more pleasant company."

9

Preston rushed downstairs, Penelope's rejection stinging, though he didn't understand why it should. One of the footmen swung the door to the dining room open for him, and he stopped and stared into it. Four other footmen stood at attention as well as the butler, Porter, a dignified man in his sixties with tilted eyes and thick, almost white hair. Porter glanced at him and then back at the beautifully decorated table with two place settings ready.

This was Spencer's dining room, where he could have been sitting with Penelope for his first dinner with her as man and wife.

And because of Preston and Lord Beckett and Penelope herself, that would never happen.

Emptiness spread through his heart like poison through his blood. He couldn't sit here, dining with the ghost of his brother and the specter of his doomed marriage.

No. He needed to leave.

Run.

"I'm not dining tonight, Porter," he said. "Tell Mrs. Brown to send something up for Her Grace."

With that, he left. He didn't know where, just away. The carriage was already waiting—he'd ordered it as he needed to go out after dinner. Despite his angry words to Penelope, when he laid his hand on the cold, smooth surface of the carriage door handle, he knew he wouldn't go to a prostitute. He had a hunger for a woman in his blood. But it wouldn't be satisfied by just anyone.

It was her, the damned vixen upstairs, whom he wanted. No one else would do.

"I will never belong to you," she'd said.

And she was right. She never would because she would always belong to Spencer. And even if she had never loved his brother and had only been leading him on for his money, Preston began to understand why Spencer had been so enthralled with her.

"Where to, Your Grace?" asked Sam, his favorite coachman, a tall young man with kind eyes. Sam had a special talent with horses, Preston had always thought.

Where to, indeed? He wanted relief, something physical to ease this anger and this unexpected desire. Should he bother his fencing instructor, Mr. Bowen? No. It was dinnertime. He didn't want to take the man away from the dinner table with his wife. Boxing, perhaps? No. The sport was too ghastly and brutal. Not sophisticated enough. He had dabbled in it but never felt the joy of it like Spencer had.

He took in a deep breath of the spring air. It smelled fresh and flowery and warm. Like a new beginning.

Exactly what Spencer should have enjoyed with the woman who was upstairs and wed to Preston now.

This marriage was doomed if the husband was looking for an escape from it on the second day—and the wife had never wanted it in the first place. He wasn't sure why he cared in any event. Marital bliss had never been his goal from this union. He'd wanted revenge and he'd gotten it.

Deep down he had always hoped the wife he'd eventually take would be a good match for him. Having seen his parents madly happy and in love, he knew it was possible, even for dukes. His best friend, Sebastian, was incredibly happy with his wife, whom he loved dearly.

Preston had botched any chance of that for himself the moment he'd decided to marry Lord Beckett's daughter.

He looked up at the first floor of Chalworth Place. Her windows were on the outer side, not on the inner courtyard. From this side, the dining room windows glowed as Porter, the footmen, and the maids no doubt cleaned away the table. The stone walls were dark, the faces of lions and dragons and angels like dark spots in the night.

It was such a contrast with Sumhall and Grandhampton. These were the places where their father and mother had loved them. Two houses full of light and love. Quarrels and games. Until the one terrible event that had landed him in boarding school.

"To Elysium," he said.

"Elysium, Your Grace?" There was an implicit question in Sam's voice, like he was checking if the duke was really sane. "The one in Whitechapel?"

"Yes, in Whitechapel," Preston barked and got into the carriage. As if the man hadn't taken him there before. Perhaps, quite understandably, Sam was surprised Preston should visit the exclusive whorehouse the day after his marriage. He really shouldn't have barked at him like that.

The filthier the better, Preston thought as the carriage moved, rattling against the cobblestones.

In twenty minutes or so they reached Whitechapel...

They rode past medieval houses with roofs half gone and stone staircases so worn out they sagged in the middle. Windows with glass panes broken and never replaced. Streets with puddles of sludge that were like sinkholes in swamps so deep, carriages got stuck there after rain. Whitechapel was the home of criminals and robbers, prostitutes and scum.

And inside it, hidden like a pearl in the mouth of an oyster buried deep under the muck, seaweed, and shipwreck at the bottom of the sea, was Elysium.

They arrived and Preston got out, eyeing the building. From the outside, it looked just like the rest of the buildings on the square—brick row houses with the windows on their first and second floors gaping black while the ground floor pub and brothel windows were alight. Inside those houses, no doubt, criminals taught children how to pickpocket, burgle, and, perhaps, even kill. Young women with few prospects and no family learned how to ply their trade with their bodies.

Like the others, Elysium was a brick building of three floors that spread the whole block to the left and to the right. The upper floor was dark—no doubt, the private quarters of the owner. Regular pane windows were aglow with candlelight on the ground floor and the first floor.

Although it was all brick and paned windows, Elysium didn't look as old as the rest of the neighborhood. Six sharp triangles were arranged in a semicircle over the entrance door, creating the sign of a sun's rays that the members knew it by.

Just like the final resting place of Greek heroes and the virtuous, Elysium was a place where one could gamble and dine and eat and drink and indulge in one's physical needs—whatever they were—as much as one wanted, without being judged, and without consequence.

Everything was possible in Elysium, which was owned by

Thorne Blackmore, the infamous Mister B, one of the most dangerous men in London.

He passed through the front gate and presented his membership card. It bore the same symbol of the sun's rays in sharp triangles, his name printed underneath. The guard, who recognized Preston, nodded and let him through. He entered the dark vestibule where a footman stood to take coats, but Preston didn't have one.

From there, he walked into the great hall. It was dark, the wood-paneled walls painted an elegant, dark teal with gaslit sconces illuminating them. Several crystal chandeliers with candles gave the hall, which was full of round tables with gentlemen of all ages dining, a soft, golden glow. The scent of something delicious wafted to him. Vichyssoise, he rather thought as he let a footman guide him through the ornate passage formed by round tables and chairs. He recognized several noble members of the ton. Others, he didn't know, though they were dressed as well as the aristocrats.

While he waited for his dinner, Lords Robbins and Mander came in and plunked into the seats opposite him at the table.

"Ah, Grandhampton!" cried Robbins. How many times had Preston spent nights of debauchery with him, Sebastian, and others? It was odd to be here without Sebastian, but quite understandable now that his best friend was married. So was Preston, but his wife hated him. "Did your wife kick you out of your marital bed?"

"Right!" said Mander, who was a shorter young man with a double chin and a round belly. "It was rather unexpected to read about your wedding this morning."

Since these two weren't members of Tyche, they wouldn't know he'd bought Penelope's hand at an auction. But he had no intention of telling them, so he said, "The reasons for the haste should be of no consequences to you."

"Right"—Robbins winked and gestured with his hand to suggest a rounded stomach—"the consequences..."

Preston found his fingers curling tightly around the wine-glass. "Do shut up."

Then their dinner was brought—the first course of vichyssoise—and the men started eating.

And Preston started drinking.

As he ate, he watched three pythons writhing in the branches of a marula. A panther paced its cage on the other side of the room.

His companions babbled about something or other next to him. He didn't really listen. Until Robbins said, "I was wondering, Grandhampton, why you never before showed any interest in your bride."

"I heard, and please correct me if I'm wrong," said Mander, "that she was for sale."

"Ah," said Robbins with a cheeky smile. He frequented brothels like a lady frequented a modiste. "Is that true, Grandhampton?"

Preston felt rage boiling in his gut. He may not love Penelope and never would, but she was still his. His wife. Spencer's love.

Before he could reply, Robbins said, "If you're still unsure about her... That is, if the marriage isn't consummated, do let me know and I'll do it for you—"

It was Preston's drunk mind. Nothing more. Surely not any desire to defend his wife's honor that made him jerk up, his arms reaching out, fists curling around the man's collar. He dragged Robbins to a standing position, brought his fist back, and slammed it into the man's face. The sound of the hard slap of flesh against flesh cracked the air, and a satisfying pain burst through his knuckles. He hit him again and again, meeting nose and cheekbone and eye. Blood burst through the man's nose.

He couldn't move his arms anymore. Several men held him by the shoulders.

"I'm sorry, Grandhampton," said Robbins, holding his nose. "I didn't mean to disrespect your duchess."

"Do not show your face here ever again," growled Preston, rage still seething within him, his vision red.

"*You* must leave, Your Grace," said one of the men holding him. "Please leave. Your membership is hereby revoked."

"Damn it," muttered Preston as he walked towards the exit with the floor swaying and tilting under his feet.

He didn't remember how he got back to Chalworth. Perhaps he'd fallen asleep in the carriage. He only remembered going to the only room he felt was a refuge, his study. Then he found Spencer's letter and cried reading it.

Then he remembered nothing.

10

Penelope beat her fist into the pillow under her head. Her room was dark, and the duke was long gone—probably in some brothel kissing another woman, since Penelope's company was so repugnant to him.

The coals must have died in the grate, and even under the thick blanket, she was still cold. She watched the shadows of moonlit tree branches dancing on the wall above the elaborate fireplace. As the wind moved them, they scraped against the window. She turned and looked at the ceiling over her head. Mahogany beams crossed in perfect square patterns with dozens of carved faces in their center, surrounded by a perfect wreath of vines, staring at her.

Unease crawled along her spine. She missed her home. She missed Alex. And, oh goodness gracious, how she missed Mama. She sent a prayer to Mama, for the hundredth time, wishing to ask her for advice, for support...for a kind word of reassurance. Anything to make her feel strong and determined again. Anything to get her through this.

But she was alone. So alone.

And she'd be alone for the rest of her life.

With only the dying coals, the scraping tree branches, and the unseeing faces to keep her company.

No.

She sat up. That was not who she was. She had hidden away in her bedchamber long enough. If this was supposed to be her new home, she wouldn't let some carved wood and overgrown trees intimidate her.

She turned in the bed and placed her feet on the soft carpet protruding from under her bed, then put on her house slippers. Then she sparked the flint and lit the candle on her bedside table.

In the dim light, she picked up her shawl from the chair by the bed and wrapped it over her shoulders, then stood up. The candlelight casting even more wild shadows against the walls, she walked towards the door separating her and the duke's bedrooms and pressed her ear to the cold surface. She listened for a while, but there was not a sound.

He must still be out.

Good. Without him present, she could do anything.

She opened her main bedroom door and walked out into the corridor. Light fought the darkness away as she bravely walked towards the stairs, ignoring the screeching of old floorboards and the whispers of the wind through gaps around the windows, and God knew what else.

She'd been told there was a large library downstairs. It must contain books on art. This whole house was like an art exhibition, the pride and joy of any art collector. It was her home now, so she ought to make it her home.

She opened the door to the library and gasped softly as her candle cast light on a large room with bookshelves covering every inch of the walls. There was a massive writing desk, two sofas standing by the dark fireplace, and several chairs for reading were spread throughout the room. It smelled like books—pungent and holy. She smiled as she went to one of the shelves and ran her fingers across the spines. There couldn't be ghosts in this room. And if there were any, they'd be friendly. She'd have much in common with them.

She briefly noted the author names and book titles as she moved along the shelves. She'd walked the perimeter of the whole room when she noticed a door to what must be another room. What could it be?

Feeling cheeky, and with curiosity bubbling in her stomach, she pushed the door open and froze. Her candle crackled softly as did another one standing on the desk by the window of the smaller room, which housed fewer shelves and fewer books. On the chair next to the desk sat her husband, his chin resting on his chest.

Snoring gently.

The sleeves of his shirt were drawn up to his elbows, exposing his powerful forearms. One arm rested on his stomach, the other hung with what looked like a letter held between his index and middle fingers. His long, muscular legs were resting wide apart, and she swallowed hard as her gaze crawled up his thighs and landed on the place between them...

She swallowed and drew her eyes away. This felt wrong. It felt like an intrusion, like she was taking advantage of the duke when he was so vulnerable.

And yet, she couldn't look away.

Gone was the scowl from his face. Gone was the ever-present expression of disdain and distaste he wore when he looked at her.

She drew closer to him, stepping softly against the wooden floor. Treacherously, it creaked. Her heart leapt, but the duke didn't move. His chest rose and fell slowly and evenly. As she stood right next to him, her skin tingled.

She felt like she was the one in charge now...in control, frozen in fascination watching a sleeping predator.

He looked so young and at peace, his forehead smooth and relaxed, his mouth soft and his lips full. So handsome, with those high cheekbones and straight features, the eyebrows so long and thick and angled, his closed eyelashes casting dark shadows under his eyes.

This must be his study. She broke her gaze away from him and looked around. There was one large window with closed curtains of a royal blue color. Three paintings hung on the walls. Two of them were of landscapes, but she barely gave them a glance because all her attention was swallowed by the third.

It was a painting of Danaë. Penelope knew of it because she had studied Greek mythology, but also, this painting was in her mother's book about art. Danaë was naked and glowing, lying in a daybed. A shower of gold coins rained over her.

According to the myth, Danaë's father had held her captive because he'd heard a prophecy that Danaë's son would kill him. For years, Danaë was in a dungeon, imprisoned and alone for something that hadn't even happened yet.

One day, Zeus heard about her imprisonment and came to her in the shower of gold, and he freed her. Of course, it was Zeus who fathered her son, Perseus, who then eventually did kill Danaë's father.

Penelope swallowed hard, her breath rushing in and out as she gazed at the smooth, voluptuous curves of the woman as Zeus rained coins over her, the hope in her face as the gold cast light into the darkness that must have surrounded her for years. Zeus had come to free her from her unjust imprisonment.

She couldn't look away, imagining how Danaë must have felt, having a god make love to her and knowing she was going to be free thanks to him. Did she love Zeus? Did she hate her father for imprisoning her?

Did Penelope imagine there was someone like Zeus who would help her break free from the tyrant sleeping in the chair?

She turned to her jailor, who was still asleep.

Before him, brown folders and papers sat in stacks across the desk's surface, with a bright red folder in the middle. Interesting. Then her gaze was drawn to the piece of paper in his hand again. What was he reading? Carefully, she walked to him and gently tugged the sheet from between his fingers.

Bringing her candle closer, she saw it was a letter.

She shouldn't pry. It was someone's correspondence. How could she invade their privacy—Preston's privacy? She sighed and tore her eyes away from it. She really wanted to know what it was.

But her fingers shook with the knowledge that she could peer behind the iron wall into something that Preston may never reveal to her. This man was a mystery, and she wanted to know more. Perhaps she could even learn something that would set her free.

And so, she read...

London, 3 September 1812

Brother,

I know we do not see eye to eye on many things. Including the subject of Miss Beckett...

She looked at Preston. Miss Beckett—her? Why did Spencer write to his brother about her? She returned to the letter...

"...I know you do not think highly of her..."

Right, of course he didn't!

"...but she is not the manipulator and flirt you think she is. I'd like to explain to you once and for all why I am so fond of her."

Manipulator! Flirt! Her? She scoffed and shook her head. So Spencer knew how his brother thought of her. She continued reading.

Grandmama is right. We fight over nothing. Mama was always disappointed in me for being too prideful to ever let you win. As you were prideful, too. I suppose, in that sense, we are more alike than we wish to admit.

It was my fault, after all, that you were sent to boarding school, and not yours. And yet you never told on me. You took my fall.

For the sake of Mama's memory, I'd like to stop fighting and become the brother you never had: the loving one.

Please come to the match in Portside as agreed tomorrow night.

Your loving brother,

Spencer

Penelope stared in confusion at the sleeping Preston. She had so many questions.

What did Preston take the fall for? Why did the two brothers argue about her? And who could have thought that Spencer felt something for her when she believed he was just being a rake?

The letter in her hand trembled. The memory of Spencer grabbed her, froze her to the core...the handsome, arrogant, powerfully built man with flawless manners. A perfect duke, they called him, and even his womanizing and his charming, rakish ways were overlooked by some. Eventually, it was assumed, he would settle down—once he satisfied his manly appetite, leaving dozens of ruined virgins and scandalized widows in his wake.

Spencer had always had something to say. With him, conversation had flowed easily. She'd found him to be a good friend and pleasant company, a seamless balance of respect and charm.

And with his approval of her art plans, she hadn't felt quite so alone.

A dark shadow rose quickly, and her husband stood before her. She gasped. He tore the letter from her hand, all his earlier softness and peace gone.

Before her stood the awakened lion.

And he was enraged.

"What do you think you are doing?" Preston demanded.

His own voice came to him like a thunderclap. Spencer's letter was in *her* hands. She had just read it, no doubt, the bloody minx.

Preston threw Spencer's letter onto the desk's cluttered surface.

This woman hadn't just stood between him and Spencer as a constant cause of arguments for months—she had just invaded the last good thing that connected Preston and his brother.

Preston's head pounded so hard, he couldn't think straight. Nausea rose in his stomach; no doubt the result of all that brandy at Elysium.

"I'm sorry..." she said, her big blue eyes glistening.

Empathy stabbed at him, but he brushed it off. He wouldn't let her manipulate him into feeling undeserved pity. If it wasn't for her, Preston and Spencer wouldn't have fought the night Spencer died. Spencer wouldn't have gone to Portside alone—Preston should have insisted on joining his brother no matter how annoyed Spencer was with him. Then Preston would have been there to save his brother from the beating. And they would have become true brothers, like they were always supposed to be.

"How dare you look through my personal things?" he growled.

"I wasn't looking for anything! I just...I didn't know you argued about me. Why did you argue about me?"

Preston shook. Why did they argue about her? Rage seethed through him. And to add fuel to the fire, she was dressed in an almost transparent nightdress. Her skin shone through the fine lace on her chest. She wore no corset—of course she wouldn't wear a corset for sleep—and he could see her beautiful nipples through the fabric, rosy and tight and puckered. His gaze dropped down the straight cut of the nightgown. No petticoats. She wore nothing underneath, just her warm flesh.

He could run his fingers up her legs and come to the apex of her thighs, and there she would be, bare and free...for him. Would her skin feel warm and smooth? He clenched his fists to stop himself from reaching and finding out for himself.

This was wrong. He should never feel this desire, this hunger for her. Spencer had loved Penelope. Marrying her was nothing more or less than Preston's desperate attempt to do right by his brother and avenge his death.

That was all she could ever be to him.

The memory of the last night they had fought over her pierced his mind like lightning. Spencer had been right to point out Preston's pride.

"You're your own worst enemy," Spencer had said. "Your quick judgment and your stubborn unwillingness to change your opinions. Your pride will drive away all who would love you. Do not come to my fight tonight."

So Preston's pride had driven away the brother who would love him. In the end, he was the reason Spencer went to the docks alone. The reason he died.

"Leave!" he roared so loudly she blinked, visibly shrinking.

"No," she said, straightening her shoulders. "I'm sorry I read your private letter. I shouldn't have. But I won't leave until I know why I am mentioned there."

"Leave!" he roared louder, helpless rage tearing at him.

"Duke, you must be hurting after his death. Did you reconcile? What happened?"

"I said, leave!"

"Not until you explain to me—"

That was it. If she wouldn't do as he said, he'd make her. He took her by the elbow and pulled her close. Her soft breasts felt delicious pressed against his chest.

"You want me to explain something?" he said right into her face. "Let me be clear. You do not demand anything. You listen to me and do what I tell you to do. You will leave and go to your room. In three days, you will dress like a proper duchess, and we will go to Lady Leroy's soirée where you and I will appear as a married couple for the first time. Until then, I do not want to see you or hear from you. Do not mention my brother's name ever again!"

With that, he dragged her to the entrance, pushed her out of the room, and slammed the door in her astonished face.

Shaking, he let out a long breath and went to sit on his chair. He picked up Spencer's letter and smoothed it with trembling fingers. His head was killing him, but it was nothing compared to the pain of guilt roaring inside him. He read the letter once again and hung his head, exhausted, aching inside and out.

Was he really furious at his wife for reading this letter...or was he terrified she'd learn what was truly going on deep inside him?

Not just his guilt over Spencer's death.

There was something else, something much worse that he hadn't noticed before. There was a small part of him that was glad it was not Spencer but he who had married Penelope.

Did that make him a horrible human being? Had he secretly wanted her all along?

11

Two days later, Penelope's dear husband barged in during lunch, reeking of perfume and alcohol, with dark circles under his eyes.

She thought he might have exaggerated his desire not to see her, but she had tried to stay out of his way. Still, she'd asked Mrs. Brown about him last night and had been told that he'd gone out.

"Ah," he said to her, lifting a piece of chicken fricassée from her plate and stuffing it into his mouth, chewing with a satisfied moan. Penelope stared. "My wife. Attempting to plaster on a smile and fake a happy appearance, I see. How typical."

She gasped. "Sir, you're not behaving like a gentleman. Are you drunk?"

He hemmed, eyeing her, and swayed. "On that, I do agree with you, darling. What else should I do rather than drink? My future is bleak. I must spend my life with the woman I'd never have married had my brother not died."

With that, he left. Penelope's cheeks flushed and burned as

she noticed sideways glances from one of the footmen who stood by the wall.

Later the same day, Calliope came for tea. It was a pleasant distraction from the conflict with Preston, and Penelope was surprised by how much they had to talk about. Calliope was very intelligent and a strong woman with a mind of her own.

Penelope set her cup in its saucer and placed both on the tea table. The sitting room was the one room in the whole of Chalworth that looked feminine. The walls were a gentle pastel yellow, and showcased paintings of the sunlit, rolling hills of an English countryside in bloom. The clear windowpanes let the sunlight in, and pastel turquoise curtains hung from the ceiling, topped by a pretty valance. A large rug of yellow and turquoise patterns covered most of the floor.

"My mother decorated this room," said Calliope with a sad smile, looking around. "The last time I was here must have been eight years ago. Spencer always came to Sumhall to visit, even when he started living here. Mama hated this house. She always said it was pretentious and cold. The sitting room was the only place she was allowed to change. It's quite feminine, don't you think?"

Penelope nodded. "It is. I must say, it's my favorite room in the house."

Calliope picked up her teacup. "Mine, as well. How are things with my wretched brother?"

Penelope swallowed and reached for a biscuit. Tears welled in her eyes, but she fought them back. "It's...it's an adjustment."

"He's not being rude with you, is he?"

Penelope inhaled sharply. "I would not want to speak badly of your brother."

Calliope sighed. "So he is. Please, be honest with me. I only wish to help. And I know he can be very stubborn."

"Still, I wouldn't want to—" Penelope lost the battle, and her eyes blurred with tears.

Calliope covered her hands with hers. "Oh, please, tell me what is the matter. Clearly, he made you upset. You're my new sister. Please, tell me."

Penelope's shoulders slumped. Calliope's eyes were so kind. And Penelope had no one to share her troubles with, no mother to ask for advice. Perhaps Calliope could advise Penelope on how to live with her new husband in peace.

"Truth is, I don't know why your brother married me when he hates me so much. He bosses me around. He tells me to my face how poorly he thinks of me. He gets drunk and goes out all night..."

Calliope sighed. "Drinking all night? He's a married man now and should be giving up his rakish ways. I'm sure he will once he adjusts to this sudden change. He can be difficult to get close to, but deep inside, he's very sensitive. He's protective. And has the biggest heart."

He hadn't forbidden Penelope from painting. Though that didn't prove anything about his kind heart. "Very deep inside, perhaps," said Penelope. "And very well hidden."

Calliope patted Penelope's hand. "The truth is, he was hurt by Spencer's death so much more than he admits. He and Spencer fought like two enraged cocks, but he almost always went to support Spencer at his boxing matches, and Spencer went to cheer him on at his fencing matches. Once, Spencer took Papa's favorite horse and went riding when he wasn't supposed to. When he returned and it was lame, Preston took the blame. And he was always the first one to protect me against my parents when I did mischief as a girl."

Penelope frowned. Could the duke really have been a selfless boy like that when all he did was jeer at her and treat her like his enemy? She suddenly remembered something from the letter.

"Were Spencer and Lord Richard sent to boarding school?" she asked, picking up the teapot and refilling Calliope's teacup, then her own.

Calliope frowned. "No. Only Preston was. Why do you ask?"

Penelope lifted her teacup and fingered the handle. "Why only him?"

Calliope bit her lower lip. "He told you about that, did he? All right. Since you already know... It happened at Grandhampton when Spencer was ten and Preston was eight. I was told about it much later by Spencer. Apparently, they fought. It was Spencer who instigated it. They were outside, pushing, shoving each other, running after one another. There was a construction site at the back of the building and new French windows had been brought in. Spencer said, in the heat of the moment, he shoved Preston quite forcefully. Spencer had always been bigger and stronger, but Preston was smaller and faster. And so Preston dodged and ran away. Spencer, however, lost his balance and plummeted right through the window, which stood leaned against the half wall. Then he fell over the wall and down into a pit."

Penelope gasped softly and set down her teacup, imagining the two brothers fighting the way they did, so dangerously. "What happened then?"

"Spencer almost bled out. It was quite bad, and Mama and Papa were traumatized. Preston didn't tell them it was Spencer who began the fight and Spencer's actions that led to the fall. He said it was his fault. I'm not sure, exactly."

Penelope gripped the handle of her teacup a bit too firmly, listening with rapt attention.

"But Papa and Mama got such a scare about Spencer," continued Calliope after she paused to take another sip of tea. "They all thought he'd die. So Papa became very angry with Preston, saying how tired he was of Preston's disobedience, of his tricks, and now he was actually dangerous. He sent him to Scotland, to the Mackenzie boarding school near Eilean Donan. The Mackenzies are our distant relatives... I think it was the eighth Duke of Grandhampton that had married a Mackenzie—perhaps that was where Papa's auburn hair and blue eyes came from. Anyway, poor Preston spent every year at the boarding school taking Spencer's punishment and never said a thing to Mama and Papa."

Despite herself, Penelope imagined Preston, a dark-haired boy with stern black eyes somewhere up north in the mountains where it was cold and dark and desolate. Missing home. While his brothers and his sister spent every day of their lives with their mama and papa who loved them.

That must have been so lonely for him.

But she shouldn't feel sorry for him just because Calliope had told her a couple of stories. Perhaps he'd been loyal to his family. But he certainly wasn't loyal to her or to her papa.

"Your testimonial does him justice," she said.

Calliope nodded. "Give it time. We were all surprised by your engagement since it was always Spencer who was enamored of you."

Penelope squinted. Right, that was what the deceased duke's letter had implied. "I always thought he only viewed me as a friend. I've only recently learned his feelings went beyond that."

"Truly? Well, he was a terrible rake, so it's understandable that you might have been confused by his attention. I don't know why he didn't speak with you and make his intentions clear. But there's nothing for it now. What matters is you and Preston. He has been struck by grief more than any of us, I must say. Spencer and Preston constantly fought about everything, but I always knew it was because, deep inside, they were too similar. That's why they quarreled. Not really because they hated each other. Because they loved each other."

That, certainly, was true according to Spencer's letter.

"Please, do not give up on him," Calliope said. "Try and see the good things about him."

Penelope nodded. "I will."

But the truth was, she couldn't. Not right now.

"There's one more matter I meant to talk to you about... Are you coming to Lady Leroy's art soirée tomorrow night?"

"Yes," said Penelope. "The duke told me we will attend."

"Well...I heard..." Calliope looked down and wrung her hands. "I heard a strange rumor," she said softly. "There was some question if you would be entirely welcome there."

Penelope frowned. "Why?"

"I'm not certain." She looked up and met Penelope's gaze, concern showing in her expression. "Perhaps it has to do with the urgency of your marriage. There was no announcement in the papers. No courting."

Penelope's stomach squeezed nervously. She'd never been a favorite in the ton, but she'd also never been a true outcast. She was already married, so the consequences to her reputation weren't as significant as they would be if she were unwed.

The only thing that truly mattered to her was her reputation as an artist, the ability to paint and sell her work. Her connection to the Duchess of Ashton and other influential people in the art community could be damaged by a poor reputation.

"Could they believe there was some impropriety between the duke and me before the wedding?" Penelope asked.

"I didn't hear anything specific," Calliope said. "But I will investigate and see what can be learned." She reached over and gently squeezed Penelope's arm, her eyes warm and kind. "Do not worry, sister. Whatever this nonsense is about, we will stand by you."

12

On the day of Lady Leroy's soirée, Penelope's new gown arrived from the modiste. Her maid helped her dress and did her hair in an intricate updo as Penelope's stomach twisted with worry over Calliope's words the previous day.

The duke stood at the bottom of the stairs when she made her way down, with gentle lavender satin flowing around her body. Preston looked up, and his eyes widened and burned, his gaze gaining intensity to the point that he looked positively menacing.

A shiver ran through her. A tiny part of her had wanted to impress him. Mrs. Newman had created a very pretty gown, worthy of a duchess, with lace and crystals sewn into the bodice in vine patterns.

He nodded to her as she reached him, and without a word, they went to the carriage. The silence as they rode was palpable.

"Your name was to be stricken from the list of invitees," Preston said. "But I refused to allow it. I beg you, do not undo my efforts and embarrass me."

So, Calliope was right. Somehow, she was disgraced. The churning in her stomach made nausea rise in her throat.

"Why?" she asked. "Because you might regret you forced me to marry you? Don't you already regret it?"

"I do not want you to dishonor the name my brother carried."

That kicked all the breath out of her. She couldn't argue with that.

She looked at him. "Grandhampton, I...I could never dishonor his name."

His gaze, still intense, lingered on hers. He swallowed, nodded curtly, and looked away.

They arrived at a pretty house on Burlington Square. It wasn't as big as Chalworth Place, but was a concise brick mansion with green ivy covering half of its facade.

When Penelope and Preston entered the brightly lit ballroom, the guests froze and stared at them just as they had when Preston entered Almack's. Penelope's breath caught at all the attention. He was right. This was their first social outing as Duke and Duchess of Grandhampton.

Preston paraded her through the ballroom with bright, modern colors and furnishings. Such a stark contrast to Chalworth with its dark interior and the grim faces of former dukes and duchesses. The duke kept introducing her to marquesses, marchionesses, earls and countesses, their sons and their daughters. She knew some of them from her previous Seasons, but normally she stayed in the background, not seeking out introductions to those above her station—apart from the Duchess of Ashton, of course.

The walls were mint green, divided into rectangular panels separated with gilded braided detailing. Oval mirrors hung in the middle of some of the panels, making the room appear bigger and brighter. Paintings hung on the panels between them, and Penelope ached to stop and look at every one of them. A string quartet played Bach in the corner of the room. Footmen slowly walked among the guests with trays of drinks.

Preston introduced Penelope to the hostess, Lady Leroy, a tall lady in her forties, who gave Penelope a quick, judgmental appraisal and then plastered an artificially pleasant smile on her face as she talked only to Preston. It seemed his efforts had gotten Penelope into the soirée but no further.

When Lady Leroy made an excuse and left them, a lady in her fifties came up to them. She had a beautiful face with big icy-blue eyes and wore a turban with long peacock feathers sticking from under a sapphire brooch—a recent fashion. She gave Preston a toothy smile, showing her rather rabbitlike front teeth.

"Grandhampton," she said as she fanned herself. "What a pleasant surprise."

"As it is to see you here, Lady Whitemouth," he replied. "May I present my wife to you."

She looked Penelope over from head to toe. "Of course, Your Grace. May I congratulate you on your nuptials? Of course, the news that a lucky lady managed to get the Duke of Grandhampton to settle down shook us all."

Was she fishing for the reason behind Penelope and Preston's quick betrothal, as Calliope had assumed? Penelope wouldn't give the woman an excuse to gossip. When Penelope said nothing while merely offering her a smile, some of Lady Whitemouth's bravado faded. "How is Chalworth, your new home? Do you find it to your liking?"

Anger stabbed at Penelope. She didn't like it, not really. It was uncomfortable and cold, and it was like living in a public ballroom instead of a real home.

Another lady and a gentleman joined their little circle. One of them was introduced as Lady Isabella, the Countess of

Whitemouth's daughter. The gentleman was introduced as Mr. Stalt.

"I love the famous Seaton family art collections," said Penelope, reaching to find something she actually appreciated about her new home.

"And what is your favorite art piece?" asked Mr. Stalt.

"Oh..." said Penelope, "certainly *Danaë* by Rembrandt."

"Why that one?" asked Lady Isabella.

Penelope swallowed hard, feeling the duke's gaze on her like a warm touch. "Even though she was imprisoned because of something beyond her control, she persevered. I love the inner glow and strength in Danaë and wish every woman in her situation had that."

She met her husband's hard gaze, tingles going through her body.

"Perhaps Danaë brought it on herself. Have you ever thought of that?" asked the duke sharply.

"Said every tyrant ever." Penelope held his gaze defiantly.

"Excuse me, did I hear you speaking of Rembrandt's *Danaë*?" said a man in his late thirties as he drew closer to their circle. He had a long face, large, narrowly set eyes, a long, slightly crooked nose, and bold, angled eyebrows.

"Yes, Mr. Turner," said the Countess of Whitemouth. "The Duchess of Grandhampton was just saying it's her favorite piece in Chalworth, her new home."

The floor under Penelope's feet sank as she stared at the most talented and famous artist in Britain. Her impossible dream would be to learn from him and be his apprentice. His paintings were spectacular.

"Mr. Turner?" whispered Penelope. "*The* Mr. Turner?"

"If you mean the artist, Duchess, he is," said her husband with steel in his voice.

“Pleased to make your acquaintance, Your Grace,” Mr. Turner said with a polite nod and a small smile.

Penelope practically felt her husband’s disapproval. Well, of course he would object. He was displeased by her breathing under the same sun as him. She shouldn’t care. She was used to male discontent—twenty-one years with her father had ensured that.

She beamed at the artist. “The pleasure is all mine, sir. I am a big admirer of your work. Your *Fishermen at Sea*, which I saw at the annual summer exhibition in the Royal Academy… I went there with my mama… I remember staring at that moon aglow, the boat full of men fighting the angry sea, and I couldn’t look away. That was one of the first moments I knew I never wanted to be without a brush in my hands as long as I lived.”

The people around her were silent, and when she saw her husband’s face, quite surprisingly, there was no scowl when he looked at her. His expression was open and relaxed, the walls of anger and hurt down.

That was when she saw what Calliope must see when she looked at her brother.

“I am grateful for your testimonial,” said Mr. Turner. “I do not know that I deserve it, but I’m most grateful. Like you, I do not ever wish to be without a brush in my hand as long as I live. That was so well said.”

“Excuse me,” said her husband without tearing away his eyes from her, “I must have an urgent word with my wife. Duchess, if you please…”

He gestured towards the direction of the exit and followed her. His gaze felt hot and heavy on her back as she made her way between talking, laughing, flirting, gossiping people. She was sure many of them looked at her, the new Duchess of Grandhampton, whispering to each other.

Once they were in the hallway and out of sight of the guests, he grasped her by her elbow, covered by her high glove, and tugged her behind a curtain in the corner, which was blocked by a large plant next to the tall window.

They were plunged into darkness, illuminated only by a strip of moonlight that fell through the window. She breathed heavily as he loomed over her, every inch of his tall, hard body pressed against hers, her own heartbeat thumping loudly in her ears.

"Grandhampton—" she started, not recognizing her own throaty voice.

He didn't let her say another word. He kissed her, hot and soft and demanding, feasting on her lips like they were a dessert he couldn't get enough of. His tongue...oh, his wicked, daring tongue glided and probed and entwined with hers.

He tasted like wine and something pungent and delicious, and his own taste that she wanted more and more of. His scent was in her nostrils, his arms around her, gliding over her back, and then moving to her bottom and squeezing it.

The onrush of hot desire that spread through her at that gesture made her legs sag, as weak as pudding.

Then his hand cupped one of her breasts and massaged it. Her flesh tingled, her nipples became as hard as marbles and ached. Pleasure rushed to her sex, which felt swollen and throbbed strangely and deliciously.

When she gave a moan right into his mouth, he groaned back, like a pained animal with as much need as was in her.

He lifted one of her thighs and dragged the edge of her gown and her petticoats up to her hips, his big, warm hand leaving a trail of fire on the flesh of her inner thigh free from her stockings.

Oh, what would he do? What could he mean with his hand—

And then his fingers were diving into the folds of her sex, and she jerked and gasped.

"Duke—" she tried, alarmed, bothered, wanting him there.

"Shh," he said, his hooded eyes dark and burning with desire. "This will be good. You will enjoy it. Come here."

He covered her mouth with his again and returned to the kiss, the kiss that left her head empty and her body full. Full of sensations, of pleasure, of need.

His fingers moved in her folds, exploring, teasing. And then he found a place that felt like the epitome of all that was sweet and good in her body, the center of everything.

She gave out the most decadent moan, not caring if a footman would pass by, or the Countess of Whitemouth, or even Mr. Turner himself. All that mattered was this throbbing that needed to be satisfied, something beautiful and wonderful that her body required—and that he could give her.

He kept rubbing and rubbing, and the sweet agony was increasing, building, bringing her higher and higher, somewhere close to the sky. She was getting broader and heavier, and her muscles as pliable as honey.

And when she thought she couldn't take it anymore, he gently pinched her in that wonderful place and tugged a little.

And something came over her...like the moon pushing away the darkness of the night clouds. Pleasure greater than that of seeing all the paintings in her whole life combined came crashing over her.

He closed his palm over her mouth as she whimpered, moving in waves, clutching at his shoulders as his other strong arm held her tight to his chest and wouldn't let her fall.

Then the ocean of pleasure was gone, and she was like a heavy sack of muscles and molten bones, saggy in his arms. She breathed against his hard chest, inhaling the scent of his clean clothes and his masculine cologne, and his body. There was something large and hard pressed against her belly.

"What was that?" she asked him as she looked up at him, meeting his dark gaze.

"A demonstration of the pleasure that I can give you when you're in my bed," he said, his voice like brandy. "In three days, you will become my wife in every sense."

"What?" She frowned, the closeness and intimacy of the moment gone. She straightened and stepped back to the wall.

"Do you remember our agreement? An heir and a spare. Then you can live your life however you want, without me."

Anger burst through her at his cold treatment. How could he be so tender and caring one moment and the next throw her away like a used carpet? And how could she have responded to his touch so?

"Life without you?" she scoffed and pushed the curtain away. "I cannot wait, Duke."

13

It was exactly one week since Penelope and Preston had gotten married.

Penelope's hand shook, and the line of the bark of a tree that she drew in her sketchbook became wavy and uneven. The summer garden she'd been sketching from her imagination looked stormier and more gothic than she would have liked.

Her husband, who sat on the sofa opposite her reading a paper, expected to bed her today.

After the world-shattering experience he'd given her behind the curtain of Lady Leroy's soirée three nights ago, he had gone cold as stone again, confusing her. How could he be ice-cold one moment and then ignite her with one touch the next?

And that release of pleasure he'd given her at the ball... She'd never known something like that was even possible. Clearly, even with his harsh and unforgiving ways, he knew what he was doing.

She thought about packing her belongings and escaping.

Despite the way Preston had made her feel, and her delicious dreams about him, the thought of any more physical closeness with him made her very nervous. She had already given him her freedom.

Now he wanted her body.

"Lord Beckett to see Your Grace," said Porter as he came into the sitting room.

Penelope's head shot up, her pencil frozen over her sketchbook.

The duke dropped the paper onto his knees.

"Papa is here?" asked Penelope.

"He is, my lady," said Porter, a fleeting expression of concern passing over his face.

Preston jumped to his feet. "Please tell him Her Grace is not at home."

"What?" Penelope shook her head. "No, of course don't tell him that. Please bring him here. And please bring us tea."

"Very well." Porter nodded and left the room.

Penelope's eyes locked with Preston's. "You forbade me to help him, but you cannot forbid me to see my own father, Grandhampton."

Preston said nothing, only glared at her in silent fury.

When the door opened and Papa came in, Penelope fought the urge to hide her sketchbook under the cushion. She didn't live with him anymore. He couldn't forbid her anything.

"Papa." She nodded to him.

Papa pressed out a smile on his reddish face. He fidgeted with his hands and rubbed his palms over his breeches as he met Preston's eyes. Her husband glared at him without a word.

He looked around. "What a marvelous sitting room you have here."

"How can we help you, Lord Beckett?" asked Preston coldly.

"Duke," said Penelope. "There's no need to be rude. Papa, please, sit down. Tea will be brought soon."

Papa nodded and briskly sat on the sofa opposite her. Surprising her, Preston walked over and sat on the same sofa as her. He picked up her sketchbook and placed it on the table between their sofas.

Papa's gaze dropped to Penelope's unfinished sketch, and she felt her cheeks blazing, expecting him to reprimand her. But he seemed to have merely noticed it.

"I came to inquire after you, daughter," he said to her. "How are you settling into your new life?"

The door opened and Porter came in with the tray of tea. He set it down and poured cups for the three of them, then retreated from the sitting room.

As she watched her papa pick up his cup and sip from it, she thought there was a mask of false politeness over his features. He tried to look pleasant, but Penelope didn't remember him being especially polite with her since Mama died.

"I'm settling in well," she said as she picked up her own cup. "Thank you for inquiring. How have you been, Papa? Is your health well?"

He waved his hand. "No, not very, my dear. Headaches... stomach troubles...this and that."

Penelope frowned. Was it from his drinking?

She had just opened her mouth to ask when he looked around the room, his gaze lingering on the marble bust of one of the previous dukes, on the paintings, on the vases.

"Very beautiful art you have here," he said. His eyes stopped on Penelope's painting, one that she'd had the footmen hang on the wall instead of an old medieval painting of a horse. In fact, she had asked to replace a few paintings in the house with her own, and, to her surprise, she hadn't heard a word of protest from her husband. This particular one was something she'd finished quite quickly, a watercolor of a vase full of peonies. It seemed to brighten the interior even more as the flowers practically glowed, sunlit and almost translucent. "Like that one. That must have cost you a fortune to acquire."

Penelope's stomach dropped. Of course her papa wouldn't recognize any of her paintings. But that he assumed it was a valuable professional painting made her heart soar.

"That one was painted by your daughter," said Preston, his dark eyes sharp and glinting on her papa.

Penelope hadn't expected her husband to say a single word to Papa. And did she hear a note of pride in his voice?

"Do you think your daughter an artist, Lord Beckett?" asked her husband.

Then Preston brought his china cup to his mouth and his beautiful lips curled around the edge to drink the tea.

Papa wriggled on his sofa. His jaw ticked so hard, the curls of his powdered wig moved. Penelope tensed. She had a perfectly fitted new gown on, the color of black pearls, that slithered over her body like liquid fog, thanks to the incredible talent of Mrs. Newman. But it suddenly felt like it had become too tight.

"Artist?" Papa's eyebrows snapped together like two opposing magnets. "Perhaps that one is a good painting, but that doesn't mean you're a true artist. Do you still have those silly notions, Penelope?"

Penelope shrank in her seat. What else could he have said when after her mother's death six years ago he had gone into her room and thrown her easel through her window and into the garden? The sound of the shattering glass had deafened her.

She should say something. But just like she'd promised her

father then that she would abandon any artistic ambitions, she pulled her shoulders deeper into herself and tucked her chin in. Her breathing became shallow.

"I do," she said, despite the desire to protect herself, her body rigid as a suit of armor.

Her husband's eyes narrowed on her. But, unlike her father's, they weren't menacing. She wished she could read his expression.

Papa scoffed, then drank his tea and dropped his cup into the saucer so hastily it clunked, threatening to break.

"You do not!" he exclaimed, focusing his milky eyes on her. "No woman should be an artist, a writer, a lawyer, or a physician. Women simply do not have brains for such professions. Their place is at home, raising children and making sure their husband is happy and has everything he needs."

Penelope put her own cup on the tea table. Grim daylight made her father's features appear grayish. Embarrassment ran through her. But why should she feel embarrassed or humiliated or at fault in any way? She had let her father bully her her entire life, had let him turn her greatest passion into a dirty secret.

"I wish you wouldn't say that, Papa," she said firmly. "I certainly have a brain. Mama had a brain, too."

That was like a blow to his midsection. He cowered into himself, his eyes dropping to the ground, his shoulders folding.

"I do not mean it in a bad way, Penelope," Papa said. "It's simply the way of things for women. The sooner you accept it the better. I only want to spare you humiliation. You should not hope to be an artist, only to be disappointed by public opinion."

How could one person be both so right and so wrong? It

was true that women weren't accepted into the Royal Academy of Arts, no matter their background or social status. William Turner was the son of a barber and his mother's family were butchers. And yet, he'd been accepted into the academy when he was fourteen years old. And now, his work had been exhibited there several times, and his were some of the most sought-after paintings in England.

And yet, she, the daughter of a baron, wasn't allowed to be a member.

Although she didn't think social status should be a deciding factor, either, and wished to be judged on the merit of her work alone.

But perhaps her father was correct about one thing. No man would love a woman who knew her own mind. None would want her for who she was.

So her choice was simple, really. Either submit to society's ideal of what a woman's life should be—sitting at home, birthing and raising children, and hosting her husband's boring parties.

Or be unapologetically herself.

But before she could firmly decide upon which of the two paths she wished to embark, her husband's voice shook her and made her jerk up on the sofa. "I have never been more glad that Penelope is my wife," said the duke coldly, and yet bringing heat to every inch of her body. "And I do not think I've ever disagreed more with anyone in my life than I do with you, sir. If my wife wishes to be an artist, I think that is spectacular. I think she has more brains than you, sir. More brains than most men I know."

Penelope's fist clutched around the carved wooden handle of the sofa. She could not have just heard such a statement of support coming from him—from the man who loathed her and thought she was a fortune hunter! She peered into

Preston's face, but his profile was as cold as always, his dark eyes firmly on her father. His mouth curved into a strange smile, and she had the helpless desire to kiss those lips.

He had uttered only a few words. But no one had ever protected her like that.

Preston met her gaze then, heat and a meaning she couldn't decipher burning in those onyx depths. This was different than before—why? She felt the edges of her lips curve up in a smile.

"Grandhampton," her father said, clearly annoyed. "If the world is ever in a state when women can do the same things as men, we will surely be plunged into chaos. It will be the beginning of the end. Who will bear children?"

Penelope stared at him, no fear this time. "Women can do both, Papa."

Papa's face turned into a vicious snarl. "You do not know what you speak of, foolish girl."

Preston's nostrils flared as he sat straight up and leaned forward, his face a stony mask of warning. "If you ever dare to speak with my wife so again, sir, I will be obliged to knock your teeth out. Do not ever think to belittle my duchess or try to humiliate her."

Penelope blinked, her body swaying in her seat. The shock of hearing him protect her left her speechless. Papa gritted his teeth, glaring at the duke.

"Please, enlighten me with the true reason for your visit. It is not to inquire after your daughter's well-being, is it, sir?"

Papa stuttered. "I-I-I assure you—"

"Spare me the pretense," continued Preston. "It is to ask her for money. Is it not?"

Papa opened and closed his mouth.

Preston stood up, towering over them both. "I'm afraid you have wasted our valuable time for far too long. My wife and I planned to take a walk. Porter will show you out." He turned his burning gaze on her. "What do you say, Duchess, are you with me?"

And while her whole mind screamed at her that she was foolish, that he couldn't be trusted, all her heart said was "I am."

14

THE BLUSTERING baron was shown out by the determined butler, and Preston returned to the sofa next to Penelope. When they were left alone, he studied his wife. Her big eyes were stormy despite the light coming from the windows. She looked positively regal in her dress with silver embroidered patterns of interwoven vines and her pastel blue spencer, a color that made her skin glow and her cheeks rosy.

Or, perhaps, her flushed face had nothing to do with the color of her clothes and everything to do with an open, calm, and even hopeful look in her eyes.

It was the first time since they had met that she'd looked at him like that, without anger or animosity.

Did he really know her before?

He hadn't known quite the extent to which Lord Beckett dared to offend and humiliate Penelope. But he shouldn't be so surprised. Was it really that astonishing coming from the man responsible for Spencer's death—a man who had auctioned off his own daughter? She really did seem quite different from the woman he had imagined her to be. Could he have been mistaken? Could Spencer have been right all along?

Preston may not see eye to eye with her on some things, but he despised how her father treated her.

"Your interest in art..." he said. "How serious about it are you?"

She frowned. "Why?"

"I had thought...in the beginning..."

He had thought she was estimating the worth of the paintings in Chalworth, not admiring them. But he decided not to tell her that, not wanting to get into another argument. She must be shaken from her father being so harsh with her.

"Never mind what I thought," he said. "Please, answer me. Is it serious?"

"Yes," she said. "It is."

"Why?" he asked.

She looked at her hands and bit her lip for a moment. "My mother started my interest in art. She was my inspiration. Every year, she took me to see summer exhibitions at the Royal Academy. When Mama passed..." Her voice shook, and Preston suppressed an urge to move closer and wrap his arm around her. "Painting became absolutely necessary for my sanity. I wasn't there when she died, being sick myself, and I've always regretted not being able to hold her hand in the last moments of her life. I miss her terribly, and painting is how I am able to talk to her...think of her...be with her...cherish her memory."

Preston nodded, guilt and sorrow crushing his heart. How he had misjudged her. That was who he was, Spencer was right, quick to judge and not so quick to forgive.

"And yet your father forbade it?" he asked. "The one way for you to keep the memory of your dead mother alive?"

She nodded, her eyes watering. "Indeed. My papa is an old-fashioned man. He can't imagine his daughter wanting to be a professional artist. I'd like to be the next William Turner. That is my dream. I didn't want to marry. I've always wanted to support my papa and myself through my art and not be restricted by the ties of marriage like my mama was."

Preston's jaw ticked. He was her jailor, just like her papa. She said she'd never wanted to be married. Could that be true?

He admired her independent spirit. A strong woman who didn't want to depend on anyone. He very much respected intelligence, diligence, and depth in women. He didn't know many besides his sister and his poor, dead mama who had those qualities.

"Except for my mama," she kept going, "I've had no one to teach me. Women aren't allowed into the Royal Academy of Arts. And I haven't had the opportunity to ask to be apprenticed by a professional artist. That would be a dream come true. But it's not possible anymore."

He frowned. "Why not?"

"Well...because of you."

"Me?"

"Didn't you say you wanted me to be a proper duchess and birth you an heir and a spare?"

"I did." Guilt weighed inside his chest like a boulder, and then anger ignited him. "So you assumed I'm like your papa?"

The thought made his stomach burn like acid. He had already told her he didn't mind her painting, but he supposed she might have thought he meant that she could paint as a hobby. Perhaps he had...he'd never really thought about his wife earning money as a professional artist.

"Well...yes. Aren't you?"

He went cold. Comparing him to that man... The man he was trying to ruin. The man who'd had Spencer killed...

No. Partly out of spite, he'd bring his daughter her dream

on a plate. She'd become a great artist and prove her father wrong, and he'd help her.

"Of course I'm not. In fact, I think you should pursue your dream and paint. And sell your paintings if you wish."

She blinked. "Why?"

There was no need to tell her about the "out of spite" part of his reasoning. He'd tell her the other part that he fully believed in.

"Because I think a woman should be able to do anything she has an ambition to do."

A smile bloomed on her face, so beautiful his heart stopped. Once again, and this time so much stronger, he didn't feel sorry he'd married her.

Because, somehow, she had brought light and life into his dark and lonely existence.

Ever since that dreadful day when Spencer had flown through the glass and lay in the pit with blood oozing from dozens of cuts, Preston had known he wasn't like the rest of his family. They were all cheerful, normal people.

He had pestered and pestered Spencer, tried his parents' patience, and rebelled, jealous of all the attention Spencer received.

And then, that had happened. Even though Spencer had taken the first swing, it was Preston who had egged him on. And Preston could have been the one to finish it, to apologize and walk away. But his stupid, stupid pride had kept him swinging his fists and pushing his brother.

So it was only fair he'd taken the blame and was sent up to the Mackenzie Boys' School. Away from his well-behaved brothers and sister. Away from his loving mother and father. Away from sunlit green fields and his mother's garden and the pond where Spencer, Papa, and he used to fish.

Instead, with other delinquent and unwanted aristocratic

sons, he was sent into the cold, rough Highlands of Scotland, where it always rained, and Eilean Donan towered somberly, a dark castle on a small island in the loch, surrounded by mountains.

Where he'd learned to protect himself by hardening his heart and keeping others at a distance.

"Fill this dark house with more of your landscapes," he said. "The peonies, the roses, the tulips. I like this place better with those old, gloomy paintings gone."

She blushed. "You noticed?"

"I noticed."

"And you don't mind? I thought you'd give me another speech about rules and such."

Didn't mind? He liked coming home to the sight of flowers instead of gray landscapes and dour portraits.

"I don't mind," he said.

"Thank you," she said, still smiling from ear to ear.

Something lightened in his heart, seeing her joyful like this. Damnation. That was another thing he liked immensely—putting a smile like that on her face.

And he certainly shouldn't.

The best thing would be to get this wild desire for her, these feelings for her, out of his body and his mind. Surely, once he tasted her, once he had her, he'd forget about her.

That had always worked with other women.

It was time. The seven days he'd given her had passed. He would deflower her tonight. She had fallen apart so deliciously against his fingers three days ago. He'd bring her that again and again. He wanted her to be his.

Porter entered the room and marched directly to him. He leaned close to his ear and said quietly, "Your Grace, there's someone at the servants' door at the back of the house waiting for you."

Preston threw a glance at his wife, who frowned at him with curiosity.

"Who?" Preston asked, keeping his voice low.

"I would never have let him stay, but the man said you'd want to see him. He's very distressed and says it's about Lord Beckett."

If this was about Lord Beckett, it could be only one person. His witness.

And if he came here, risking his own confidentiality, it must be serious.

His stomach sank. As much as he had looked forward to this night, as much as he burned to make Penelope his, it may need to wait. He may need to leave and wouldn't know when he'd return. He didn't want her to wait for him and then be disappointed. He wanted to take time for her. Take it slow. Make her ready.

He looked at his duchess. "You should not wait for me. I'll need to deal with something tonight, and I'll see you tomorrow."

He saw her disappointment. "Are we to dine separately tonight again?"

Regret twinged in his gut. He liked the newly established peace between them. He wanted to know more about her ambition for painting and about her childhood, and anything about her. But if this was about Lord Beckett, it may take a long while.

He stood up and went to her. Taking her hands in his, he had her stand and looked deep into her eyes. "Yes. But if you don't mind, I might come to see you after dinner."

"See me?" She frowned.

"Yes. In your chamber."

"Oh..." Delicious color filled her cheeks.

He stepped closer to her and did what he'd ached to do since her father left. He brushed his knuckles against her jaw.

"You don't mind...do you?" he asked.

Their eyes locked. Heavens, he could get lost in the depths of her blue-gray eyes, like the sea in a storm. Eternity passed before she answered, "I don't mind."

Lightness filled his stomach. He nodded, three of the most common words in the English language making his blood seethe and boil. Only because they came from her.

With Porter, he left the sitting room and went through the servants' door, downstairs into the servants' quarters. At the back door, he saw Noah, the servant from Tyche who had signed the testimony against Lord Beckett. He was a tall, scrawny young man with large eyes and an acute sense of honor. Preston guessed that was why the man had come to him; he couldn't stand to see injustice done to an innocent man.

Only, Preston didn't want justice. He wanted revenge.

"Your Grace," said Noah by way of greeting.

"Are you all right?" asked Preston, looking the man over.

"I am, yes, Your Grace. Only, Lord Beckett went to see Mr. Eastbourne last night and told him one of his employees must be spying on the guests. Mr. Eastbourne started questioning us one by one. It won't be long until he finds out I helped you. I don't know how, but he will. He's a dangerous man."

Preston nodded. One of the most important principles of Tyche was secrecy, and Noah had broken it by coming to Preston. Eastbourne might punish him himself or he might go to court and have Noah tried for petty treason because he had betrayed his employer—a possible hanging offense.

Preston said, "Do not worry, Noah. I'll protect you. Don't return to Tyche." He reached into his pocket and gave the man several bank notes. "I'll arrange for a carriage, which will take you to Grandhampton. You will start working for me as a footman there. I'll write to Mrs. Liddle, the housekeeper, and Harney, my butler there."

Noah nodded. "Thank you, Your Grace. I'm most grateful."

"It's quite all right. We knew it might come to this, but I will see that nothing happens to you."

Preston nodded to man and turned to go and look for Porter, to ask him to arrange a carriage for Noah, when a figure came out from behind the corner of the servants' hall.

His wife...pale, wide-eyed, and furious.

"What did that mean? Why does my papa search for a servant who spied on the guests of Tyche? And why did that man come to you?"

Anger hit him like a blast. She'd snooped after him! "Don't you dare get into my private affairs. This does not concern you," he said as he brushed past her.

"It's my papa!" she cried after him. "Of course it concerns me!"

Part of him wanted to tell her everything. But he had to protect her from the truth. Her father was a bad man who had gotten Spencer killed.

"Trust me, Duchess," he said. "It is best you don't know. Not from me."

"You know what, Your Grace?" she said with a bitter grimace on her face. "Do not come to my room tonight. Or ever."

Her rejection stung him like a whip. Furious with her and yet unable to stop wanting her, he turned and marched back, glaring down at her. But she didn't retreat.

"*Ever*, madam?" he said through gritted teeth. "May I remind you, the seven days I gave you are up. You will be mine tonight, however disconcerted you may be with me."

Her nostrils twitched, her upper lip trembled. Oh, she was livid.

"And may I remind *you*, sir," she replied, her voice trembling with rage, "that you said you wouldn't take anything a woman wouldn't willingly give."

Indeed. He took one step closer, now standing just two inches away from her beautiful face. "And I meant every word," he said quietly. "Only, Duchess, you will give me everything I want willingly. More than that, you'll ask me to take it."

He brushed his knuckles down her smooth cheek.

"Because I know how to make you shake and tremble with pleasure," he said. "I already have."

Her pupils broadened and darkened even more, and he knew she wanted him. Despite her rage, despite the secrets between them, she still wanted him.

"Go to hell," she said. "Do not dare come to my room. I mean it."

She stormed past him this time, leaving him staring after her.

15

THE DUKE SENT a piece of cold roast beef into his mouth and chewed, his eyes never leaving Penelope's. She met his gaze head-on, but she wouldn't let him win. Whatever that meant.

For two days after their argument, she'd been furious with him, because of his deception, because of the secrets he kept from her. Because of his power over her body. He was right, blast it. She wanted more of his touch. Her treacherous body ached and trembled for him, and for the past two nights she'd stared at the door connecting their bedrooms, both anxious and excited for him to barge in, although she'd forbidden it.

Despite the four footmen who stood at attention by the walls to serve their luncheon, all her senses were on alert, with his eyes following her every move. The sun shone brightly through the paned windows of the breakfast room onto a luncheon table that held cold meats, pastries, cheeses, and plates of fruit.

As Penelope touched the glass of red wine, more to soothe herself than out of desire to drink, she noticed there was something playful in the dark depths of Preston's eyes. What did he have to be so cheerful about when she felt like she was about to burst? It seemed no one in her life had this effect on her usually good-humored disposition but him.

"Do not make any plans today," he said.

She stilled with the glass of wine halfway to her lips. "Pardon?"

He cleared his throat and chuckled. "That is, do not make any plans today, please. I have invited someone I'd very much like you to meet."

Penelope nodded. "You intrigue me."

He tried, and failed, to hide a smile of male satisfaction. "I like to intrigue you."

Excitement bubbled in her stomach, curiosity making her forget her anger for now.

After luncheon, they went into the sitting room. This was their ninth day of marriage, and it was the first time they'd had a luncheon together and gone into the sitting room together like husband and wife. Just as Penelope took her seat, Porter came in and announced, "Miss Enrica de Luca."

Penelope jumped to her feet, unable to believe her own ears. With her mouth wide open, she stared at the duke.

"How did you manage to invite the most talented female artist in England?" she blurted out.

Her husband stood up from the sofa to greet their guest with all the grace and confidence of a born aristocrat, while she felt like a child, everything inside her bouncing up and down from excitement.

Enrica de Luca was Penelope's inspiration. Originally from Italy, Miss de Luca had learned from her father and other masters in Italy before coming to England and setting up her studio here. She wasn't married; she didn't depend on a rich and powerful male patron. Her paintings spoke for themselves.

Penelope had seen several of her portraits at a spring exhibition last year.

They were simple, yet full of inner light. All of them allowed the viewer a glimpse into the subjects' souls. They were also open and sensual. It was as though, through their bodies, Miss de Luca revealed her subjects' true selves. Her work didn't just portray noble ladies and gentlemen, but also tradesmen, cooks, servants, and even farmers.

Penelope was still trying to catch her breath when Miss de Luca entered. Behind her, a footman carried an easel, a canvas, and a wooden case. She was a beautiful, short woman in her early forties, with big green eyes and dark hair. There was a look of detached amusement on her face, which, Penelope suspected, could be her natural state. Her eyes, sharp and observant, quickly scanned Penelope up and down, then the duke.

Penelope's breath stopped, her feet sinking. Why had Preston invited her? Why did her footman have the easel and the canvas and the case smudged with paint?

She forced herself to speak. "Miss de Luca, what an honor. Please, come in."

"Thank you," Miss de Luca said with a slight Italian accent, which made her sound even more beautiful and elegant. "But would you not like us to proceed to your studio, Your Grace?" she asked, her eyebrows rising. "I thought that was why I was here."

Penelope swallowed and met her husband's eyes. The twinkle there suggested he was covertly enjoying her surprise. "You are quite right. Please forgive my wife's astonishment. You are a surprise for her."

"Ah," said Miss de Luca, chuckling. "A pleasant one, I hope."

Penelope's throat contracted. "Oh, very. So very. For whatever purpose you're here, you're so welcome."

"I was asked here to teach you, Duchess," said Miss de Luca.

And while Penelope worked on finding her breath and trying to keep herself on the firm ground, her husband gestured to her in the direction of the doors, and they went. Being taught by a real artist was a dream, always far away and unattainable.

And now, it was right there, and only for her.

Penelope followed them to a room she'd never been in before. There was an easel with a canvas standing in the middle and more canvases leaned against one wall. Watercolor and oil paints lay on the table, as well as brushes, palettes, cloths, aprons, graphite pencils, and paper. The curtains were pushed all the way to the sides to let in as much light as possible. The walls, unlike any other room in the house, were painted in a neutral, light beige, giving an impression of even more light and air in the room.

Against one of the walls, there was a table with a white cloth on which sat a large bowl full of apples, grapes, and peaches.

As Miss de Luca and her footman proceeded into the room to set up her easel and her tools, Penelope stood at the doors, unable to move.

"This is for you," said the duke, standing by her side and looking at the room. "Your own studio."

She looked up at him; the stern profile she'd hated from their first dance looked soft and dear now. She fell in love with him a little then, despite all that had happened, despite knowing that he was hiding something from her.

But before she could reply, Miss de Luca turned to her. "If

only every woman was lucky enough to have such a supportive husband...”

Penelope walked into the room and went to stand by Miss de Luca’s side, her eyes still on her husband, who leisurely came into the room. “I suppose I am lucky. The deeper I look, the more I like what I see.”

Miss de Luca smiled. “In that case, how about we capture the wondrous man in question?” she said so everyone in the room heard her. “Would you sit for your wife, Your Grace?”

The look on the duke’s face was precious. All relaxation and quiet satisfaction evaporated. He looked positively horrified.

“No,” he said, stepping back. “Forgive me, no.”

Miss de Luca marched towards him and passed her arm through his. “But sì. Yes. Your wife would love to paint you, wouldn’t you, Duchess?”

Penelope’s heart trembled in her chest. She had drawn his face over the past few days over and over in her sketchbook. It was her attempt to understand him, to grasp him. To uncover his secrets.

But even more—to understand her own fascination with him. The fascination she shouldn’t be feeling if she had any hope of protecting her heart from him.

But she had torn each portrait out and burned it. Even worse than being fascinated by him would be him finding her work and knowing she couldn’t stop thinking about him.

And now, studying his gorgeous features under the guidance of a master, maybe she would come to understand why he had such power over her—how she could hate him and yet keep him in her thoughts.

“I would, actually, Your Grace,” Penelope said. “I would like that very much.”

The duke’s jaws tightened, and his Adam’s apple bobbed.

"No. I assure you, this bowl of fruit is much more captivating—"

Miss de Luca laughed and pushed him towards the wall. "My dear sir," she said. "I assure you, there is no sentence in the English language that is more false than that." She released Preston and pushed the table towards the corner. "You are the most captivating subject in this room. Except for your duchess." She winked at Penelope.

"Please," Penelope said and smiled at him, and then she said something she hadn't even considered saying before. "Please, Preston."

For a moment, he looked like he had been slashed by a saber or burned on a stake. Creases appeared on his forehead between his eyebrows, and there was a haunted, pained look on his face. Then he nodded.

"I will." And then swallowed hard, and added, "Penelope."

Her Christian name pronounced by him, with his voice, with that touch of ache was like a brush of a gentle hand against her naked back.

Miss de Luca was practically beaming, glancing between the two of them. "Excellent!" she exclaimed and clapped her hands once. "Now, Your Grace, would you please stand like this?"

She showed him a pose that Penelope saw often in Miss de Luca's most recent portraits, with his back straight, one arm propped against his waist, the other hanging down his body. One leg straight, the other relaxed and slightly bent.

Miss de Luca stepped back and looked him over. "Beautiful. Please, keep this pose."

Then she came to stand next to Penelope. Together, they made a rough sketch. Miss de Luca taught her that it was first about seeing the general forms—circles, triangles, squares.

"See how his body is a triangle," she mumbled as she

corrected Penelope's sketch on her canvas. "His shoulders are broad. His waist and hips are narrow. Look at his chest, it's more like a large rectangle."

"Yes, I see," said Penelope as she continued to draw the shapes outlined by Miss de Luca. She was right. There, underneath those clothes, Penelope could almost see the powerful muscles of his chest, like two rectangles. There must be a dip between his pectoral muscles, going down to his narrow waist. His stomach, if it was as hard as she remembered from when he had her pressed against him, must be all muscles, too. He was like one of those Greek statues, with six squares for muscles...and then down—

She pressed too hard against the canvas, and the graphite of her pencil broke. She gasped and Miss de Luca giggled, seeing at what place in the sketch it had broken.

She handed Penelope a fresh pencil. "Do not press hard, Duchess. Especially not in that area."

Penelope's face burned. "I didn't—"

"Glide your pencil over the lines of his body like a lover," said Miss de Luca. "Love him with your pencil as you would with your hand."

Heat burned Penelope's whole face, right to her hairline. She nodded, and when she caught Preston's eyes again, it felt like he didn't see anyone or anything else in the world but her.

She kept drawing, gentler this time. It felt like she was caressing his body with every touch of the pencil.

When Penelope started drawing his facial features, Miss de Luca came to stand behind her shoulder. "Very nice. Look into his eyes. The glint of light against the dark. The little dips and hills that form his eyelids, his eyebrows. Eyes are the windows into a person's soul. He's letting you in. What is it behind those eyes?"

Penelope's pencil moved, and what came from it was magnificent.

He was magnificent.

Despite his hatred, despite his actions towards her and her father, now, looking at him, she saw none of that. What she saw behind those eyes was a man with a beautiful, wounded soul.

And in his eyes, she didn't see animosity anymore. She didn't see her enemy.

She saw a grieving brother, helpless in his rage. She saw a kind man. She saw a man who loved his family. She saw an incredible strength of character.

And then she was done, and the sketch on her canvas looked like him.

Like the true him—not the one hiding behind a mask.

Even though in her drawing he wore clothes, the depiction made him seem bare and vulnerable. Defenseless.

"Congratulations," said Miss de Luca quietly behind her back. "You captured him better than anyone could. Better than I could."

Penelope chuckled and looked at her. "Thank you. I'm sure that's not true, but—"

"You are talented, Duchess," said Miss de Luca with a warm smile. "I see the potential of a great artist in you. Next time, I'd like to show you how to paint with oils, if you let me."

"Oh, I would absolutely love that!" said Penelope warmly.

Miss de Luca nodded. Penelope glanced at the sketch that the artist herself had done of Preston, and she was right. Perhaps hers was more technically perfect and bore more physical resemblance, but Penelope's was full of light and love.

"May I see?" came his voice, and Penelope suppressed an urge to cover her work, like she had every time her papa came near.

But she didn't need to anymore.

"Yes, of course," she said, stepping back. "But it's not finished."

Preston stood in front of the easel and studied her drawing for a long time. Miss de Luca and her footman busied themselves with packing her things. But instead of congratulating her or being pleased, Preston's face became somber.

"It's beautiful. Clearly, you're very talented," he said and met her gaze. "But I don't deserve to be portrayed so well."

"Don't say that," she said, taking a step towards him.

"I don't deserve a portrait like that because I'm not a good man. And you know that, too. More than anyone. That is why I'm surprised that this is the way you drew me."

"I do see you as a good man," she said, taking another step to him and laying her hand on his shoulder.

He drew her to himself like a force. She knew now what Calliope had spoken of. She saw the real Preston, the man under the social mask and the layers of anger and grief.

The man she was ready to give herself to.

He met her eyes and their gazes locked. For a brief moment, she imagined she could have it all. Her art. A happy marriage. Perhaps there was hope for her after all. Perhaps she didn't need to feel so alone.

"In fact," she told him, "come to my room before dinner. I'll show you exactly how I see you."

16

Preston knocked at his wife's door. The knock came out gentle, almost shy. He let his arm drop and suppressed the tremble in his hand, clenching it into a fist. Light footsteps approached from the other side. Then the door was flung open, and she stood before him.

Her eyes were bright and sparkling. And her dinner gown was a soft blush color, almost the exact shade of her lovely skin, with shining crystals and intricate silver embroidery. The image took his breath away. It wasn't exactly that she looked naked, but his mouth went dry at the sight of her, and heat rushed to his groin. His gaze dropped to her bust, and he didn't know where her body ended and the dress began. He could just imagine her rosy nipples.

He swallowed hard and forced himself to look at her face. "Here I am," he said hoarsely. "I have come before dinner, to your room. As instructed."

She nodded and stepped aside to let him pass. Inside her bedroom, before the fireplace, there was a small table set with a light supper of bread, butter, cheese, pigeon pies, cold tongue, and fruit, and a carafe of wine with two glasses. There were no footmen to serve them, no maids, and no butler. No one to observe and watch over them.

She stood in the middle of the room, clutching her hands. “I thought it would be nice to dine here, together, just the two of us.”

He nodded, his skin prickling with heat. “I like that, Penelope.”

Penelope... Heavens, he loved her Christian name on his tongue. It tasted divine, like ices on a summer day. As round and as refreshing, and as pure.

Pure...was she pure, indeed?

As he sat down at the round table, he watched her take her seat and select a slice of the cold tongue, her eyes warm and her lips curled in a soft half smile.

Preston stabbed a piece of cheese and sent it into his mouth. “I confess, you’re not what I thought you were.”

Penelope’s eyebrows rose in an amused expression. “I daresay. You thought me a superficial fortune hunter. What do you think me now?”

Knowing her better now, it was hard to imagine that she had been intentionally leading his brother on, encouraging him in his feelings while only thinking about his fortune and his status. Could he really abandon his previous convictions regarding her and stop thinking about her as an enemy?

But he already had, he realized, and he hadn’t even noticed. She wasn’t the enemy anymore. But she couldn’t be a friend, either.

He didn’t know what she was.

But he couldn’t allow himself to have any feelings for her, even if she was his wife. Because even if she may not be his enemy anymore, even if he assumed she was not at fault in

Spencer's death, she'd always be the only woman his brother had ever loved.

"No," he said. "I do not think you a fortune hunter or a superficial woman. You have a strong and independent spirit. You're very talented in the arts. You have wit and a kindness of heart."

And an amazing body; he still couldn't forget the feel of her writhing against him in ecstasy. Neither could he forget the scent and the taste of her on his fingers after he had pleasured her, and how her soft and hot flesh felt quivering against his palm... He'd have to fuck that memory and his need for her out of his system.

Tonight.

After that, he'd get bored of her and would return to his normal life, only lying with her until she was with child. An heir and a spare, that was all he needed from her. She'd have all his support to pursue her arts. He'd help her with his connections and pay the best artists to tutor her, and he'd make sure she got into whichever art exhibitions she wanted. Mostly, to show her father how wrong he was about his daughter. But also because she should have a happy and fulfilling life. He had taken away her choice to marry, and now he realized she was just another victim in this scheme. He'd do his best to make it up to her, even if he could never love her.

"Why, thank you, Preston," she said. "I noticed you my first Season. But I have always been so intimidated by you. If you thought all those things of me, why did you never ask your brother to introduce us and find out for yourself if they were true or not?"

"Because I knew I was right. I'm always right. And I didn't want to be wrong. It's my pride."

"But why did you think me a fortune hunter at all?"

"As I mentioned that night at Almack's, everyone in the ton

knows your father's situation, how poor he is. How he looked for a rich husband for you and failed to find one."

"Everyone except me," she mumbled. "I knew we weren't rich, but it was only when we came back from Almack's that he told me how bad things were."

"That is why he was desperately looking to marry you off."

"Marry me off? But he never mentioned anything to me."

"Nevertheless, he did. We are in the same circles. Men talk and gossip as much as women do."

"Then why did no one propose?" she asked.

"He was looking for the best candidate. The richest one. I heard one time, he found someone, but the agreement was broken off because of my brother."

"Your brother?"

"You were flirting with him. Don't deny it. You were. I saw you two. The smiles. The batting of eyelashes. You two giggled like two children. Because of his reputation and you two being so close, there were concerns about your purity."

Eventually, those concerns had led to Spencer's death.

She frowned and put her fork and her knife down. "My purity? Most of what we talked about was art. He told me about his childhood. About you. He was a good friend. I never flirted with him—I was only enjoying his company. Nobody else wanted to have anything to do with me."

"But tell me, honestly, swear that you never thought he was interested in you as a woman."

"I suppose you can call me naive, but I didn't. Have you seen the kinds of women Spencer was interested in? Gorgeous widows. Sophisticated, beautiful, perfect married women who were bored with their husbands. And me...clutching at a wall in the ballroom, burning from embarrassment if a man threw a glance at me? I always believed he thought of me as something like a younger sister."

Preston had never noticed how she burned from embarrassment. Whenever a young man had come to talk to her, she'd given one of those gorgeous smiles that lit her up from the inside, that lit up the whole room like a small, personal sun. She'd never looked shy or embarrassed.

"Little sister?" Preston scoffed. "He already had one. That night, when he went out to the docks and got beaten to death... that night, we argued about you. He was sure you liked him. He loved you. He wanted to propose. That was what we argued about."

Penelope froze, her eyebrows drawn together in confusion, her big eyes wide. She shook her head. "He wanted to propose?"

"He did. But I told him he was making a big mistake. Just from watching you, it was clear to me you did not return his feelings. I was sure that the affection you showed Spencer was false."

Preston remembered that doomed night as if it were happening in this moment. It had happened in this house, in Spencer's study.

The room smelled like brandy, Spencer's cologne—peppery and crisp—freshly washed clothes, and him.

Spencer threw back his brandy and placed the glass on the desk. "You only say she is fake because you're judgmental. You have never even talked to her. But you're wrong. No one understands me the way she does. She sees me for who I am. Not as a rich duke."

"You're delusional!" cried Preston. "That is exactly how she sees you. All I'm trying to do is save you from a life of unhappiness. She has not a penny in her dowry, so she needs a rich husband to pay off her papa's gambling debts. The thing she loves best about you is your fortune."

"Go to hell." Spencer stormed out but stopped at the door and turned. Little did Preston know, this would be the last time he'd see

his brother alive. "You're your own worst enemy," Spencer had said. "Your quick judgment and your stubborn unwillingness to change your opinions. Your pride will drive away all who would love you. Do not come to my fight tonight."

Preston should have insisted. He should have shoved his pride aside and insisted on going along to support him despite their disagreement. But his brother had just told him to go to hell.

"Very well," said Preston despite a heavy feeling in his stomach. "I have better things to do anyway than sit in your sweaty, dirty boxing pit."

And then Spencer had left. And that was the last thing Preston would ever tell his brother.

If Preston had gone with him that night, he would likely still be alive. Perhaps he would have proposed, and Penelope would be his wife. And Preston's sister.

So shouldn't he feel a horrible remorse for being glad that he had her now? Wasn't it as though he wished his brother dead?

"I was never interested in your brother that way, Preston," she said gently. "I did not know he misinterpreted my friendship as romantic affections. I'm sorry I gave him the wrong impression, it wasn't willingly. And I'm glad we didn't marry because we both would have been unhappy."

Preston's skin was covered in sweat. This shouldn't matter. Her words shouldn't matter.

But despite himself, he searched for the hidden meaning... *They*, Spencer and she, would have been unhappy.

"Out of all Seaton brothers," she said, "it was always meant to be you."

Heat scalded him whole. *It was always meant to be you...*

Preston and she...could they be happy? She had noticed him a long time ago.

No, he should stop this train of thought. Imagining her happy smiles every day because he caused them. Her quivering with pleasure under his touch. Coming back home to her, warm and gorgeous, in his bed. This lightness in his chest, this burning and yearning for her, satisfied. Turning from delight to happiness.

A life with her, a happy marriage...

He shouldn't think like this. This was sin. This was wishing Spencer's death because it was only possible due to his death.

And yet, the words were out of his mouth before he could stop them. "Do you think you could be happy with me?"

She swallowed and looked at him. A century passed before she finally replied, "There was a time I didn't think I could feel anything for you but hatred. I don't feel that anymore."

Neither did he.

Her words were his undoing. The yearning for her won.

He stood up, and in one step crossed the distance to her chair, pulled her up to stand, and kissed her.

17

His lips brushed against hers—surprisingly soft and yet insistent, urgent. They asked her with their velvety touch, and there was just one answer she wanted to give.

Yes.

She parted her lips in reply, and a masculine groan of relief...of need...issued from back of his throat. He wrapped his strong arms around her, bringing her close to him, so close, every inch of their bodies was pressed against each other. He kept kissing her, his wicked tongue dipping into the depths of her mouth, coming to her like he was desperate and she was his only salvation.

He tasted like wine and like something sweet and pungent —like him. He was so hard and so warm and smelled so good, she wanted to rub herself all over him like a cat. Soon, she felt a warmth inside of her that had nothing to do with the burning coals in the grate.

He deepened the kiss, and she shuddered. Her breasts ached, and only the feel of his body would soothe them. She clutched her hands around his neck in a desperate need to bring herself closer to him, as close as humanly possible.

His hands dug into her hair, her perfect updo that her very skilled lady's maid had done for her, and held her head, angling his face to kiss her even deeper. And she allowed him, opening up, arching into him, needing him to be hers.

She wanted him so completely, she couldn't feel the ground under her feet. All she was aware of was him against her, and how strange and unnatural her clothes felt, digging into her expanding chest and her swelling breasts.

She knew he must feel that, too, based on something hard and long that was pressing against her lower belly from the vicinity of his trousers. She wanted to bring him as much pleasure as he had brought her the night of the soirée. She ran her hands down his waistcoat and undid his buttons, then slid her hands under its edges and pushed it towards his hard shoulders, and then down his arms.

He chuckled into her mouth. "How eager you are, Duchess. As eager as I am to look at you."

"To look—"

"Oh, yes," he said, his gaze dark and smoldering under his hooded eyelids. "Come here."

He resumed kissing her, but this time, his hands worked at her back, opening the long row of hooks just as proficiently as any maid would. He pulled her dress down until it fell onto the soft carpet, pooling around her feet. Next went her petticoats in a stiffer heap around her ankles. Heat rushed through her. A man—not just any man but *this man*—would see her naked in a moment.

He stopped the kiss and stepped away and looked her over as she stood in only her chemise and her corset. Was she pleasing to him? His eyes dragged over her body slowly, taking in every inch of her.

"Turn around," he said, his voice low and rough.

She obeyed, turning her back to him. She felt the pull of her corset when he began undoing the lacing. Soon, he dragged it over her head, and she was left in only her thin chemise. He took her by her hand, sending a jolt through her arm, and turned her around to face him.

"Take it off," he said, his Adam's apple bobbing.

She inhaled in a sharp breath. Her nipples tingled and puckered against the light fabric. She was the sole object of his attention; he looked at her as though nothing and no one else existed but her. He was the duke and her husband, and she belonged to him in front of God, the king, and the court. He could command her as he pleased—as he did. And yet, something about his voice, about the almost pained, intense expression of his face, made her feel powerful.

Without taking her eyes from his, she undid a small lace holding the front of her chemise together. His eyes dropped to her hands, his nostrils flared, and his chest rose and fell faster. As she pushed down the broad straps of her chemise, exposing one shoulder, his gaze darkened and became predatory. She pushed down the other strap, and then let the whole chemise drop to her waist. It hung on her hips.

"Heavens..." he cursed as he stared at her breasts like a starving man. "All the way down, Penelope."

She obeyed. A cool whoosh of air brushed her whole body, and there she stood, naked except for her thin woolen stockings held to her legs by delicate lace garters and her shoes. She stepped over the pile of clothes at her feet and took another step to him. She was burning hot despite being naked.

His gaze crawled down her body, his breath coming faster and the bulge in his trousers growing even bigger.

"By God, Penelope," he said in a gravelly murmur. "How beautiful you are... How you tempt me..."

A jolt of happiness rushed through her, making her blush. He thought she was beautiful... He was the one who was handsome, who was striking.

"Wait here." He went to the bed and took the quilt from it, then went to the fireplace and spread it on the floor before the grate. "I want to see all of you. The whole time. I want to see you when you climax over and over and the moment when you become mine."

A shiver of need rushed through her at his words. He took her hand and brought her to him and kissed her again, only this time, he didn't stop at her lips, but made his way down her neck and her chest and to her breasts. He cupped one breast and took the other one into his mouth. The lash of his tongue against the sensitive bud was almost more than she could bear, and she clenched from the intense pleasure of it.

"Oh, Preston," she whimpered.

"Do you like that, love?"

"Yes."

Her knees became as soft as jelly and buckled, but he caught her and laid her on the blanket. The heat of the hot grate warmed her from one side, the quilt soft under her back and buttocks. He knelt over her, still looking into her eyes, and removed his waistcoat, then undid the buttons of the placket of his white shirt. They landed in the same pile as her own clothes, and Penelope stopped breathing at the glorious body of a prime male before her. She'd seen Greek statues before, knew the perfection of a male figure, but never a naked man.

His strong shoulders were broad and his chest was muscular, with soft black hair and dark nipples. His biceps bulged. His skin was darker than hers and glowed golden in the light of the fire. The hard relief of his stomach led to a region with which she wasn't familiar at all—apart from what she'd seen in paintings and sculptures. The region he was about to uncover...

His trousers dropped, and something long and thick sprang forth...the male organ! Could it really be so big and stand like that, pointing upward? She'd never seen that on a sculpture! There were dark curls of hair at the base, and below that, his thighs were thick and muscular and beautiful.

"Preston, you are so much more magnificent than I could ever have imagined..." she whispered. "You must let me paint you nude."

He chuckled and then smiled.

Smiled!

The view was so unexpected and so breathtakingly beautiful that she ached to touch his lips to make sure she wasn't dreaming. For the first time since she'd first seen him three years ago in one of the ballrooms, he looked carefree. The ever-present scowl was gone, and he was young and boyish, and so handsome her chest hurt.

"Only you could think of painting at a moment like this." He chuckled. "Let me see if I can make you think of something else...or not think at all."

He went back to kissing her breasts. He cupped them both in his hands and alternated between teasing one with his mouth, and then the other, while rubbing and rolling her nipple between his fingers. Sweet pleasure was shooting through her. She arched her back to give him more access, to be closer to her. Then he kissed his way down her stomach, leaving traces of fire behind. And all the way down, past the hair at the apex of her thighs...

His fingers had worked magic there last time.

Oh, heavens, she was burning. Was he going to—

He spread her folds and sealed his mouth with her sex. She

gasped and jerked with a shock of intense pleasure, and with the scandalous decadence of it.

"Preston, I—"

"Shh..." he whispered. "You taste like heaven. Better than I've ever imagined."

She lay back on the quilt, her cheeks blazing as he proceeded to kiss her there as if he were kissing her mouth. He'd *imagined* kissing her there—think of that!

But after a few moments, she couldn't think at all, as his tongue teased, licked, glided, and his lips sucked and nibbled on her sensitive flesh. She was expanding, swimming in the sensations, in the pleasure that rushed through her in delicious waves. Then his finger went in...just a little. It didn't hurt exactly, but it felt like a small invasion.

"How soft you are, darling," he mumbled. "How warm and tight. How wet you are for me."

Wet? Oh heavens, was she embarrassing herself?

"It means you're ready," he said softly. "Are you ready?"

"For what?" She looked up at him.

"To take me in," he said. "That's how you become mine. How you stop being a virgin and become a woman."

She wanted him inside. She wanted him as close as two human beings could be. She wanted him everywhere.

"Yes," she said.

"It might hurt, might be uncomfortable," he said. "It's only because it's your first time. But I promise I'll make it wonderful for you in the future. As wonderful as you feel now...and better."

She knew nothing of any of it. There was no one in her life who'd prepared her for it. And his care for her, his willingness to teach her and to show her warmed her heart and her soul. She wanted him. Today. Tomorrow. Forever. Even if it hurt. Her stupid heart was falling for him.

"Yes, Preston," she whispered, her chest rising and falling.

He positioned himself between her thighs and spread them as he lowered himself to her. His hard member nudged her at her entrance, and she moved her hips, urging for him to enter her aching, throbbing, needy body. There was a fire burning, and only he would do to soothe it. Her heart pounded hard. How would she ever fit him in when she'd never had anything inside her body before? He looked deep into her eyes. There was such tenderness in his gaze, such care for her that her throat clenched with emotion.

"You're perfect," he said to her, setting a flock of little starlings into a flight inside her stomach. He kissed her, gently and deeply, and started to make small thrusts inside her. With one arm supporting himself, he slid the other one between their bodies, and with his finger he found the center of her pleasure between her folds and began gently rubbing it. She spread her thighs, wanting more of him, deeper.

And then, suddenly, there was a pinch inside her, and he slid halfway in. She jerked slightly and he went completely still. The burning was unpleasant—but only a little. He appeared to be almost in pain. "Are you all right, love? Do you want me to stop?"

He was so thick and expanding inside of her, and she felt like she was stretched almost to the limit. And despite the discomfort, she still wanted him. She was still aroused and not nearly finished. Droplets of sweat beaded under the locks of dark hair that fell over his forehead.

"Don't stop," she said, running her hands down his muscular back. "Please don't stop."

He swallowed. "Good. Because you feel so amazing, I think I'd have an apoplexy if I had to leave the heavens of your body."

He slowly pushed deeper into her as his hand kept rubbing

the center of her pleasure, and soon the pain dissolved into this intense wave that was part of her pleasure.

She moaned and arched her back when he was deep inside her. He was part of her now, and she was part of him, and as he started moving faster, still gently pushing in and out of her, the intensity built. He removed his hand and angled his hips so that he was still stimulating that wonderous point, and now there was another pleasure deep within that was building, too.

He started thrusting in and out with vigor, emitting deep grunts that bordered on cries of agony.

"How good you feel, Penelope," he groaned. "Heavens, you're so tight... Do you like this?"

"Yes... Please...please..."

"Please what, love?"

"More... More..."

"I feel you clenching me so tight... Are you close to your release?"

"I'm... I'm..."

She didn't know what she was. She knew there was this tension building inside her, as inevitable as a carriage being driven at full speed. It felt different from the first time. Full. All-consuming. It felt like her whole body would burst like a firework. He held the fire. And he would be her undoing.

And then she did.

"Ah, Preston!" she cried out as her body clenched in a delicious moment of ecstasy.

It washed through her like a giant wave in a storm, making her blind and deaf and brainless for a moment. He bucked and tensed and groaned some sort of wolfish sounds, and then she thought he was with her, too, as he jerked and twitched inside her.

For several moments, they were like this, he losing himself in her, and she rocking on the waves of bliss.

And then he collapsed on top of her, moved to the side, and cuddled her onto his shoulder. They both panted hard, sweating.

Why had no one told her how incredible things could be between a husband and wife? Maybe this pleasure was not the same for everyone. Maybe it was only because it was Preston.

She was falling for him. Her silly heart didn't care that he held some threat over her father. She didn't even want to think about it.

Because nothing would be the same after this night.

And no matter how good it felt with him now, they still had secrets between them.

Secrets that may destroy this fragile sense of happiness and shred her heart into pieces.

18

Preston lunged forward, a fencing sword in his right hand. His sword clicked against Richard's as they parried. The locks of Richard's auburn hair fell on his forehead as he did a riposte, then grunted and launched into a counterattack.

Other gentlemen trained in the fencing club, Olympus, facing each other and swinging their swords in several lanes in a large room. The room was filled with the metallic clicks of swords, the shuffling of feet, and the grunts and sharp commands of the trainers. Most gentlemen were dressed in fencing jackets—simple white garments made of thick material with hooks on the sides of the torso. Paintings of horses and landscapes hung on wood-paneled walls. And tall windows opening onto Old Bond Street in Mayfair let in plenty of light.

Preston's body savored the physical exercise, the strain of muscles, to make himself forget. Forget the night before, with his wife.

Because the plan to fuck her out of his system hadn't worked. The moment he'd sunk into her sweet, tight depths last night, it had become very clear to him that he'd never have enough of her. He'd never stop wanting her.

Her sweet body, so responsive, so hungry for him. Last night, he'd gotten a glimpse of how it would be, just him and her. Of the happiness. Dinners alone together. Falling asleep with her in his bed. Waking up and seeing her face.

But none of that was possible. She would always be Spencer's beloved, and there would always be his brother's death between them.

Preston did a counterriposte and slashed his sword against Richard's, but it was a weak thrust and directed too much to his right, and Richard easily unarmed him.

Richard walked to Preston's sword. "What are you doing, brother?" he asked as he bent down and picked it up. He handed Preston his weapon. "Why are you so distracted?"

Preston's hand wrapped tightly around the handle of his sword. "It's nothing to worry you."

"Is it Penelope?" he asked.

He didn't need to talk. He needed to distract himself. "No. It shouldn't concern you. Come on. En garde!"

Preston followed his example and stood with his knees bent significantly and his elbow bent with the sword pointing up.

"She's the only woman Spencer ever loved," said Richard. "That must worry you."

Richard knew him way too well. He was always the peacekeeper. Not as competitive as his brothers, he had keen skills of observation and always seemed to know what was on one's mind.

And while the whole ton thought Richard was yet another Seaton rake, Preston knew it was only a façade. Deep down, Richard was a true romantic, and as much as he tried to indulge in meaningless connections, he couldn't go through with them.

Preston had always thought that Richard would be the one from the three Seaton brothers to end up happily married as he was popular among women and was a man of true honor.

But since his former betrothed had broken off their engagement, Richard had closed his heart to romance and sworn to never marry.

Preston attacked again, just to distract Richard, with his sharp eyes and his keen mind.

"Come on," grunted Richard as he blocked Preston's attack. They sparred in several lightning-strike attacks.

"If it worried me"—Preston slashed—"it would signify that she means something to me."

Richard parried. "Doesn't she?"

Preston advanced. "It does not matter. Because she shouldn't."

Richard lunged, and Preston was too slow to block his sword. The tip of Richard's blade touched Preston's chest.

"But she does," said Richard, standing straight. "I can see that."

Preston stared at his brother for a while. Was it even worth denying it when Richard knew him so well? What would be the point?

"She does," Preston said.

Richard walked up to him. "I'm sure Spencer would have wanted you to be happy."

Preston sighed. "I'm sure he would. But not with her. He loved her. She was supposed to be his."

"Weren't you the one who always said she didn't return his affections?"

"Yes."

And she had told him she'd never been romantically interested in Spencer.

Preston nodded with his chin at the changing room. As they walked, a footman handed them each a cloth.

"I treated her poorly in the beginning. I regret it now."

She deserved to be treated well every single day.

"I suspected so. I never liked your decision to marry her to exact revenge upon her father."

Preston wiped his sweaty forehead. "Well, don't you want revenge?"

"I want… I want Spencer to be alive," said Richard. "I want this to never have happened to him. But I do know that revenge is not going to bring him back. And I daresay, it might destroy your marriage."

Only a week ago, Preston would have replied that there was nothing to destroy anyway. Unfortunately, for the past few days, his stupid, stupid heart had begun hoping. Feeling. He couldn't get her out of his head. Part of him wanted to return to the time when he had just hated her and there was no hope for them.

But he had gotten to know Penelope. The real Penelope. He had learned how wrong he was about her.

They entered the changing room, and Preston went to the wardrobe and started to undo the hooks of his fencing jacket.

Richard stood facing him, one shoulder leaning against the wardrobe. "Haven't you already had enough of hatred and anger? If you want to be happy with your duchess, you'll need to let go of revenge and forgive her father. It's impossible for you to both hate him and be happy with her."

Preston's chest quivered. He did not like how right Richard was.

"Eventually," Richard added softly, "you'll have to choose love or revenge. Can you do that?"

Preston began removing his jacket. Love? All he felt for Penelope was lust. Yes, he liked her enough, and yes, she touched something deep within. But love?

He grudgingly admitted to himself that there was a tiny part of him, the one that had seen that love and happiness in marriage were possible, that had begun hoping. Begun imagining a life where he could have a happy marriage.

What a silly part. It was only an illusion, and it would only lead him to pain and heartbreak.

No. There would never be love.

However, there *would* always be the hole in their family that was Spencer's absence. He'd never sit at his place at Christmas. He'd never argue with Preston again about something insignificant. He'd never beat him when they'd race their horses across a field in Grandhampton.

Preston dropped the jacket and shoved one arm into his coat. "I cannot. I'll never be able to forgive my brother's murderer."

Therefore, he should not develop feelings for his enemy's daughter. He should stop the growing closeness between them before he completely fell in love with her.

Or she fell in love with him.

He should let her go and live on one of his estates, away from him. He could support her while she painted and leave her alone.

But he couldn't. He needed an heir. And he was too weak of a man, and she was too big of a temptation.

19

"Calliope, are you thinking about marriage?" asked Emma, the Duchess of Loxchester. "Look at the way Lord Chapman is eyeing you."

Hyde Park bloomed as Calliope, Emma, and Penelope walked the gravel path. The air was cool and fresh after the rain, and a strong breeze, so typical of April, sent the locks of Penelope's hair into her eyes from under her bonnet. The park was full of elegant ladies and gentlemen as they strolled between the bushes of fresh, young green leaves, glistening with the droplets of rain that had stopped not an hour ago. Occasional riders rode through the rolling hills of cut grass. Open carriages drove along horse lanes, showing off the attire of the fashionable ladies and gentlemen in them.

The three of them nodded in acknowledgment to a horse rider who passed on the other side of the path. He was short, but quite handsome and dashing in his dark navy tailcoat against his round, pale face and raven hair.

"Please, Emma," said Calliope. "Please, don't join my

brothers in this. I have no intention to ever marry. Become my husband's property? No, thank you."

"I'm not joining your brothers," chuckled Emma, her remarkable big green eyes sparkling. "I'm on your side. I just asked if you were interested in marriage. Because marriage can make you very happy."

Calliope snorted in a very unladylike manner, her pale cheeks reddening, her bright blue eyes blazing as she stared ahead. "I have other plans for my life than to have a *Lord Chapman* command me to make his babies and entertain his friends."

"Why, are Preston and Lord Richard talking about marrying you off?" asked Penelope. "Preston never mentioned anything to me."

Both ladies looked at her sharply. "*Preston?*" asked Calliope. "Do you call my brother by his given name now? Does it mean you two have made up?"

Made up, loved up, and essentially merged into one being every night as soon as they were alone in her bedchamber. Three nights of little sleep, but of many activities that made her body ache and glow...activities she couldn't in good conscience talk about with an unmarried young lady like Calliope.

Three nights that, she dared not hope, may be the beginning of a lifelong happiness.

"We did," said Penelope, trying and failing to hide a smile. "And you were right, Calliope, I only needed to give him a chance." She thought of how much she loved her daily painting sessions with Miss de Luca, and how much she had improved. All thanks to him. "He's a wonderful man."

A wonderful man who still had something over her papa that could destroy him.

A secret that she hoped she would get out of her papa

today. She glanced around, looking for a short, stout figure wearing a powdered wig. But he was nowhere to be seen.

"So there's a chance of happiness," said Emma, as delighted as Calliope. "I'm so glad. Our husbands are both stubborn grumps, but we love them for it, don't we?"

"Did you know right away?" asked Penelope. "That you loved the Duke of Loxchester?"

Emma sighed and smiled. "No. But quite soon. I thought he was not a good man at first, because of the way he treated me, but he saved me. Multiple times. I think that's what Grandhampton is doing. He seems like a coldhearted man only interested in his own affairs, but deep down, I believe both of our husbands are very warmhearted indeed. But they are wounded souls that need to heal. As soon as I saw that in Sebastian, I fell in love with him."

A wounded soul... Yes, Preston was one. Penelope knew Preston was still grieving Spencer's death, and he'd opened up that he'd blamed himself in that, and that he'd even blamed her because he was sure she had led Spencer on.

And yet, none of that explained why he was so set on destroying her father... Suddenly, she spotted his white powdered wig about fifty feet away as he slowly walked along with his stick.

"Ladies," she said, "do you mind if I talk to my father? I see him walking over there."

Both of them looked at him. Calliope nodded, a puzzled frown on her face. "No, of course not, please go ahead and talk to Lord Beckett. You don't need our permission."

Penelope cleared her throat. "I know...it's just...don't mention me seeing him to Preston. Please."

Calliope and Emma looked at each other. "If you don't want us to, we won't," said Emma.

Calliope added, "Though I fail to see why Preston would mind you seeing your own papa."

"There's a small disagreement between them. I couldn't tell you what it's about, but I'd like to get to the bottom of it myself. I'll rejoin you shortly."

"Of course," said Emma.

They nodded and she hurried forward. Quickly, she caught up with him. He turned to her, his face puffier and redder than she'd remembered from last seeing him. Dark circles under his bloodshot eyes made her stomach clench in worry.

"Papa," she said. "Here you are."

"Ah, Penelope," he said, his gaze darting away from her. "A little chilly for a walk, don't you think? I do not have much time."

As they walked slowly, his walking stick dug with squelching sounds into the wet path.

"Have you been well?" she asked carefully. A whiff of alcohol, a long unwashed body, and stale sweat reached her. Was this really him, the baron? Could he have fallen so low?

"How can a man be well without money, Penelope? What a silly question. Use your brain. I'm scraping by. But keeping up appearances is hard without a full staff of servants to keep the house."

"Alexandria sends her regards," she said. "She wrote me from the country."

"Ah. Please send her my regards back. If only her papa could lend me more money."

The Duchess of Ashton turned the corner of the path ahead, accompanied by two younger ladies, and Penelope's heart skipped a beat. They had now been introduced. They were of equal standing. Would this powerful woman recognize and greet her?

The duchess looked stunning in her emerald green spencer

and a tall white bonnet decorated with red poppies, puffed emerald green gauze, and elaborately placed peacock feathers.

"Ah, Your Grace," the duchess said as she stopped. "Congratulations on your wedding and many happy years with your new husband."

Her sad eyes grew even sadder as she said that.

"Thank you, Your Grace," said Penelope. "May I present to you my father, Lord Beckett."

"Of course," said the duchess with a stilted smile as Papa squeezed her hand. "How do you do, Lord Beckett? I hope you're finding your walk satisfactory. I couldn't sit at home a moment longer after two days of rain. With good fortune, we'll have many sunny days to enjoy the park."

"Certainly," said Penelope. "I hope to come here to paint *en plein air*."

"Ah!" said the duchess, the sadness disappearing from her eyes. "That is right, you mentioned something about art at Almack's."

Papa cleared his throat unhappily at that but, mercifully, kept his mouth shut.

Penelope smiled. "I did, Duchess. Your memory does you justice. I paint quite often. Recently, my husband hired Enrica de Luca to teach me."

"Miss de Luca?" The duchess's eyes glinted with curiosity. "Your husband must love you very much, and she certainly doesn't teach just anyone. She must have seen something in you. Now I am curious. Please, you must allow me to see some of your works."

Penelope's heart did a flip. The whole park brightened around her. "Of course, it would be my honor, madam. Nothing would make me happier. Please, you must call on me."

"I will," said the Duchess of Ashton with a pleased smile.

"Nothing gives me more pleasure than to see new talent. Good day to you both."

With that, she and her companions continued their stroll. Penelope and Papa resumed their walk as well, her heart drumming so hard, she felt it in her ribs.

"Well, you didn't marry too poorly after all," said Papa with a smirk. "All those high connections. Even the Duchess of Ashton wants to butter you up."

Of course. Because Papa could never imagine the duchess actually thinking that Penelope may have any talent. She swallowed the bitter, angry thought.

"You look thinner, Papa. Are you eating enough?"

"Of course not." He glanced at her, and there was such a plea in his eyes, her heart squeezed. "Penelope, please, help me."

She had come to ask him about his conflict with Preston, but seeing him falling so low, she couldn't take it. Yes, one of Preston's rules was that she was never to give any money to Papa. But she couldn't stand her papa being degraded like this. He was still her father. She had no mother anymore, but she still had him.

They stopped. With her hands shaking, she went into her reticule and took out her two-week allowance for dresses and various expenses. It must be two hundred pounds. She pressed it into her papa's hands and looked over her shoulder. Had Calliope and Emma seen her? She wasn't sure. They weren't on the path behind her and Papa.

Papa shoved the money quickly into the pocket of his coat.

Heavy guilt sank in Penelope's stomach. She was helping her papa but betraying her husband. The husband with whom she'd just started to be at peace; the husband with whom she'd spend the rest of her life.

"Please, Papa, do not gamble it. Use it to pay the servants what you owe and to buy provisions."

"This is not nearly enough, Penelope," he said. "I need more. Can you give me more?"

"How much do you owe exactly, Papa?"

He didn't reply for a bit. Instead, he resumed walking, his steps slow. "Ten thousand pounds."

She gasped, the ground careened under her feet. "How could you have gambled away such a fortune?"

"It was the thing that made me feel good after losing your mama. I loved her. She and you...were the only light in my life."

Penelope's heart squeezed for him. "Of course I'll get you more money. I can give my whole monthly allowance to you. But, please, tell me, what does Preston have over you?"

Papa stopped again and turned to her; his Adam's apple bobbed as he looked around. When he'd made sure no one could hear them, he leaned closer to her, his eyes soft and kind for the first time in years. "Thank you, Penelope. You have a good heart. Your mother's heart. That is why you must help me. I do not know what it is exactly myself. But you could find the piece of evidence that he has and bring it to me. Then it all would be over."

Penelope didn't like what she heard one bit. She'd betrayed Preston when she gave her papa the money, but she couldn't betray him even further by stealing important documents... could she?

"What is it, Papa?" she asked.

"A red leather folder, Penelope. If you find it somewhere in the house and bring it to me, I'll be free of the yoke Grandhampton has over me. Moreover, you'll be free to leave him."

Leave him? No. That didn't feel good or right at all. She didn't want to leave him. She didn't want to betray him. She wanted the truth, and she wanted to love him and live her life happily with him. She wanted more nights like they'd had, more of his hot, hard body pinning her to the mattress in the most delicious way possible. More soul-to-soul conversations that made her feel loved and understood and important. More painting his handsome, chiseled face. More admiring his body as she painted the outlines of his arms and his muscular chest.

More of him. Every day.

"Papa, I can't steal my husband's documents."

"Well, can you let your poor old papa die in a debtor's prison?"

"You won't go to the debtor's prison. You're a peer."

"Then die at the hands of the men I'm indebted to?"

A bone-deep chill ran through Penelope. "What?"

"Yes. It has come to that." His chin shook as he looked around, his eyes watering. Penelope closed her eyes, her heart bleeding with pity for her papa.

"There must be another way. I'll tell Preston, I'm sure he'd understand and help—"

"No! Do not dare. Who do you think wanted me to be in this terrible situation? I almost had a solution in my hands, and he took it from me."

Penelope exhaled sharply. A lord and lady passed by them, laughing and smiling in the sunshine. When they were out of earshot, she resumed walking and so did Papa. She was thinking. If the document in question went missing, Preston would be furious. But it would not only help Papa, it would also remove the very means of Preston's revenge. So perhaps, with that out of his hands, he'd stop his menacing plan. They'd be able to move on, and she'd finally have her happily ever after with him.

"Very well, Papa," she said, a shiver running through her blood. Resentment towards him pinched at her. She was not a thief. She was not a liar. All she wanted was to help. But it seemed her papa was always pushing her to do things she didn't wish to do. "I'll do it."

After her talk with Papa, Penelope returned to Emma and Calliope and walked with them for a bit. An hour or so later, she was back home.

She gave her bonnet and her spencer to Porter and asked him to tell Mrs. Brown to come and see her in the library. A few minutes later, Mrs. Brown entered, as always very professional, with her face stretched out in a polite mask. "Your Grace, may I be of service?"

"Mrs. Brown…" Penelope said, eyeing the door to Preston's study. How would she ever be able to go in there to actually steal something? "I just wanted to discuss the menu for the next week."

"Of course, madam," said Mrs. Brown. "What would you like?"

"I thought something lighter than usual. Something more fitting for spring. It's so wonderful to feel summer approaching, and I think His Grace would enjoy the change. I'd like to cheer him up. Radish salad, perhaps. Asparagus would be nice, as well."

"Of course," said Mrs. Brown. "Let me write that down."

She went to the desk and took a piece of paper from a small, elegant folder and began writing. They added artichokes and green peas to the list as well as dill, chives, and parsley.

Now that Preston had given her her own studio and allowed her to change the paintings to lighter, more colorful ones, she'd started to feel more at home here. But the biggest transformation was, of course, her husband. He had changed from a cold and unfeeling man who hated her into someone who made love to her and talked to her, listened to her, and shared some very deep secrets.

And yet, she had agreed to betray him. Heaviness sat in her stomach. She wanted to make up for what she was about to do in some way. She wanted to make Chalworth her and Preston's true home. She wanted to brighten it up for him. Dissipate the gloom and darkness and make it more hopeful and full of light.

"I'd also like to order a few pieces of new furniture," said Penelope when they finished discussing the menu.

Mrs. Brown straightened her back. "Oh, Your Grace?"

"It's just all so dark. I'd like more light in the house. Can you give me an address for a good carpenter? I'd like modern furniture with light colors."

Mrs. Brown didn't reply for a bit, seeming to look for words. "Very good, Your Grace."

There was an edge to her voice, which Penelope chose to ignore. She understood Mrs. Brown was loyal to the family's history, but it was long past time for a change. Penelope was doing this for Preston and for herself. Perhaps even Mrs. Brown would feel less sour in a more cheerful space.

"Also, if you could please make sure the curtains are drawn as much as possible?" asked Penelope. "The windows are small and don't let much light in."

"Very good, Your Grace," said Mrs. Brown coldly. "I'll make sure the maids know. Anything else?"

"Yes, I'd like the bed linens to be washed weekly. I've been here for almost two weeks, and I like to sleep in a fresh bed. As does the duke, I'm sure."

"Of course, Your Grace."

"And sometime next week, I'd like to give a dinner for all the Seatons and the Duke and Duchess of Loxchester. Something simple but delicious. Just family."

"But the duke and the duchess aren't family...are they?"

"Well, they're almost family."

"Yes, ma'am."

"Thank you, Mrs. Brown," said Penelope warmly. "You're a wonderful housekeeper. Thank you for making my life and my husband's life so easy."

A surprised twitch of her brow revealed a fleeting expression of being touched, then the old mask of detached servant was back.

"It's my pleasure, Your Grace."

"Thank you," said Penelope again. "Do you know if His Grace is back yet?"

"Not to my knowledge, ma'am."

When Mrs. Brown left, Penelope looked at the door to Preston's study, clutching her hands. She walked briskly towards it, full of determination, but her stomach was dropping inside. *This is for Papa,* she kept saying to herself as she flung the door open. *This is for Papa.*

It was empty. The painting of Danaë still hung there, as beautiful and as eerie as before. A stab of empathy for the woman made Penelope bite her lip. She needed to hurry. The servants would have no reason to suspect her of anything if they found her here...she was the lady of the house, after all.

But Preston...

She hurried to his desk and looked through the pile of documents that lay on top. Then another one. Only brown leather folders and papers. Some books. Heavy ledgers.

She opened one drawer in the desk after the other. There were more documents. Letters. Pens and a closed jar of ink.

Then in the third bottom drawer, there it was—a red leather folder lying on top of other letters and documents. She remembered seeing it on his desk the night she'd found him asleep in here. The night she'd read Spencer's letter... She went completely still, her pulse drumming in her ears. She swallowed and laid her shaking fingers on the smooth, tightly stretched leather.

This was the answer to her father's troubles and the revelation of Preston's secrets. She clasped the folder and picked it up, feeling like it may be a snake about to bite. She held it before her, the leather dully reflecting the light from the window.

She had it now. All she needed to do was to leave with it and hide it and then to deliver it to Papa...

Should she look inside? But how could she betray Preston so completely and irrevocably that the fragile trust and peace between them would forever be broken?

She remembered Preston's words as he'd protected her against Papa's harsh words... *If my wife wishes to be an artist, I think that is spectacular. I think she has more brains than you, sir. More brains than most men I know.*

Preston, being giddy and excited about hiring Enrica de Luca for her.

Preston, getting down on his knees and having his mouth on her...there... Preston, telling her about his deepest pain and deepest guilt...

Preston, the trust with whom was so fragile and precious now.

No. She couldn't look inside or steal it. She was not this person. She loved her papa, but there must be another way to help him than to betray her husband.

Just as she moved to put the folder back into the drawer, the door creaked open.

She looked up.

Standing in the doorway with a shuttered expression was Preston.

20

Preston soared through the house as if on wings. A fresh bouquet of yellow, white, and pink tulips stood in the vase on the sideboard as he entered Chalworth. The scent in the house had changed from dusty and old to flowery and fruity, like bergamot and lavender.

Penelope.

The reason he felt so light—something he hadn't felt like for at least seven months, if not years—was because he'd convinced William Turner to tutor Penelope. Preston couldn't remember ever being so excited as he was for his wife at this moment. She came to life when she painted. And seeing that light in her eyes, that enthusiasm, was like having his own soul heal.

"Mrs. Brown, where is the duchess?" he asked the passing housekeeper.

"I spoke to Her Grace in the library just now, Your Grace," she responded with a polite bob.

Preston rushed there. The room was empty, but the door to his study stood just a little ajar.

Worry tightened his gut. What reason would Penelope have to enter the study when he was away?

Cautious, he opened the door, and his world came crashing down.

She stood frozen with the red leather folder in her hand, guilt in her eyes.

He had told her not to snoop around. He had specifically forbidden her to come here and yet...

And yet it was not anger that he first felt. It was hurt. Hurt as painful as stepping on a thousand pieces of broken glass. Because he knew exactly why she had that red folder in her hands.

"Penelope," he said, his voice sounding as though he had swallowed a handful of gravel.

She dropped the folder onto the desk like it was white-hot. "It's not what it looks like..." Her tender throat moved as she attempted to swallow. "I...I was just about to put it back."

Slowly, very slowly, he shut the door behind him. Then walked to her, the floor like a swamp under his feet. "You betrayed me."

She stepped back, her eyes filling with tears.

Goodness gracious, pain stabbed at him. He should hate her. It was he who should be in tears. And yet, seeing her sad made him want to suffer any wound if only she would smile again.

"I didn't!" she cried. "I'm sorry."

Lies. And more lies, he told himself. She wasn't sorry. She was just pretending.

"Were you going to steal it and take it to your father?" he demanded, walking around the desk to stand right in front of her.

He towered over her, trying and failing to ignore her delicious scent. She was so delicate and so small, and yet no one in his life had such a powerful ability to hurt him.

She straightened her shoulders, her blue-gray eyes never leaving him. "No."

His lip crawled up. "Do not lie to me. Do not dare take me for a fool. You searched for it in the desk and took it out!"

"I didn't even look inside!" she yelled back.

"Well, good then that I came home so early. Had I come a minute later, you'd have already left with this."

She picked the folder up again. "What is it anyway, Preston?"

"It's best you don't know." He snatched it out of her hand and shoved it deep into the upper drawer of his desk. The slam of the drawer was a cannonade exploding around him. "Don't you understand? Your ignorance is your peace of mind. I'm protecting you!"

She took one step towards him and softly laid her hand on his chest. His mouth went dry. One innocent touch and tingles showered through him.

"You don't need to protect me, Preston," she said quietly and gently. "I'm a grown woman. A duchess, no less."

"Penelope, of course you're a grown woman. I just don't—"

He just didn't want to break her heart, he wanted to say, but she interrupted him.

"I admit it. Papa asked me to bring him a red leather folder. Yes. But, Preston, he was so poorly. He isn't doing well. He's much thinner."

Pity for the old man tickled his chest. Lord Beckett was hungry? Damnation, that couldn't be easy for Penelope to witness. Did it really need to come down to this?

But no. Preston needed to stay focused.

Lord Beckett wasn't doing well? Neither was Spencer—he was dead.

"And you decided to betray me," he said, his voice a rasp.

"I didn't decide anything. All I wanted was to help Papa. But I changed my mind, just before you came in. I was about to put it back. And I must tell you something else..."

His stomach dropped. "What?"

"I gave him money."

She had broken his rule. She had deceived him. Preston stepped back, his whole being in agony. He hadn't anticipated his enemy's daughter could ever have the ability to hurt him like this. Like a cannonball had landed right in the middle of his chest, and torn, ragged pieces of his flesh ached and bled. "You need to decide right now, your father or me. Who has your loyalty?"

Penelope exhaled sharply, her eyes watering. "You're forcing me to make an impossible choice, Preston! He's still my father. He was hungry, unwashed. I think his health is rapidly declining. I'm worried about him. He's the only parent I have left."

Her only parent who had been ready to sell her like an animal. And yet, she had a big, warm heart. How could he both be so hurt by her and love her for caring so much about her unworthy papa?

"He may be the only parent you have left, Penelope," he said. "But you have more people that care about you. I'm your husband. You have me now."

Their eyes locked for a long time, and he sank in the depths of her eyes the color of a stormy sea hit by a beam of sunlight.

"Do I, though?" she asked. "Will you be able to ever fully trust me?"

"How can I trust you when you go against my rules, when you betray me in our own home?"

His jaws tensed to the point of pain. Yes, he was disappointed by this betrayal, but it was more than that. Trusting her, fully trusting her, meant pulling down the defenses and layers of protection he'd built around his soul piece by piece. Like the walls of Eilean Donan Castle, built from the granite of the mountains around the Mackenzie Boys' School, flanking the flat, silvery-gray surface of Loch Duich. It was at that school that he'd learned he really was always alone.

And people who were alone couldn't trust others, especially not with their feelings. Because if you trusted people, they hurt you. They sent you off to school like a traitor, like an unwanted dog. Like there was something wrong with you.

How could he take down the stones of his walls one by one, with bleeding, bruised fingers, and show her that behind them was not an almighty duke, but just someone who didn't think much of himself?

"What did my father do to make you distrust me so much?"

He said nothing. He couldn't contradict her. It wasn't just his insecurities that made trust impossible. She'd always be his enemy's daughter, and as long as Preston craved revenge, this war between him and Lord Beckett would never stop.

And she'd be entangled in it forever.

Richard's words rang in his head. He either had to choose love or revenge. If he wanted to be happy with his wife, and love her, he'd have to forgive Lord Beckett.

And that wasn't something he could ever do. Was it? Wouldn't that mean endorsing Beckett's actions? But even if he could never forgive her father, it wasn't Penelope's fault. She was just caught in the middle. Regret stung him, and any remaining anger slid away.

"I have something for you," he said.

He went into the inner pocket of his tailcoat and fished out Mr. Turner's letter. With shaking hands, she unfolded it and read. Her eyes brightened, and a smile spread on her lips, making his dead heart melt like wax.

"William Turner?" she breathed. "*The* William Turner?"

How could she think he was the one with all the power in this relationship, the one making all the rules, when he was ready to turn the world upside down for just one of her brilliant smiles?

She was the one with all the power.

The power to be his absolute bliss or his complete destruction.

"Yes, Penelope," he said. "*The* William Turner. For you. Anything—for you."

Anything but letting down the five-foot-thick granite walls around his heart.

21

In the following week, Penelope didn't think she could ever be so happy and so miserable at the same time.

Preston barely looked at her. Barely talked to her. Which was so much worse than if he had kept yelling at her.

Every day, Penelope painted and worked on her craft. William Turner came to tutor her, and it was a dream come true, seeing the great artist at work and having him guide her and help her improve.

She kept dreaming that she was Danaë, entrapped in Preston's study, waiting for her Prometheus to come and free her. Only, he didn't come. And with the shower of golden coins, the red folder dropped right into her lap. She held it in her hands, knowing that if she opened it, it would be the end of the shower of gold and the beginning of her freedom. Only, she didn't want the shower of gold to end. She was so happy in it. She'd never been so happy.

But she opened the red folder. And inside was a dark, bottomless cavity into hell. It began sucking her in, dragging her lower and lower. Every time, she'd wake with a jerk, to see

Preston's side of the bed empty and feel her heart aching for him.

In the back of her mind, she kept wondering what was in the folder. What had her father done that Preston had such power over him? It ate at her while she painted, managed the house, and did her best to please Preston, hoping he might truly forgive her and things could go back to how they'd been before he caught her in the study.

His secret was still a dark cloud that hung over both of their heads. And she knew one day that dark cloud may turn into a devastating storm. All she could do now was enjoy the sunshine she had.

On the third day, she went to see her papa and told him she wouldn't help him with the red folder, but she gave him the rest of her monthly allowance. For the last time, she vowed, hating that she was going against Preston's wishes yet again. But her papa was desperate, and the money would mean food on his table. When she asked him, once again, what was in that envelope, he said, "If you won't help me, you should just burn it."

At the end of the week, after the family dinner, the Dowager Duchess of Grandhampton, Calliope, and Emma went with Penelope to visit the Duchess of Ashton's art salon while Preston, Richard, and Sebastian stayed home for port and a game of billiards.

The drive was full of chatter. Penelope rode in the carriage, smiling and laughing with the three women who had become her friends and family so quickly she couldn't remember a time when they weren't in her life.

When they stopped before Neverton Place and got out, Penelope's breath caught. She had thought Chalworth Place was impressive. But Neverton was as grand as a royal palace. A long façade stretched to the left and right, with four grand marble columns shooting up to the roof, three stories above. Several Greek statues of the pantheon lined the roof. The walls were all painted in a brisk cream color that glowed against the darkness of the night. Large fire torches and braziers illuminated the gravel pathway towards the grand stairs, and lights played behind the tall paned windows of the ground floor.

The dowager duchess gave the butler their calling cards, and they proceeded to the salon. There were many ladies and gentlemen in the room already, but Penelope didn't notice any of them as her eyes went immediately to the many paintings and portraits that occupied every inch of the walls in the richly decorated room. There must have been hundreds of candles, their warm glow illuminating the gilt frames of the artwork.

A large part of one wall held several portraits of one man. He was tall, in his fifties, with a balding head of dark hair showing only a little gray. He was athletic and quite handsome with a straight nose, small, narrowly set eyes under stern eyebrows, and a square jaw. He had a prominent chin with a dimple, a broad mouth, and the piercing gaze of someone who knew what he wanted.

He was portrayed in different poses and against different backgrounds: landscapes, interiors with columns, bright bordeaux-colored drapes. There were portraits of him hunting with hounds, sitting on a proud stallion, standing next to a vase of flowers, and so on.

The man himself stood under the paintings, dressed in a rich dark green waistcoat, his back straight, his head held proudly. The Duchess of Ashton stood next to him, and they were talking to a man of medium height with a large belly who was dressed in a waistcoat with rubies, diamonds, and emeralds sewn into it.

Looking at them, the dowager said, "That is the Duke of Ashton. You know the duchess, of course. And they're both talking to the prince regent. The duke is His Highness's right hand in all things."

They approached the duchess, the duke, and the prince.

The Duchess of Ashton wore a distant, polite smile that didn't touch her eyes as she listened to the prince and her husband talking. As always, she was striking, wearing a gown of dark green silky muslin that matched her husband's waistcoat.

When her eyes fell on the dowager and on Penelope, a genuine smile spread her lips.

"My dear," said the Duchess of Ashton. "How lovely to see you."

"Your Highness." The Duchess of Ashton looked at the prince briefly, then at her husband. "Your Grace. You both know the Dowager Duchess of Grandhampton, no doubt. May I introduce the new Duchess of Grandhampton."

Penelope's heart sank as the prince looked her over. He was an overweight man, not very handsome, and Penelope supposed that all the rumors about him and all the caricatures of his overeating and excessive drinking were true. He had a puffy face with meaty cheeks, a longish nose, and a very fashionable windswept haircut. He was dressed like a real dandy, with a clawhammer dress coat and long dark trousers, his crisp, high white cravat pushed up his puffy cheeks like a corset did with breasts. His translucent blue eyes studied her with a lewd glimmer as he slowly nodded to her. Penelope wanted to shake off the slimy feel of his gaze.

"And of course, the Duchess of Loxchester," said the Duchess of Ashton as she nodded at Emma. Emma did a low curtsy. "And the granddaughter of the dowager duchess, Lady Calliope Seaton."

Calliope did a low curtsy, as well.

"What pleasant company you have gathered here, Your

Grace," said the prince with a quick glance at the Duchess of Ashton. Then his gaze returned to Penelope. "I should attend more art soirées if they attract such pretty ladies."

"Why, yes," said the Duchess of Ashton. "Not just pretty ladies. The Duchess of Grandhampton paints."

"Is that so?" said the Duke of Ashton. "How do you find the exhibition, Your Grace?"

He brought a glass of port to his mouth and drank. Penelope looked over the wall with the paintings. "Her Grace has impeccable taste in art. I look forward to studying the paintings in detail. I've heard great things about your collection, Duchess."

With a bright smile, the duchess opened her mouth to say something, but the duke interrupted her without noticing. "Turner's paintings are here, too." On the other side of the wall, Penelope saw *Sun Rising through Vapour*, his 1807 painting of the River Thames and with the sails of several fishing boats, the early sun rising from behind the violet clouds, spreading its golden light over the calm water of the river and the cerulean skies. On the shore, fishermen weighed the catch from the early morning.

Her palms tingled, and she ached to go to the painting and study its every detail, then ask Mr. Turner about his process in two days when he'd come to tutor her. "He did my portrait, too," said the duke proudly, waving his arm towards the wall of his own portraits.

"Beautiful," said Penelope with a stiff smile. They were all great portraits, but Penelope wondered what man really needed fifteen portraits of himself. "They all do you justice."

"Duchess of Grandhampton," said the prince as he narrowed his eyes at her. "Now I know why I remembered this name."

"Oh?" asked Penelope, frowning.

"It's a silly rumor, no doubt." The prince chuckled. "But quite a funny one. Perhaps with your talent in art it makes more sense. But I'm sure it cannot be true."

"Perhaps it's best we make a tour and see the paintings," said the dowager, her blue eyes suddenly worried. She stretched her arm out to Penelope. "Come, darling. Let us indulge in the pleasure of seeing the portraits of Ashton."

But the dark cloud that had lingered at the back of Penelope's psyche since she'd first learned of the rumor made itself known, and there was a heaviness that spread at the bottom of her stomach. "I'd like to know the rumor, Your Highness."

The Duke of Ashton cleared his throat. "Certain rumors are, perhaps, best kept from gentle female ears."

"No, no," said the prince regent. "I'm sure the duchess would be able to deny it once and for all. Wouldn't you?"

Penelope held her back very straight against the feeling of an impending disaster, like an unstoppable carriage driving towards her at full speed. "Once I know what it is."

The prince chuckled and licked his thin lips. They reddened and glistened in the light of the candles. "Apparently, they say that the Duke of Grandhampton bought you at a secret auction held by your father."

Penelope paled. Silence fell on their small group as she felt the eyes of six people on her. The walls of the grand room began closing in, and all air disappeared from her lungs.

There it was. The secret. The red folder. It must be. The secret that would hurt her, like Preston had said. The knowledge he was protecting her from.

That her father would sell his only daughter to pay his debts. She could even guess the exact price... Ten thousand pounds, no doubt.

Only, if Preston had bought her for that amount at the

auction, why was her papa still ruined? Why was he still in debt?

"Well?" asked the prince. "It's not true, is it?"

Her eyes burned with tears, and she commanded herself to keep calm. To keep up appearances. She plastered the biggest smile on her face and chuckled gently. "No, Your Highness, it's not true. Could you imagine? How barbaric."

Everyone chuckled with relief. The prince took a large sip of his champagne. "The Earl of Whitemouth told me he witnessed it. But he must exaggerate. You're right, Duchess. What peer would sell his daughter at an auction in these modern times? That's unheard of. No. We are far too civilized in England for such things."

But if he really knew her husband, he wouldn't think that. With a dark premonition, Penelope knew she had a hard conversation with Preston awaiting her once she got back home.

22

JOEL, Preston's valet, grasped his dress coat and helped him remove it from his shoulders. His dressing room was quiet, with only the coals crackling in the small fireplace. The dark navy, almost black walls of the room had given him the sense of being in a tomb before, but not tonight. Not after such a very pleasant evening with his family that his wife had organized.

And not when standing leaned against the back of the chair was his portrait by Penelope, finished now. Joel had brought it in earlier, as he explained, at the request of Her Grace.

Preston stood staring at it, speechless. It was even more impressive than when he'd first seen it, now that she had added the finer details. He was struck, again, by the way she'd managed to capture his true essence, something even he could no longer see in himself.

No one saw him like that. With softness in his eyes. With that loneliness and pain he'd thought he'd hidden behind his walls so well. He thought he remembered looking like that when he was six or seven years old. Still undamaged, still himself. When was the last time he'd felt like that?

Right. When he had been in her bed. When they had talked. When he had made love to her.

Despite his anger with her, every day Chalworth felt more and more like home.

"Was the evening to your satisfaction, Your Grace?" asked Joel.

Joel, now in his forties, had been his valet ever since Oxford. Preston trusted the man. It was Joel who'd seen Preston fall apart after Spencer's death, sitting and bawling into his hands back in his dressing room in Sumhall. It was Joel who made sure Preston dressed and had his hair cut in the latest fashion because Preston couldn't care less about such things. Joel was a hardworking Scotsman, and Preston knew how fortunate he was to have a valet like him.

Preston raised his chin to allow Joel to undo his high cravat. "Yes, Her Grace and all the servants went above and beyond to make it a great success."

Preston was looking forward to seeing Penelope. He'd had to push back against the rumors that kept going around London about her. Had he still been indifferent to her, he wouldn't have cared. But now, thinking that his kind, talented, well-bred wife would be denied entry made him sick to his stomach, and he did everything to protect her and her reputation.

He hoped the Duchess of Ashton would introduce her to the right people, and he had no doubt they'd see Penelope's talent like he'd seen it, admire her as he admired her.

When she returned from the outing, he'd ask for her forgiveness. He'd tell her he didn't want to fight anymore. He'd ask her if they might forget about their last fight and move on.

And then, she'd tell him all about her brilliant, fabulous evening. Then he'd make love to her.

Heavens, how much he wanted to make love to her... An

entire week without her had been agony. He'd kept himself away only because of his damned stubbornness.

But he was ready now to push away the guilt that he dared to be happy with his brother's beloved while Spencer was dead in the ground.

Joel laid the cravat carefully onto the dressing table. "I'm glad to hear it," he responded to Preston's comment about the dinner.

Just then, sharp, quick footsteps approached from the corridor. Then the door swung open, making the candles' flames jump wildly.

Penelope stormed into the dressing room, and Joel's hands froze as he and Preston both stared at her pacing the length of the room.

Preston took a step towards her. "Sweetheart, what's the matter?" She looked distressed and agitated, her eyes wide and so dark they were pure steel. Her cheeks were flushed, her chest heaving. Then a dark thought bolted through his mind. "Did someone offend you? Damnation, I should have come with you."

"What's the matter? Who offended me? I'll tell you what's the matter. You. You offended me. What is all this about some auction you bought me at?"

Joel, who had been neatly folding the cravat, stilled and looked at Preston. Preston's face burst with heat. He had known that one day the truth about the auction would come out. That their happiness had an end date. That he couldn't be happy with her forever because he didn't deserve her.

And of course, sooner or later, she'd know what her father had done and why Preston was after revenge.

"Joel, that will be all. I'll manage."

"Very good, Your Grace," said Joel with a nod. "Good night."

When Preston and his wife were alone, she stood still and stared at him with her blazing eyes, her pretty, perky breasts, supported by the corset into two half orbs he ached to lick and suck. He went to her, but she took a step back.

"Is it true?" she asked, her voice low and slow. "That you bought me at an auction like a cow? That my father sold me?"

Well, he guessed there wouldn't be any gentle lovemaking tonight. Instead, tonight would be the beginning of the end.

There was no point in denying it. Neither was there a point in continuing to lie to her and postponing what she would inevitably find out in any case.

He lowered his chin onto his chest and said, "Yes."

She sucked in a shaky breath. "And I had to find it out from the prince regent himself. The prince knew before I did!"

A cold slap of shock had him curse under his breath. Rumors in the ton were incredible. Still, why was he surprised? Any sense of secrecy in Tyche was an illusion. The real place where things were buried and would never be revealed was Elysium.

Penelope started pacing again. "Do you understand how humiliating this is?"

"I do—"

"How hurt I am?"

"Yes, darling..."

He watched the light hem of her skirt waver in the air behind her. "Clearly you didn't pay any money to my papa, or he wouldn't have been in such a state. So then how did you buy me?"

How could he tell her? How could he tell her and see her fall apart even further?

"What was more important to Papa than money?" she insisted. "Is it whatever is in that red folder?"

He wanted to tell her. He wanted there to be no more secrets between them. He wanted her to stop hating him, wanted to stop their feud forever.

But for that, he had to let go of revenge.

And he couldn't. His brother's murderer deserved vengeance. It was the least he could do for Spencer.

But still. He couldn't bear to tell her what kind of man her father really was. She had said he was the only parent she had. How could Preston destroy her image of the man so completely?

"Yes, Penelope, there was an auction. Yes, I bought the right to marry you. What does it change between us?"

She stopped and looked at him, her beautiful eyes wide, her mouth opening and closing as she tried to find words.

"Nothing," she said finally. "And that is exactly the problem, isn't it? Because you still won't tell me the truth. What was my bridal price, Preston? What are you holding over my father?"

"You already hate me," Preston said somberly. "I don't want you to hate him."

She stopped pacing. Tears filled her eyes, and she slowly shook her head in disappointment. Seeing her like this broke his heart all over again. Without saying another word, Penelope stormed out of his dressing room, but in two large steps, he caught up with her and grasped her arm, turning her to him.

He couldn't let her leave, so hurt, so vulnerable. He would hurt her even more, he knew. His secrets would destroy her heart.

And their chance at a happy future.

But just for now, she was his, and she was still in his arms. She stared at him with her big eyes full of tears, so incredibly beautiful.

"Please, Penelope," he said. "Don't go."

"You cannot keep this information from me and yet expect me to—"

"I don't expect you to do anything. But just for now, just for tonight, don't leave. Please."

She didn't say anything. But she also didn't move. And that was all the invitation he needed. He kissed her then. Scooped her into his arms and carried her into his bedchamber, never allowing his lips to leave hers for a moment.

When he reached his desk, he dropped to his knees in front of her and slowly raised her skirts up, exposing the most beautiful legs in the world, wrapped in thin white cotton stockings. Her breath hitched and her hands clutched his shoulders.

"Preston, what are you doing?" she asked, her voice hoarse.

"I wanted to thank you for the portrait," he said as he placed a tender kiss on the inside of her thigh. "And tell you I don't want to argue anymore. I want to make up. I want to ask you to please forget our differences, just for tonight."

"Preston..." she said, her voice protesting.

"Did you miss me?" He licked the bare skin above her stocking on her other leg, and noticed with satisfaction as a tremor went through her. Her divine scent had his head spinning. "Because I missed you like a severed limb. It killed me not to come to you every night."

"I did miss you," she whispered softly, and his stupid heart lurched in his chest.

"De Luca," he said, pushing her crisp petticoat higher to her belly. "Turner. Rembrandt's paintings. Any gallery in the world. Whatever you wish."

There it was, the small gathering of her hair at the apex of her thighs. The entrance to his own personal paradise. He leaned down and kissed the naked flesh of her thigh above the stocking. She shuddered and gasped softly. Good. She still liked that. She couldn't fake it.

"I am on my knees in front of you," he said and pressed his lips higher. He could feel her soft hair on the side of his face. "Whatever you desire is yours."

Then he gently spread her folds and kissed her soft, hot flesh. She tasted divine, sweet and fresh, and the scent of her arousal, the feminine scent of her body got his blood boiling. When she clenched her fingers around his shoulders even tighter and wavered, he picked her up, hooking his arms around her thighs, and placed her on his dressing table.

"Preston—" she said, her voice throaty and alarmed.

"Shush, love," he said, spreading her legs and lowering himself to kneel on the floor again. "I'm just getting started. I've been hungry for you for days."

She gave out a whimper of sweet distress when he sealed his mouth with her folds once again and lifted her legs to rest over his shoulders. He was having a feast with her. He licked and teased her with his tongue, knowing exactly where she liked it the most. He ran the tip of his tongue up and down and around and around her inner lips.

He gently took in her clitoris and sucked on it until she was calling his name. Oh, how he wished that she called it with love and admiration, and not just because he brought her pleasure. But she never could love him, could she? Not when because of him, her papa suffered.

And yet, he couldn't stop.

He couldn't stop his revenge. And he couldn't stop wanting her. Adoring her. Giving her the world just to see a smile on her face.

Or hear her scream his name in ecstasy. Or clench around him rhythmically as she found her release.

He inserted a finger, then a second one, and hooked them

both so that he reached that one pleasure spot inside her. While he kept licking and sucking, and gently nibbling at her clit with his lips, he moved his fingers inside her in a circular motion. When she cried out, he wanted her fingers on him, clutching him, while her inner muscles tightened around his cock as he pounded in and out of her.

He was hard and his trousers were too tight, but he wanted this to be about her. He wanted to give her orgasms because he needed to see her come. To feel her come.

He wanted her to have all the pleasure and for himself to have nothing.

Perhaps Richard was right. By focusing on revenge, he could never be happy. And so he was punishing himself.

She was growing tighter and tighter around him, her entrance becoming wetter and wetter. The whimpers of distress grew louder and faster. He felt her thighs shake and tremble around his face. And with another stroke of his fingers, she cried out, clenching so tight, her walls held his fingers like a tight fist, and then she was coming.

She shook all over as she kept calling his name, clenching and unclenching against his lips, and around his fingers. Ah, that was music to his ears. Music he wanted to hear all day. Every day.

His name had never sounded so good as it did called out by her in the moment of her greatest ecstasy.

And he was a bastard who didn't deserve this woman.

But he had to try.

He wanted to give her the world.

He brought her to his bed and plunged into her tight, wet, hot depths with a cry, greedily unable to deny himself in the end. Heavens, how good she felt, just perfect for him. She arched her back, panting, moaning as he began slowly easing in and out of her. Without thinking, he whispered, “I do not want there to be anything between us...”

She didn’t say anything at first. It was when they both lay sated and warm and heavy in each other’s arms, and he was drifting to sleep, that she whispered, “It’s impossible, Preston. There will always be something between us. I’ll always be your enemy’s daughter.”

Penelope woke with a strange sensation. Her chest burst with pain as she heaved, trying to cough the burning smoke out of her lungs.

Dark smoke filled the whole room, red-orange flames consuming the curtains. There was a hole in the floor next to the window and fire burst through it. The air was so hot it scalded her skin.

Fear hit Penelope like a slap. She grabbed her chemise. “Preston!” she cried as she hastily put it on.

“Preston!” She shook him, but he didn’t move. Good God, did he even breathe? “Preston!” she yelled right into his ear and shook his shoulder hard.

But he wouldn’t wake up. She coughed violently, her lungs cooking. “Preston!” She ran over to his side of the bed and grasped him by his arm and pulled. She had to get him out of here. She pulled, but he was so heavy, and he barely moved on the bed. “Preston!”

The door burst open, and Joel ran in in his dressing gown. “Your Grace!” he cried. “Are you all right?”

“Oh, Joel, thank God!” She let out another racking cough. “His Grace isn’t waking up! We must get him out of here!”

“Of course.” Joel ran to the bed and hauled the naked duke onto his shoulders like a sack of wheat. He was much shorter than Preston but strongly built. "Come, Your Grace, you must leave the room!"

She nodded as Joel ran out. She grabbed the blanket to cover poor Preston's nakedness and ran after Joel. The footmen appeared from the stairs with buckets of water. But none of that would help with such a great fire raging in the old walls.

"Go outside," said Penelope. "Please, do not try to fight the fire. It's pointless. And I don't want you to risk your lives. We'll call on the fire brigades. Leave!"

A minute or so later, Penelope was outside, breathing the blessed fresh air through her scorched lungs. Her throat felt like it was on fire, and she couldn't stop coughing. Preston lay on the ground, with his head in her lap, wrapped in the blanket. With one third of the great house enveloped in flames now, she could clearly see his face, so peaceful and so dear. He was breathing, which was good.

"Please, wake up," she whispered in a rasping voice. "Please, just wake up."

And as the fire kept raging, she looked at the windows of his study.

Everything inside was gone. *Danaë*. The books. The documents.

And the red leather folder.

23

Preston's chest burned, and he found himself coughing. His throat felt like it was on fire. His eyes felt full of sand.

Above everything was the sound of roaring and crackling, and below that were voices crying and yelling. The acrid smell of smoke was heavy in his nostrils... He lay on something very hard and stone-cold, apart from his head, which was cushioned. All that stirred uneasiness inside him. Something was terribly, terribly wrong.

He felt a cool and soothing touch on his forehead. He opened his burning eyes. Penelope's face was above him, lit with an orange-red glow against the absolute blackness of the sky above.

"Preston," she said with a big smile and teary eyes. "You're alive! You woke up! Thank heavens."

He coughed and tried to sit up but failed. Through the pain in his throat and chest, he found his voice to ask her, "Penelope, are you all right?"

"Yes, I'm fine," she croaked. "How are you feeling?"

"What in the world is going—"

But she didn't need to reply. His gaze fell on the burning building...his burning home. He lay in the middle of the inner courtyard, watching fire consume the London home of twelve generations of the Dukes of Grandhampton. Flames burst through every window of the right wing and even through the roof. The entrance was aflame, but some of the furniture and art stood in the inner courtyard. Myriad sparks flew into the dark sky. Ladders were put against eight windows that were not yet in flames, and his loyal footmen and other servants were saving more furniture, paintings, vases, rugs, and anything they could put their hands on before the fire engulfed the building.

Three fire engines—big wooden constructions on wheels, like carriages without windows—stood in the courtyard, and firemen in the green uniform of his insurance company, Lindsay and Jensen, pumped the handles to get water into the hoses, while six or seven firemen stood with hoses that shot water into the fire.

But with a fire like this, everyone knew not much could be done. It was too late, Preston feared. The men were wasting their time.

"I sent word to Sebastian and the Duchess of Ashton," said Penelope, "asking them to send the fire engines of their insurance companies and their men. I don't know when they'll arrive."

It could take hours to gather a brigade. Volunteers and firemen would need to be summoned and gathered, then horses would need to be readied, and then it would still take a while to get the heavy and poorly maneuverable engines through London's streets.

He sat up and felt cold. The blanket fell from his shoulders, and he realized he was naked.

Three hoses from each of the engines were connected to

holes dug in the middle of the courtyard. The firemen must have dug into the ground to chop into the wooden water pipes. When the fire was out, they'd plug the holes before burying the pipes again.

More people ran in and out of the courtyard with buckets of water. Where were they getting it from? Preston wondered distantly. Perhaps the neighbors, the Viscount of Kitson or the Marquis of Cornforth, not wanting the fire to spread to their properties, had sent their servants with water from their troughs and cisterns.

But nothing would stop it, Preston knew. The fire raged like an unstoppable giant, completely consuming the wing of Preston's and Penelope's bedchambers, the library, the study... And soon the rest of Chalworth Place.

"Is everyone out?" he asked.

"Yes, everyone's safe. The horses are being brought out of the stables. Sam is preparing a carriage to take us to Sumhall."

"Good," he said, trying again to sit up and finally succeeding.

Then a thought hit him like a blast. "Damnation!" Wrapping the blanket around himself he scrambled up to his feet, coughing, his head reeling. "Penelope, your studio! Your paintings!"

"Forget about my paintings. Everyone's alive. That's what matters. I'll paint more."

"But the *Danaë*...and *The Shipwreck*...and Spencer's collection..."

And Spencer's last letter to him. And all those little mementos of his brother that were left in that burning hell, never to be returned.

"I'd like to help," he said, walking to the fire brigade chief. Ice-cold cobblestones dug into the bare soles of his feet. "What can I do?"

Penelope tugged him by his hand, and to his shame, his head spun so much he staggered. "Nothing, Preston. You cannot do a thing. You will go to Sumhall where a physician will examine you."

As though hearing her words, hooves and the rattle of wheels sounded behind them, and Sam pulled the carriage to a stop nearby.

Preston set into a coughing fit. Penelope was right. He couldn't do a damn thing like this. He just wanted everyone to be safe.

Mrs. Brown and Porter hurried to him, seeing that he was standing.

Mrs. Brown, still in her nightcap and nightgown, tugged the edges of her shawl around her shoulders. "Your Grace, thank heavens you're awake."

When his coughing eased, he rasped, "I'm glad everyone seems to be safe, Mrs. Brown. Look, besides Her Grace and myself, there are at least two seats inside the carriage. More if someone wants to sit at the front and stand at the back where the footmen ride. Mrs. Brown, perhaps you'd like to come along and bring those servants who aren't feeling well with us to Sumhall. Then Sam will return for the rest of the staff."

"Certainly, Your Grace," said Sam.

"No, Your Grace," said Mrs. Brown. "That is, I am fine and would stay here to watch over things. Kitty, the kitchen maid, is coughing quite badly. And Peter, the groom, cut his arm when he broke the window in the sitting room to carry the furniture out. They can ride in the carriage."

"Good," said Preston. "Let them come. And anyone else who will fit. I leave it with you."

"Come," said Penelope, supporting him at the elbow. "Let's get you inside the carriage."

He threw a last glance Chalworth, flames shooting into the

black sky like moving, living walls. His heart shrank at the loss of this ancient mansion that had so recently begun to feel like home.

After everyone was gathered, they drove to Sumhall. The streets of Mayfair were full of the reek of smoke, but it was only a ten-minute drive.

When they stopped before the tall, pristine white walls of Sumhall, Preston thought how this house, with its fashionable classic architecture, always felt so starkly different compared with Chalworth Place, which was dark, cold, and medieval. The house was big, with four stories. The front façade of the building boasted a series of elegant bow windows, each one gracefully curving outward. These distinctive windows were positioned one atop the other on each floor, creating two striking vertical lines. They were placed twenty feet away from either side of the entrance door, which was under a long portico supported by a row of six thick columns with scroll-like ornaments on top and bottom. The triangular roof structure above had decorative motifs of garlands of flowers.

Two figures burst from the shadows under the portico. "Preston! Penelope!"

As Preston got out of the carriage, his feet burning against the icy cobblestones, he saw it was Calliope and Richard who hurried down the stairs. Their butler, Teanby, followed them in a brown dressing gown and with a gas lamp in one hand. Even from here, Preston could see the butler's face wrinkled in worry, his perfectly combed, thick white hair in disarray. Teanby had joined the household when Preston's papa was an adolescent. He had seen all the Seaton siblings grow into the people they were today. And Preston knew Spencer's death had aged the man as much as it would have aged a grandfather losing his grandchild.

Behind him, Mrs. Girdwood, the housekeeper, followed.

Her white nightcap sat askew, revealing her tangled pale red hair. She wore a dark blue nightgown and carried a gas lamp, as well. She had joined the household only five years ago, but was already beloved and respected by everyone. Behind her, two maids and three footmen hurried, everyone in their nightclothes.

"Jason, Finley," barked Teanby over his shoulder at the footmen, "help His Grace!" Then he stopped before Preston and looked him over. "Your Grace, may I inquire after your well-being?"

Preston coughed, then nodded. "I'm all right. Thank you."

"And Your Grace?" he asked Penelope.

"I'm fine, thank you, Teanby," said Penelope. Thankfully, her voice wasn't as raspy as it had been when Preston woke up seeing Chalworth Place burning. "Could you and Mrs. Girdwood please make sure the servants from Chalworth are taken care of?"

"Of course, Your Grace," said Mrs. Girdwood with a kind smile and a sharp, worried look over Kitty and Peter. "Your room is already prepared, the Sapphire Room for you and for His Grace—"

"One room will suffice," said Preston before lapsing into a coughing fit. "We'll take my old room," he said when the fit passed.

Mrs. Girdwood nodded. "Of course, Your Grace. It's all ready for you."

"Here, brother," said Richard as he stood on Preston's left side and put his arm around Preston's back. "Let me help."

Richard looked so much like Papa, Preston's chest squeezed. While Spencer and Preston had their mama's coloring, Calliope and Richard had inherited their slightly darker skin tone from Mama, but their auburn hair, their bright blue eyes—they were from Papa.

"Thanks, brother," said Preston as he gladly accepted Richard's shoulder.

"The physician is on his way," said Calliope, taking Penelope's hand.

They entered the familiar interior. Inside, the house was all Mama. When she'd said she didn't like Chalworth Place and wanted to live in another house, Papa had bought Sumhall, and she'd redecorated it like she wanted. She'd brought the Mediterranean here. The large entrance hall had pale turquoise walls with golden and terra-cotta ornaments, paintings of Spanish landscapes with palms and sunlit pale rocks against the bright sea. The drapes on the windows had patterns of palm leaves and oranges.

Sumhall was much smaller than Chalworth, but it was warmer and cozier than the duke's grand London house, which always felt to him much more like a museum than a home. And now it was burning down, and who knew if it would even be possible to restore it.

"How did this even happen?" asked Richard as they walked through the foyer towards the grand stairs that led to the first floor and the bedrooms.

"I have not the slightest idea," said Preston. "Do you know, Penelope?"

She breathed out. "Yes. Sam told me they think the fire started in the study. And he saw someone running away from the house."

Worry brushed an icy hand down Preston's spine. "Who?"

"I don't know. He couldn't see. But since the fire started soon afterward..."

"Arson?" asked Richard, his voice deadly flat.

"No," said Preston. "That cannot be. Who would do such a thing? And why? I'll talk to Sam."

When Preston and Penelope were left alone in his old

bedchamber, he lay back on the pillows. Mrs. Girdwood sent a maid with hot tea, a decanter of wine, and a platter of bread, cheese, cold meat, and raisins.

Tea soothed Preston's throat as he sipped from the cup, sitting upright in the bed. Penelope cuddled into his shoulder, and the feel of her, warm and heavy, was divine. She smelled of smoke, a dark reminder that they both could have died there.

"I didn't want to say in front of Richard and Calliope," said Penelope, "but Sam said it was a short man in a powdered wig. He was stout and ran slowly like he was old...or older."

Preston put his teacup on the bedside table and cleared his throat. The soothing feeling evaporated. Anger and resentment hit him like a thousand knives.

"The fire started in my study," he said slowly. "Where I keep the red folder your father asked you to get for him. And then Sam saw a man in a powdered wig running away. Penelope, there's only a handful of men in London that still wear wigs."

Penelope sat up. "It cannot be him," she said, her eyes filling with tears. "I can't believe he'd set fire to our home."

Oh, but Preston could. He could believe it so easily. Because he knew the truth—Lord Neville Beckett was very much capable of harming people to get what he wanted and to save his own skin. He had already caused Spencer's death.

And now he'd almost killed Penelope?

No. That was it.

Preston threw the blanket off his legs and stood up. His head still spun, but he went to the bell handle and pulled it. He needed clothes and he needed a carriage.

"What are you doing?" asked Penelope, standing up.

"Making sure something like this will never happen again."

"Lord Beckett!" Preston banged the brass lion's head knocker on the door on Vine Street. "Lord Beckett!"

He coughed, painful, dry spasms making him double over. He hadn't waited until the physician arrived. He was so furious and so terrified, he couldn't see straight.

Just a few more minutes, and he could have lost Penelope.

He was less terrified of his own death than he was of hers.

He kept banging on the door while Carl, Sumhall's coachman, waited, sitting at the front of the carriage, throwing sideways glances at him. What could have possessed a duke to bang on the door of another peer at three in the morning? The street behind him was quiet and dark, just the wind rustling the crowns of blooming acacia trees.

"Lord Beckett!" he yelled with the remnants of his voice, his chest and throat bursting with pain.

Finally, there were shuffling steps behind the door, and it was unlocked. Lord Beckett's wigless head of sparse gray hair protruded from the opening. Dressed in a yellowish nightgown, he peered at Preston over the candle in his hand, and his eyes widened in fear.

"Your Grace..." he mumbled. "What is the matter?"

"You know what is the matter," said Preston, straining his dying voice to sound loud and clear. It refused, the rasp making it almost incomprehensible. "Did you do it?"

"Do what?"

"Did you commit arson in my home?"

Lord Beckett's face fell. "Arson?"

"Yes. Arson. Chalworth Place is in flames. The fire started in my study. Did you steal the red leather folder and set my home on fire, almost killing your own daughter?"

Lord Neville's eyes widened in real fear, the whites bluish in the night against his pale skin. "Is Penelope all right?"

"She is."

Lord Beckett quickly shook his head. "No. I'd never do that to her."

Preston narrowed his eyes. "I don't believe you. Penelope told you she wouldn't help you anymore, and I think that is strong enough motivation. You wanted the proof of your crime gone, and you wanted revenge."

"No. I would never. It is you who are mistaken, sir. You are so set on your own revenge that you think everyone is capable of it. The only thing I can say is that Penelope is now finally free from your horrible clutches. You do not have anything on me anymore."

Preston's chest rose and fell painfully. He commanded the burning tickle in his throat to calm down. He would rather die than show weakness in front of this man. "So you admit it? You burned it?"

"I admit nothing. It is gone thanks to the fire, of course."

Preston shook his head, revulsion curling his lip higher. He couldn't believe he had considered if he could one day forgive Beckett. This man wasn't even sorry that his daughter almost died.

"I can get another testimonial," Preston said coldly. "But a life taken cannot be returned. What I won't tolerate is having my wife associate with a father who'd risk his own daughter's life to protect his interests."

Neville paled. Good. Every last ounce of compassion for him died in Preston's chest. He would not fail to protect another person from Lord Neville Beckett. Never again. Or he wouldn't be able to live with himself.

"Prepare yourself, Lord Beckett. I will not tolerate you killing my brother or my wife. This is a fair warning. I'm going to Eastbourne and I'm buying out your debt. Then I will take this house, your country estate, and every last thing you own and throw you out on the street. And then the Bow Street Runners will come for you."

Lord Beckett blinked fast. "Please... Sir... Your Grace..."

Preston took a step closer, glaring down at the monster. "You will be nothing. All of London will hear of your crimes and of your humiliation. Forget you have friends. Forget you have family. Forget you have a daughter. You will not contact Penelope ever again. Remember well her face when you last saw her because that was the last time in your miserable life. All you have in front of you is the life of a beggar on the streets, and if I'm successful, you will pray for the noose. At least you won't harm anyone else."

24

THE MATTRESS DIPPED BENEATH PENELOPE, and she opened her eyes. Preston slipped beneath the blanket and rested his warm, hard body along hers. He slid his arm under her head, and she sighed, inhaling his scent mixed with smoke and the scent of the outdoors. He kissed her forehead, and she relaxed against him.

"Where have you been?" she asked sleepily as she laid her hand on his bare chest.

He cuddled her closer to him and rested his head against the top of hers. His bedchamber was dark and quiet, the dark navy walls almost black in the night. Coals crackled softly in the grate. A little light from the gas streetlamps came through the paned windows, creating a square pattern with shadows of moving branches and leaves on the paneled ceiling.

She suspected she knew the answer to her own question. Her heart broke about her father. She hadn't said so, but she secretly agreed with Preston. It must be Papa. And she blamed herself for it. Had she taken the red leather folder to him, she wouldn't have brought Preston into mortal danger. His home wouldn't have burned down. But he never would have forgiven her betrayal...

"Don't you worry about that," he said in his raspy voice.

Heavens, he could have died! The thought—a thought that had been circling through her mind repeatedly for hours—made her shiver, and she clutched her arms around his neck, pulling herself even closer to him.

"How are you feeling?" she asked, looking into his dark eyes. "Did you see the physician?"

"Yes. He examined me just now when I arrived. He says I'm fine. He recommends rest for the next couple of weeks."

"Splendid idea," said Penelope, cupping his jaw. She could feel the beginning of stubble on the side of his face. "I'll make sure you're all rested."

He kissed the tip of her nose. There was so much love in his eyes her chest tightened. "I'm so glad you're unharmed. I don't know how I could keep living if you were hurt."

"It's me who's glad," she said, love filling her whole being with light. "When I saw you unmoving, the flames coming closer, I must have died a thousand times."

He inhaled deeply and smiled. It was such a rare occasion, to see a smile on his face, that she stilled, marveling at the creases at the corners of his mouth, at the wrinkles at the corners of his eyes, his teeth, white and beautiful. He was so gorgeous when he smiled, he looked like an angel straight from heaven.

And he didn't just look angelic. He was a kind man through and through. Despite his grumpiness and his dislike of her in the beginning, he'd given her everything her father hadn't. He'd given her a studio and private lessons with great masters—it was her dream come true. He'd given her freedom to be who she wanted to be. His family had welcomed her with their arms and hearts open, as though she'd always belonged.

The only thing he hadn't done was tell her what horrible deed her father had committed.

"Preston, can you not tell me what my father has done? Not even after he set your house on fire?"

His smile fell, and she was ready to kick herself for that. "Our house," he corrected her. "And I do want to tell you. But not here and not now. Our home is gone. Let us go to Grandhampton and stay there until my barrister is able to buy us a new home in London."

"Go to the country?" The idea was exhilarating. It meant leaving all their troubles behind and spending time together, just the two of them.

"Yes." He tucked a strand of her hair behind her ear. "What do you say?"

"I'd love to. You'll be able to rest your lungs there and recover faster."

"Sounds wonderful."

There was not much to pack, only borrowed clothes from Calliope and Richard. Preston got the news that the fire was finally contained. Chalworth hadn't burned down completely, but it would require significant time and money to rebuild it. While Penelope prepared for the journey, Preston told her he was going out for business.

Instead, he went to Tyche, where he made an arrangement with Solomon Eastbourne that would ensure his threat to Lord Beckett was realized. He bought the man's debt.

Finally, they set out. The roads were still muddy even in spring, and the trip took a full day, so with their late start they were forced to stop at an inn overnight.

But it was all worth it.

When they arrived, Penelope's breath was taken away. Grandhampton Court was so much grander than Chalworth. It looked like something that should house a royal family. The house was breathtaking. Tall and long, built in the Palladian style from large, perfectly square pieces of sandstone, it had an impressive portico so large, it could host a ball. Twelve fluted columns three stories high supported a roof structure that held twelve statues of the Palladium. To the left and to the right, the building stretched farther and could envelop two Sumhalls.

Round-arched windows lined the ground floor, and perfectly rectangular windows lined the first and the second floors, each with a triangular ornament above. Grand stairs one story high led to the entrance door under the portico.

Before the building, a beautiful, well-maintained natural park spread with cut grass, neatly pruned bushes, and flowers. There was a large fountain. Trees and small groves grew here and there. A herd of sheep grazed on a pasture two miles or so away.

When Penelope stepped out of the carriage, she breathed in the sweet air, full of the scents of leaves and earth, and closed her eyes. Sunlight fell on her face and wind kissed her cheeks. She held her bonnet as she raised her chin towards the sun.

"Welcome to Grandhampton," said Preston, and when she looked at him, she didn't recognize him.

The stern mask of a London lord was gone, and he was someone else. The tension around his eyes melted away, and a soft smile bloomed on his lips. He was so handsome her heart burst, and it was that moment that she knew she was utterly and completely in love with him.

The realization struck her like a blow. She went momentarily numb, unmoving, as if suspended in air. How strange was it, to know it was her heart that slammed hard against her ribs, but that it didn't belong to her anymore.

It was his.

After the servants were introduced and Preston gave her

the initial tour around the house, he led her outside, around the back. Hidden by a grove of trees were the entrance for servants and deliveries, the stables, a cow shed and a chicken coop as well as a garden. And at the side of the house was a natural pond with a jetty and a boat.

Willows grew on the other side, their branches trailing in the water. Reeds and grasses framed the shores. Flies and bees buzzed by.

"We used to swim here as children," Preston said and pointed at an inviting little meadow before the pond with cut grass and daisies popping up here and there. "We spent most of our time here. That is, until I was sent to Scotland. After that, I came here only in summers, but those were the happiest months. Then when the time came for Spencer to be introduced into London society, we started to attend the Season every year in London. That's when I knew that my father had a different side to him. In London, he was the perfect duke. Here, he was my papa. Someone domestic and simple who went to fish with all of us, even Calliope. Who taught me how to swim. Who playfully tickled my mama when he thought no one was watching. This is where Mama ran after us children with squeals of delight and tickled us and wore such a warm smile on her face that it was impossible not to smile back."

Penelope saw how that must be true. Preston here was not the Preston she knew in London. She got glimpses of him like that when they were alone and in bed. But there was more to him, and she couldn't wait to find out what. Only...she had a sinking feeling she'd only fall further in love with him. And that terrified her.

He showed her the meadow where they played cricket. A pasture a mile away where Spencer had taught him to ride his first pony. The grove of trees where they had fenced with sticks. He told her Calliope had had a favorite dog, Butterfly, who had sadly died a few years ago.

As they passed by the portico where two footmen stood waiting for them at attention, Preston leaned to her. "Richard was always the servants' favorite."

Penelope chuckled. "I can easily see why."

Preston shook his head softly. "He charmed them. Always had a smile for any of them. Not only did the little devil know each of their names, but he also knew what each of them liked to eat. Up to the age of eight, he hid portions of his food in napkins for them—to both the pleasure and irritation of Mrs. Liddle, the housekeeper, because they left fat stains that were very hard to get rid of."

Mrs. Liddle, the housekeeper, and Harney, the butler, came down the stairs, a footman following them with a tray in his hands.

"We thought you and Her Grace would like some refreshments, Your Grace," said Harney.

He was a man in his seventies, with a bald head in the front and sparse hair at the back. He was tall and broad, with a wide mouth and an impressive straight jaw. His wrinkled face had a kind expression. The liveried footman stood proudly next to Mrs. Liddle, with two empty glasses and a decanter of wine and another with something stronger. Alongside the drinks sat a small platter with toasted slices of bread rubbed with something red and drizzled with some sort of greenish oil.

"Pan con tomate," said Mrs. Liddle proudly. She was a sweet woman in her sixties, with plump cheeks and translucent blue eyes. Both Mrs. Liddle and Harney looked like they could barely maintain their polite masks. Penelope had the impression they had to restrain themselves from dashing forward and hugging Preston. "Just like your dear mama, God rest her soul, taught Mrs. Norman."

Preston's face spread in a broad smile that warmed Penelope's heart. When Harney poured wine into two glasses, Preston took one of them and handed it to Penelope. He then took the other glass and a slice of red bread. "Please, thank Mrs. Norman. Mama always loved her pan con tomate." He looked at Penelope. "It's a Spanish dish Mama insisted on having. It means tomato bread. It's a traditional peasant dish, but Mama tried it once back in Spain when she was little and loved it."

Curious, Penelope picked up a piece of bread and sniffed. It smelled strong and pungent, like something from faraway lands. "What's in it?"

Mrs. Liddle smiled at Penelope. "Toasted bread is rubbed with tomato and garlic and drizzled with some olive oil. There's also sea salt."

"Oh," said Penelope. "Does your gardener grow tomatoes?" She sipped some wine, then bit into the pan con tomate.

The crunchiness of bread, the sweet-tart flavor of tomato, and the pungent bite of garlic were delicious on her tongue. She suppressed a moan of delight because, of course, duchesses didn't moan in company. Preston chewed with his pose stiff and upright, but she saw the delight dancing in his eyes.

"He does," said Mrs. Liddle. "Ever since Her Grace started living here. The tomatoes on the bread are preserved as they're out of season. We still plant them every year because the children... Beg your pardon, Your Grace, I still refer to you four as children. Well, they all enjoy the Spanish cuisine their mama introduced here."

Penelope nodded. "I look forward to tasting more Spanish cuisine. All I've known my entire life are regular English dishes."

She wished she'd known Preston's parents, just as she wished her own mama were still alive and he could know her.

When they finished their slices and their glasses of wine, Preston thanked the two servants.

"How long will you stay for, Your Grace?" asked Harney.

"Two weeks at least," said Preston. "You couldn't have heard, but Chalworth Place burned down two nights past. We're here to recover from the shock. Get some fresh air."

"Is everyone all right, Your Grace?" asked Harney with a tone of worry. "Are you?"

"Yes, thank you, Harney," said Preston. "Thankfully, no one was harmed badly. Of course, there are cuts, burns, and bruises on the brave servants and firemen, but everyone's alive and will recover. Now it's a matter of finding us a new home while Chalworth is being rebuilt."

"Was much lost in the fire?" asked Mrs. Liddle. "Would you like me to arrange sending some furniture to Sumhall to store until you find a new home?"

"Not for the moment," said Preston. "But it reminds me." He looked at Penelope with a twinkle in his eyes. "Do you know where Mama's old watercolor paints are, Mrs. Liddle? Her paper, pens, brushes... You see, Her Grace is a talented artist, but most of her art and art supplies were lost in the fire."

"Oh, of course, I know exactly where they are. Let me get them for you."

While Mrs. Liddle, Harney, and the footman returned back into the house, Penelope wrapped her arms around Preston's neck, and he pulled her into his embrace. He kissed her, his lips soft and tender, making her head spin and the ground shift under her feet.

"Are you sure you don't mind me using your mama's paints?" she asked when he pulled away.

"Of course not," he said. "She would have been the first to offer them."

Later, while Preston stood on the jetty before the pond with a fishing pole in his hands, with the most serene and nostalgic expression, Penelope painted. She painted the picture before her—the idyllic pond, the jetty, the boat, only she added a family, too. Four children, two parents, a picnic blanket, and a picnic.

She painted the deceased Duke of Grandhampton standing on that jetty with a fishing pole, small Preston and Richard looking at the fish in the bucket. Little Calliope with her auburn locks next to her beautiful mama with her dark hair and her pretty white dress, making a dandelion wreath.

And Spencer. She had painted everyone and the whole landscape except him. He was a white silhouette standing next to his papa with a fishing pole, the tallest and the largest of the boys.

Spencer's absence was a gaping hole in that painting. And as she began painting him, the hole in the painting started to fill.

But would the hole his death had left in the family ever be filled?

And would her and Preston's happiness ever be complete with that vast chasm of Spencer's absence between them?

25

"PRESTON..."

Penelope's sweet voice broke through his sleep, and he felt soft hair tickling his naked chest. He inhaled a lungful of her scent—clean skin and the lavender soap she'd used when she bathed last night.

Blindly, he wrapped his arms around her and pulled her onto him, her naked, soft breasts brushing against his torso. She giggled, and he grinned, opening his eyes. She gazed down at him, smiling from ear to ear, bathed in the sunlight coming from the window of his old bedroom, her uncombed hair glowing in a halo. Heavens, after three days in Grandhampton, just the two of them, he could not stop wondering how he had gotten so lucky with this woman. He had no notion. All he could do was be thankful for every moment she chose to be in his arms, every moment he was fortunate enough to hold her.

He kissed her lightly, even though his cock was already semihard, just from feeling her thighs on both sides of his hips and her warm and soft sex pressed against him in exactly the right place.

"Yes, Duchess?" he said.

"I have an idea."

"If that idea involves you and me naked, I'm all yours."

"Well, it does involve *you* naked."

"All right, then." He shifted his hips up, which caused the most delicious friction against her body, and groaned. He leaned forward to kiss her properly, but she avoided him.

"Not like that."

He frowned and narrowed his eyes at her. "Pardon? How else do you want me naked?"

"I'd like to paint a nude portrait of you."

He couldn't speak for a moment. He imagined himself frozen for hours in one of those Greek postures while she painted him... A bark of laughter burst from his throat. In a quick movement, he pressed her to him tighter and flipped them both over. She gave a small squeal, and he chuckled. There she was, his beautiful wife, pinned to the mattress under him, her thighs spread and his hard cock pressing right at her warm, tight entrance.

"No," he said. "There's a much better use of my naked body, and it's to make you come over and over. Allow me to give you a demonstration."

She bit her lower lip as he moved his pelvis, caressing her clitoris again and again with his cock. She arched her back, her head lolling.

"Do you like it?" he asked. "Am I pleasing you, love?"

"Oh yes..."

"See how much better this is than you and me five feet apart and me standing in one pose for hours? If I can move, I can do this..."

He plunged into her, sliding easily through her delicious wetness. He groaned in pleasure as her tight walls took him in. She gasped and wrapped her legs around his hips, her arms around his shoulders, clinging to him, urging him closer to her, deeper.

He obliged and sank into her, angling his hips in that way he knew would allow him to rub against her clitoris at the same time. Then he had an idea and stopped for a moment. "Do you trust me, love?"

She blinked and nodded. "Of course I trust you."

That broke his heart a little because he still hid a terrible secret from her; she still didn't know why she was married to him.

He pulled out of her and kneeled in front of her. "Lift your leg." He grabbed her ankle and put her leg over one of his shoulders, then the other one. Her smooth thighs were spread before him, high and wide, giving him full access to her. Oh, the sight in front of him had his erection tighten and tingle and ache with need for her.

"Heavens, how much I want you. Have you any sense of how incredibly beautiful you are?"

She exhaled softly, leaning back on her pillow. Her lips were red and swollen from desire, her hair spilled on the pillow. A little seductress, what was she doing to him?

"No," she said. "But I know how incredibly handsome you are and how much I desire you."

He groaned and lowered himself on top of her, penetrating her sweet depths once again. How he loved it when that little gasp came out of her lips every time they connected like this, flesh to flesh, skin to skin, as deep as two humans possibly could. He started moving then, he was bollocks-deep in her, and kept plunging in and out of her. He watched color come to her face, and her hooded eyes, heavy and dark with pleasure, her white teeth biting her lower lip as she arched her back and moaned.

That was right. He looked down at her pretty round tits

bouncing as he drove her higher and higher towards the peak of pleasure. He didn't think he'd ever been so deep inside her, and he loved it, being enveloped by her so completely.

Just him and her.

Soon, he was wild with desire. He fucked her, driving her deeper and deeper into the mattress. Her head rolled, her chest reddened, and the thin sinews on her neck strained. He felt her suck his cock tighter, deeper inside her. She was about to burst with pleasure, and then she froze, and her internal muscles squeezed him like a fist, and that was his undoing. As she clenched and shook around him, fiery pleasure crashed through him like a tidal wave. He bucked and gave animallike groans, and was lost in emptying himself into her.

Then he collapsed on top of her and rolled to the side, panting. He lifted her onto his chest, and they both breathed hard.

"Tell me I'm right," he said when he finally found his breath. "Is this not a better use of my nakedness?"

Penelope gave a low moan and looked straight into his eyes. "Preston, I love you and I want to commemorate how beautiful you are..."

They both stilled. Preston swallowed a painful knot in his throat. Her eyes went wide as she stared at him without moving a muscle.

"You what?" he asked.

She could not be serious. She couldn't love him. He didn't deserve her. He was not a good man; his way forward was destruction. And all she was was pure and beautiful and everything that was good and right in the world. How could she love him? There was nothing to love about him.

"I love you," she said. "All of you. Your gorgeous body. Your kind heart. Your beautiful soul. And I want to paint you like I see you when we're like this."

Something within him began unravelling. He was more open to her than he'd been to anyone. Not even his siblings. Not even Sebastian, his best friend, knew him like she did. He'd always been the second best. The "spare." Born just in case, so that someone could continue the noble name. All his life he'd tried to prove to everyone, but mostly to himself, that he was just as worthy as Spencer.

While deep down, he didn't believe he was.

But he didn't feel like he needed to prove anything with Penelope. She was in his sacred place, and she fit just right. She was healing something inside of him. Her light broke through his walls and shone directly into his heart. His grief for Spencer, the guilt and self-loathing he'd hidden from everyone his whole life, the way he protected his fragile nature with a gruff, prideful, uncaring exterior.

This woman knew.

And she said she loved him.

"Say something," she said.

He loved her. The realization hit him clear and hot. Tears prickled his eyes, his chest heaved, and he felt hot and shaking. Through all of this, he had managed to fall in love with his wife.

I love you, Penelope. You are the best thing that has ever happened in my life. You're healing my stupid dark heart. You make me feel like I may be a worthy man. You make me so happy...

The words were on his tongue. He opened his mouth to say them. She looked at him with her eyes as blue as a winter sky.

But he didn't say them. He said none of that.

"I don't want to do a nude portrait, Penelope," he said, his whole body feeling pricked with needles. "What I want is you and me in this bed. If I'm nude, I want you nude, too."

She hid the hurt in her eyes and pressed out a smile. "This is not the end of this discussion."

He freed his shoulder from under her head and rolled to sit up, putting his legs over the side of the bed. "It is for now."

As he stood up and put on his dressing gown, he didn't look at her.

He was a fool if he dared to hope for a lifelong happiness, like his parents had had. There couldn't be true love between them. They may be in love now, but sooner or later it would end.

Love terrified him. It was possible, he knew, for good people. Like his parents. Like Sebastian and Emma.

All that happy future he could almost see and feel—it would never be. Deep down, he didn't deserve a happy life and the love of this woman. She had started to break down his walls. He could see cracks in them, see how low and thin they had become thanks to her.

But it terrified him that she could see the real him... She couldn't love the jealous, prideful boy who'd become an arrogant, stubborn man. She loved some version of him that she had constructed in her head.

Wrapping the belt of the dressing gown around his waist, he went to pull the servant bell. He knew he was guilty in Spencer's death. She was mixed up in the middle of it all. And she was still his enemy's daughter. And while he should be staying indifferent to her and simply making her pregnant, he'd somehow managed to lose his mind, his heart, and his soul to her.

This whole marriage had been a big mistake.

She loved him. He went to the window and looked out over the beautiful sunlit park in front of Grandhampton. He had just betrayed his brother even further. Not only had he married Penelope, but he had fallen in love with her and she with him.

Spencer didn't deserve that betrayal.

Besides, would she even want to be with him if he hadn't

forced her? Like many women, she must be just trying to make the best of the situation she found herself in.

And so should he. Until it all came crumbling down.

Because his choice was the same. Love or revenge.

And he was still set on the latter.

26

Penelope wove her fingers through Preston's on his lap. From the window of the carriage, she could see that apple trees had blossomed like white clouds and magnolia trees were covered in gentle pink flowers, and the crisp scent of lilacs filled the air. London was in bloom.

As was Penelope's heart. Two blissful weeks in Grandhampton had been heaven. Preston's lungs had recovered quite well, she felt much better, and Preston's solicitor had written to inform him that he had found a potential new house for them. Preston and Penelope had a meeting today at the house to view the property and decide about the purchase.

The only cloud that darkened Penelope's happiness was that she had blurted out to Preston that she loved him. And clearly, she had spooked him.

He hadn't said it back. Which meant he didn't love her. Not yet.

Or he did, but was afraid to admit it.

She was not sure how she could love the man who held her father's destruction over his head. She must be a masochist.

But he did promise he'd tell her the secret. In Grandhampton Court, she hadn't insisted that he tell her because she didn't want to ruin the peace of that place. Besides, stressing him while he was injured had seemed cruel. But, perhaps, the main reason was that she was terrified the news he held would completely destroy them.

Now Preston was better, and they were about to make a decision on their home together. They couldn't start the next chapter in their lives with a secret like that between them. She had to know.

She looked into Preston's warm, dark eyes. He smiled as he met her gaze—as he had often in the past two weeks.

His hand in hers, she said, "Preston, we're going to our new home. A home that won't be Spencer's. A home that won't hold the memory of generations of Grandhampton dukes. A home that will be a clean slate."

His smile fell and he nodded, looking down at her hand. "That is all very true."

"Well... Don't you think we're now past the things that we held against each other in the beginning? Don't you think we ought not to have any secrets between us?"

He didn't look up at her, but his Adam's apple bobbed as he swallowed. "We ought not to."

"You must know what I want to ask you, Preston. What was in the red leather folder? What did my father do that you must treat him so? What did you have that was big enough to buy me without money?"

Preston nodded again, his face stern and somber. The mask of London Preston was on, with his straight jaw and his hard eyes and his mouth pressed into a straight line. The carefree, happy, relaxed Preston she'd had for two weeks was gone.

He inhaled sharply and looked at her. All traces of warmth disappeared from his eyes. He removed his hand from hers and rubbed his chin. "I will tell you. I had intended to tell you, but, weakling me, I couldn't bear to destroy the blissful existence that you had miraculously transformed my life into."

She hadn't expected that. "Did I?"

He looked at her like she was out of her mind. "Of course you did, Penelope. Before you, I thought my future would include marrying a cold, perfect lady who'd I never be able to love and drinking my way through the days until I died. I thought I'd feel lonely till the end. But then you came and showed me what I had been too blind to see."

She swallowed hard. "I know that exact feeling, Preston. I've always thought I'd be alone if I followed my dream to be a professional artist." She squeezed his hand. "But you showed me I don't have to be. And I'd like to show you neither do you. I love you for who you are—a kind, loyal, slightly obsessive soul." She chuckled. "I don't know why you set out to get revenge against Papa, but somehow I know it comes from your deep loyalty."

He sighed and shook his head, his black eyes watering.

"You may change your mind once you know. If Spencer wasn't dead...if your father wasn't involved in all that...I'd be the happiest man alive. Because I have you."

Cold shock washed over her. "Spencer dead..." she murmured. "My father involved—in what exactly? What are you talking about?"

He brushed his hands through his hair and leaned forward towards her, his eyes so dark they looked bottomless. "There's this club called Tyche. Have you heard of it?"

"I have heard of it," she said. "Everyone in the ton has. A sinful place for gentlemen."

"Yes. A gaming hell. Your father gambled all his fortune away there."

Penelope felt pained, even though she already knew about her father's folly. All she could do was nod. "Right."

"That's where you were auctioned. Bad deals are done there. That's where gentlemen can make connections with men who do bad things for good money. Things a true gentleman wouldn't involve himself with."

Her hands shook. "What things?"

"There was a servant at Tyche, Noah, who told me something about your father. He broke the rule of secrecy, so he's in danger now."

"Goodness gracious." Penelope clutched at her neck. "What was it?"

"He overheard your father inquiring after a man to—" He exhaled sharply and shook his head once. The next breath he took was shaky. "—to beat Spencer up."

The world shrank around Penelope. Her chest constricted; she couldn't breathe. "No. That can't be right. Not my papa. Why would he want to harm Spencer?"

"Tyche's owner, Solomon Eastbourne, threatened him and pressed him to repay his debts, and your father felt like he didn't have anything else left of value but you."

Penelope was going to be sick. She laid her hand on her stomach. "Me?"

"Your hand in marriage," he explained.

"But how is that connected to Spencer's death? You said, if Spencer wasn't dead..."

Preston closed his eyes for a few moments, then opened them and said, "The men your father hired beat him up so viciously that Spencer died of his wounds."

Her hand shot to her mouth and covered it. Her eyes blurred with tears. Her chest burned and squeezed the breath out of her. She understood.

Preston thought her father was to blame for Spencer's death.

And therefore, she was to blame, as well.

Preston covered her hand lying on her knees with his. "I'm sorry, Penelope. If I could take this pain away from you, I would. Do you want me to stop?"

She shook her head, still holding her hand to her mouth, afraid she was going to be sick right on Preston.

"But what did Spencer ever do to Papa?" she finally managed.

"You know about Spencer's reputation."

She nodded. "And Papa thought he'd only ruin me because he would never marry a baron's daughter..."

Preston nodded. "And ruin his chances to find a rich match for you."

"Oh no," Penelope breathed. "Oh no!"

The worst thing was, she understood what she really was to her father. He was never there for her. She'd always tried to impress him, but in vain. He'd only thought of her as another possession to be sold off.

"As far as Lord Beckett was concerned, Spencer hadn't had serious intentions towards you. He couldn't risk you being dishonored only to be dismissed by one of the oldest ducal lines in England."

Penelope felt the waves of shock thunder through her.

"At that time, your father had been anticipating a wedding proposal from the wealthy Duke of Woodley."

"Right. He did come to visit often and danced with me and talked to me at the balls."

"But then that fell through when the duke learned the extent of Lord Beckett's debts. After that failed, he had hoped for another match, but eventually he got desperate. It took a few months for your papa to resort to auctioning you off."

Preston barely appeared to breathe as he waited for her response.

She sat there stunned, her mind reeling through all that she had learned and somehow returning to that night in his study, the letter from Spencer, the first time she'd realized he'd felt more for her than friendship. He had asked Preston to go with him that night. The night he died. "You didn't go with him," she said, realization jolting her. "You think that's why he's dead. You blame yourself. You blame my father. You blame me."

She felt like she was an executioner holding the noose.

"Yes."

The single word blew up her world like a bucket of gunpowder lit on fire. That was why they were married. She was nothing but revenge for him. To punish her father, to punish himself, and to punish her. He had thought she'd been leading Spencer, that she'd wanted to marry him for money.

The carriage stopped, and they both looked out of the window at a beautiful, dark-bricked, sunlit town house behind a wrought iron fence with elaborate friezes. An oval fanlight sat above a large chocolate-brown entrance door surrounded by a white reeded architrave. The very fashionable large paned sash windows had iron grilles along the bottom for safety. Violet wisteria bloomed above the door.

It was gorgeous. Homey. Inviting. After the cold and mausoleum-like Chalworth, she had wished for a home exactly like this one—for Preston and for herself. Warm. Cozy.

Happy.

But grief and pain weighed in her chest. The three of them—she, Preston, Papa—were all entangled in Spencer's death. That was what had plagued Preston this whole time. Part of her regretted she'd ever asked Preston to tell her the truth. She now wished she didn't know it.

The door opened, Preston stepped from the carriage, and the footman offered Penelope assistance as she climbed out. Without a word, they proceeded inside, where the butler showed them around. The house was spectacular. Light and modern, with a water closet and a shower installed. It was not too big but allowed space to entertain and even throw a ball. There were plenty of bedrooms for guests and to convert into a nursery.

When she stood in the room that could be their bedroom and looked outside onto the quiet Mayfair street with petals of magnolia flowers sweeping the ground in the wind, Preston came to stand next to her. She tensed. Her chest felt like it had been slashed open, and ragged pieces of her bled.

It was hard to watch the sunlit street and know that happiness had been within reach but now would never be. Even though they didn't hate each other anymore, their story was tainted. Her father was a horrible man, after all, and Spencer's death would always hang between her and her husband. If Preston had wished for a punishment, he'd gotten one.

"The house belongs to a viscount who needs money," said Preston without looking at her.

"It's beautiful," she said, watching a carriage pass by.

"It is."

There they were. Two people forever locked together in a marriage that may never work. Except...

She turned to him, and he met her gaze, his handsome eyes solemn. "Thank you for telling me the truth," she said. "And I'm so sorry for what my father has done."

"Do you believe me?" he asked. There was a painful edge in his question.

"I believe you," she said. "Why wouldn't I?"

"I thought perhaps you wouldn't believe your papa was capable of something like that."

She touched the pale blue curtain with golden patterns of interwoven vines. "Unfortunately, I do. It hurts to know he's capable of harming an innocent man like that. It also hurts to know he'd sell his own daughter."

"I'm sorry, Penelope. I tried to shield you from this knowledge. At least it's a relief there are no secrets between us any longer." He took her hands in his, and his warmth scalded her cold palms. "And this is our new house. If you like it, I'll sign the offer today. I can see a future for us here. Can you?"

Could she? Had he asked her an hour ago, she would have said yes. Now...she didn't know.

"But as long as I'm who I am and you're who you are, your brother's death will always lie between us. No matter how much I love you."

An expression of the most agonized pain disturbed his features. "No. No. I...I love you, Penelope."

The words thundered like a cannonade in her head. *He loved her...* While all this time she'd thought he was just indulging with her to conceive an heir, like he'd told her he would.

"You love me?" she asked stupidly.

"Yes, I love you. You're my wife. I love you. I want all of you."

Suddenly, she felt very, very cold and began shaking. Part of her felt like she was about to float right to the ceiling from joy. He loved her back!

But with a sinking sensation she realized this wasn't enough.

"All of me—but no matter how much you love me, you still hate my father. You still married me for revenge. Not for love. So which is stronger, Preston? Because you can't have both. Do you love me enough to stop with your revenge? Or do you hate him more than you love me?"

Preston looked like he was being drawn and quartered. With pain thundering behind his eyes, he opened his mouth to say something, but there was an urgent knock on the door and the viscount's butler came in.

"Begging Your Graces' pardon... This is most unusual. A boy from Lord Beckett just arrived with a message."

Penelope let go of Preston's hands and hurried to the butler. "From my father? How did he know where to find us?"

"The boy said he went to Sumhall first, and they told him you'd be here for the viewing."

"What's the message?" asked Penelope.

Preston marched to stand next to her. "Penelope—"

"What's the message?" she insisted, her heart thundering.

The butler swallowed. "Lord Beckett called for your help. His house is being repossessed."

Penelope gasped, the floor shifting under her feet, and turned to Preston.

"Is this your doing?" she demanded. He looked lost and guilty, his eyebrows drawn together. "Is there something you haven't told me?"

Preston shot a look at the butler, who stood with his face straight and impartial. "Yes," said Preston.

"I thought there wouldn't be any more secrets between us."

Preston let out a quick sigh. "I bought Lord Beckett's debt from Solomon Eastbourne. I couldn't stand your father hurting another person that I love. You."

Hurt burst through her like a gunshot. "So you're forcing him out? You're continuing your revenge?"

Preston held her gaze for a while, then nodded his head, his eyes wet.

"Stop this, Preston! He'll be on the streets. He'll be a beggar!"

He said nothing.

She couldn't believe this. Her own husband would condemn her papa to the lowest state to which a human being could fall. She guessed this was the answer to her question, whether he chose love or revenge. Tears blurred her vision, and he was nothing but a beige and black spot against the pale blue of the bedchamber. She was burning inside.

"If you don't stop this, I'll leave you, Preston. If you choose revenge, you don't choose me. You don't choose our happiness. Which will it be?"

He stood, shaking, his jaw muscles working, his chest rising and falling quickly.

A tear rolled down her cheek.

She couldn't let him destroy the only parent she had left, no matter what her father had done.

"So this is what I was for you all this time, a means to an end? I was nothing to you, while I fell in love with you."

"No, Penelope, please. I love you!"

She shook her head slowly. Her life was falling apart. She had just lost the father she'd thought she had; she had just lost her husband and her lifelong happiness.

"You may think you do. Or you may say so to make me feel better. But you don't love me, not really. Or you wouldn't have hurt my papa like that. I can't leave him alone. And I can't be with a man who chooses destruction and hatred over me. I deserve better. So do you, Preston. Buy the house or don't. I won't be living in it."

With that, she walked out to save her poor, old, misguided papa.

No matter what he had done, she knew Papa couldn't have meant to kill Spencer. He was a wounded person, but not an evil one.

27

Three days later, Penelope furiously embroidered some sort of flower in the sitting room of the hotel suite she had rented for her papa and herself using her allowance.

The sitting room featured paneled walls that were decorated with oil paintings of country landscapes and a view of the city over the Thames. Vases filled with peonies, lilacs, and tulips brightened the corners of the room, providing a pleasant fragrance.

The large paned windows were dressed with violet-fringed curtains. Candles, placed in ornate holders, stood unlit. And a carpet with patterns of red flowers and green vines covered a wooden floor.

It was a pleasant enough suite, with everything she needed...except for the man she loved.

Penelope sat on a comfortable sofa, with plush cushions and soft upholstery. Emma and Calliope sat to her right on the sofa, teacups in their hands. A tea table stood nearby with a delicate tea set.

"Dearest," said Emma. "Would you take care? I'm afraid you're going to miss the cloth and stab yourself."

Penelope stopped and breathed out sharply.

"What is that supposed to be, anyway?" asked Calliope, craning her neck.

Penelope stared at the mess of yellow, orange, and black threads. "A sunflower," she said sadly.

Emma put her cup on the saucer, slowly leaned forward, and gently took the embroidery from Penelope's hands. Penelope's fingers shook as she craved a release of emotion: the fury she felt towards Preston and towards herself for having fallen in love with him, the sadness of the greatest loss of her life, the hurt of her husband's betrayal, and the frustration at her father.

"What happened?" asked Emma.

"You know what," said Penelope, taking a cup of tea.

The cup rattled against the saucer, and she put it back. Apparently, she couldn't stop shaking.

"We know you and Preston are no longer living in the same house," said Calliope. "But we don't know why."

Tears welled, burning Penelope's eyes. "I'm not sure I should tell you."

"Why not?" asked Calliope.

"Because you would never see your brother in the same light again."

Calliope chuckled. "I do not think that is possible. Preston can be a scoundrel if he's hurt and may not see things clearly if those he loves are in danger. But he means well. He's loyal, and he'd die for every one of us." She paused, then added softly, "Especially for you."

Especially for her... He may be willing to die for her, but his vengeance was even more important.

"You both must promise this will not leave these rooms.

Because it doesn't just concern my husband, it concerns my papa, too. And I care for both men dearly."

Calliope and Emma exchanged puzzled glances, and Penelope began talking. She told them everything. What her papa had done. What Preston had found out. About the auction. About the horrible start of their marriage, and how Preston blamed her, her father, and himself for Spencer's death. His revenge plan. Her giving Papa money. Her papa trying to get the evidence. The fire.

And then how Preston had bought out Papa's debt and forced him onto the streets.

And how, when she'd told him to choose her or his revenge, he hadn't said anything. He hadn't said he chose her.

"Your father—" whispered Calliope. "He did that?"

Penelope nodded, her chest tight and painful. "I am ever so sorry, Calliope."

"It's not your fault." Tears welled in Calliope's eyes. "It was an accident. I don't blame you. I blame your papa...a little. But not so much as to want to destroy him."

It was an accident, but had she not been involved, had she not been so friendly with the deceased duke, Papa wouldn't have sent the thugs after him. And he'd be alive.

"You know what I think?" said Emma, her intelligent steely-blue eyes narrowing on Penelope slightly. "I think you love your husband."

Penelope swiped a tear that rolled down her cheek with the back of her hand and sniffed. "I do. Silly me. How could I have fallen for my father's tormentor? For my father's victim's brother?"

"How could you have not?" asked Calliope, wiping her own damp cheek. "You two are perfect for each other. You're meant to be."

"No, we're not," said Penelope. "There's no future for us,

even if we're married. We'll forever live separately and be one of those couples where the wife prefers the country and the husband the city, and they never see each other. We all know them."

Emma cocked her head. "Look, darling. I've gone through something similar. That is, I thought all was lost with Sebastian, but it wasn't in the end. I wonder if it's truly so for you. It seems Preston needs to let go of his desire for revenge. But it also seems to me you're angry with him, as well. Could you ever see it in your heart to forgive him?"

"I don't know. It is true. My father's deed cannot be undone. Spencer cannot come back. What's happening now with Preston is destruction. It's poisonous. It's hatred. If we are to have any future, my husband and my father must move past this. And so must I. I must also forgive my father for harming Spencer...for selling me...and for setting fire to our home."

"And do you?" asked Calliope.

"I think so," she said. "But I won't forget, and I don't excuse what Papa did. I know I can't trust him, but I don't want him to be put out on the streets, either. He's my papa. But I won't let him behave like that again. I must stand up for myself."

The ladies talked a bit longer, making Penelope feel so much better. She missed Alex, her best friend, but now she knew she had two more great friends here in London. And they felt like family.

Later that night, when Papa returned to the hotel room for dinner, Penelope observed him with different eyes. He looked better, with the fresh clothes she'd ordered for him and a new powdered wig that looked as white as snow. He didn't stoop anymore and didn't smell, as she had hired a new valet who made sure he bathed regularly.

They sat down at the dinner table, just the two of them. A hotel footman served them the first course of soup.

After eating in silence for a few minutes, Penelope asked, "Where have you been, Papa?"

He lowered his spoon. "Huh? I was out. Why?"

"Because I'm afraid you're going to go gambling again."

He didn't say anything, then looked at his plate.

"If it wasn't for your gambling and your debts, none of this would have happened. Do you understand what a destructive habit it is? Not just for you. But for your family. For me."

"I didn't play cards," he said quietly. "But I went to Tyche. I must keep up appearances. Must keep up with my acquaintances and friends. I'm still a baron."

"Barely," she said as she put down her spoon. "Our London house on Vine Street got repossessed along with anything else of value that was left there. The only thing that keeps your title is Beckett Manor, but it's falling apart without any hope of being repaired. And had it not been for me, you'd be begging on the streets now. Surely, now I deserve some gratitude from you along with respect, which is long overdue."

He lowered his head, his shoulders stooping. "I didn't intend to burn your house down, Penelope. It was an accident. I came to take the red leather folder, but I heard some footsteps, and as I turned, the lamp fell, and the papers in the study became engulfed by fire. I tried to put it out, but the more I tried, the more it spread. And so I ran."

Penelope sighed. "You ran without alerting anyone, leaving people in mortal danger. My husband almost died. How many more need to suffer because of your selfishness, Papa?"

Papa nodded, his eyes watering. She'd never seen him like this. His eyes found hers, and they were so sad and so broken.

"You're right, Penelope. You're right. I did make many mistakes. What you're wrong about is that I don't respect you. I do. You're a strong, kind, and talented woman, like your mama was. I am sorry I failed to see that, but I see it now. And I couldn't be prouder."

Penelope listened to the words she'd craved to hear for years. Had he told her that when she was growing up, when he saw her painting, she'd have been a much more confident woman. She would have started her education as an artist and perhaps even have sold paintings by now.

Hearing him say such things now did buoy her spirits. But, strangely, she didn't need his approval to feel good about herself anymore. She was proud of herself, too. She'd never given up on her dream; she'd been ready to live it, and she had sacrificed it for him.

When all he ever was was selfish. She pitied him, in fact. He was supposed to be her father, protecting her and taking care of her, but he had ruined his life and almost ruined hers.

"You need to make amends for the harm you've done, Papa."

"You're right. I do."

"Good."

She needed to choose herself first. She had chosen Papa first when she'd agreed to marry Preston instead of running away and starting her life as an artist. And her papa had never chosen her.

But neither had Preston. He was still choosing vengeance over her.

And she wanted more. She wanted to be in a marriage where her husband put her needs and their love above all other considerations.

She wouldn't settle for anything less.

28

Preston sat alone in his new house alone. It was empty. It was dark. The shutters on all the windows were shut as per his command three days ago, when the love of his life left him.

He sat on the floor of the room that was supposed to be Penelope's studio with a bottle of brandy in his hand. His elbow was propped against his knee. A candle flickered, illuminating the watercolor paintings and two oil paintings that stood leaned against the opposite wall. The room still smelled like dust as it hadn't been cleaned. It was also cold, since there were no servants to light the coal grates. And it was so quiet. No footsteps, no distant voices muffled by the walls and doors, no sign that there was another soul here.

He gazed at Penelope's paintings—landscapes of Grandhampton Court with its lively forests, brooks, and rivers that meandered through the rolling hills. The house itself, the place where he'd been happy. Where his brother had been alive. She had such a talent for this. And the painting she had started where his whole family was there, including Spencer, made his heart shatter into a million little pieces once again.

As if it had ever been whole since she'd walked out.

He brought the bottle to his mouth and took several large gulps. More. More of this, to make himself numb, to make himself forget that he was the author of his own misfortune. Of his own unhappiness.

And yet, he couldn't have done it otherwise.

He stared at Spencer's oil portrait that Penelope had started back in Grandhampton Court from memory and using several other portraits of him that hung in the hall. There he was, his brother, so alive, with his black eyes glistening as he looked right at Preston. With his high cheekbones and his olive skin and that perfect bone structure. The fashionable, windswept haircut that so many dandies wore these days with long sideburns. Dark colors suited him, and the contrast of his perfectly white high cravat against the dark navy tailcoat was striking.

"Cheers, brother." Preston raised his bottle an inch higher. "Devil, I miss you. Please, forgive me that I've fallen in love with her. I understand now why you did. I wish I hadn't been so opposed to your marriage. I wish I'd had more sense to see that she's a true gem. That there isn't a selfish bone in her body. That she is genuine and pure and so, so kind."

Spencer's portrait didn't reply. What would Spencer have said? Was there even a chance for a trace of forgiveness? Not only had Preston not protected his brother from death, he'd also married the woman his brother had loved. He'd taken Spencer's home and his role as duke. He'd taken everything that once would have been Spencer's, as though his brother's death was to his advantage.

When the truth was that Preston would have been glad to meet death in his brother's stead if it meant that Spencer could live a full and happy life.

But it was too late for that.

He drank more, then closed his eyes and leaned his head back against the wall. There was a large, gaping hole in his chest. But it wasn't from Spencer's absence. It was from missing his wife. The wife who now felt like as much a part of him as his hand or his leg.

Three days and he was a half-dead man. He had watched the servants pack the house and remove the furniture, and only an hour or so ago, they had left the house for Preston and his family to move in.

But there wasn't a place in the world that would feel like home without Penelope.

A loud bang of the door knocker burst through the silence. He ignored it. There was no butler or footmen to open it, and no one knew he was here. The knock, however, repeated.

"Preston!" He heard a muffled roar. "Preston, we know you're here!"

He groaned. He knew that voice very well.

Richard. Always stepping in to help. He'd always been the peacemaker in the family. And by "we" he probably meant Seb was with him.

"Preston! Open the door!" Right. That was definitely Sebastian.

Preston stood up with another groan. Why wouldn't they leave him alone?

He marched through the corridor and into the front hall, then turned the door handle. Blinding daylight made him wince and turn his head. Two tall, broad-shouldered figures were dark against the light. But as they barged in, he could see that they were indeed Richard and Sebastian.

"Preston, what the devil?" asked Sebastian, looking him over.

"You look terrible," said Richard.

Preston offered the bottle to them, but they shook their heads. "How did you know where to find me?"

He took another gulp of brandy. He'd drunk so much in the past three days that the alcohol wasn't doing much anymore.

"You weren't anywhere else," said Richard. "And when we heard Penelope rented a hotel suite for herself and for Lord Beckett, drastic measures had to be taken to find you. Clearly you're unwell. I don't quite know how to soothe a man whose wife has left him. But I know a man who has experienced the same."

Preston looked at Sebastian. It was true, Emma had left him right when he'd almost secured their lifelong happiness together, but it was because she'd had no choice. Still.

"Well, old chap," said Preston, putting his hand on Seb's shoulder. "I remember you in an even worse state last September, so I am not sure you're the right person to help me. Please, take no offense."

"You're right," said Sebastian. "I'd thought I wasn't going to get past her abandoning me. I almost got myself killed in the boxing ring and drank myself half to death without Emma. But you don't have to."

"Oh, I think I do." Preston chuckled drunkenly. "She's disappointed in me. And rightly so. I'm just glad she finally sees me for who I am. A selfish bastard. She shouldn't have fallen in love with me."

"And you love her, too, don't you?" asked Sebastian.

Richard watched them both with a frown.

Preston felt his head hang until his chin rested on his chest. "I do. I bloody do. Nothing makes sense without her. I can't breathe. I can't take a step and not hope I'll see her around the corner. I can't sleep in the bed because she's not by my side. Her paintings...they torture me because she made them. Because they're a glimpse into her beautiful mind."

"Then go to her and beg her to come back to you," said Richard. "You two love each other. What seems to be the problem?"

"The problem, brother," said Preston, "is that I've done wrong by her papa. He's my enemy. He should be your enemy, too. He got our brother killed. Why aren't you on the warpath for him?"

Richard lowered his head. "Because Spencer wouldn't want it."

The words hit Preston like a cannonball. Spencer wouldn't want it... How right Richard was. He'd always had this ability to understand others, as though he could read their minds. He was able to put himself in their shoes and feel what they felt. And what Preston had not considered for all these months that he'd planned his revenge was how Spencer would feel about it. If he would want to be avenged.

And, knowing Spencer...no, he would not.

"It won't bring him back, Preston," Richard said quietly. "Nothing will. Spencer wouldn't want his legacy to be a multiplication of the evil in the world. He'd want you to if not forgive Lord Beckett, at least make peace with him. He's your family now."

Preston's feet refused to support him. The ground sank from beneath him, and swaying, he walked to the single chair in the front hall and dropped into it. Gently, he put the bottle on the floor. Now he wished he hadn't been drinking; he wanted a clear head.

"I finally ruined my enemy, only to lose the love of my life," he said.

"You didn't lose her, old chap," said Sebastian, slowly walking to him. "You can still go after her."

Preston leaned forward and pressed his face into his palms. The possibility of giving up vengeance and making peace with her father freed something in his chest. It felt as if the shackles around his heart opened, and with all that tension gone there was suddenly so much space within him.

Sebastian was right. He could still choose love. Choose her. Give up his pride. It was his pride that kept driving him to destroy Lord Beckett, even when he was a fallen man who needed help. Penelope saw that, but he'd failed to because of his stubborn pride. The same stubborn pride that had made him fight with Spencer over her.

"I'm still responsible for his death," he said as he stood up and started pacing the room. "How can I allow myself to be happy with the only woman my brother loved? How can I live with myself?"

Richard said, "You can't blame yourself for Spencer's death. You didn't know what was going to happen that night. And the thugs would have simply found another way, another time to get at Spencer if you had been with him. Or maybe you both would have been killed." Suddenly, Richard walked to him and placed his heavy hand on Preston's shoulder, stopping him. Preston looked into those blue eyes so like their father's. "I would not trade your life for Spencer's, as much as I loved him and wish he were still with us. I love you just as fiercely, as does the entire family."

Preston was stunned. How could his brother's words have reached right into that achy, old wound in his soul? The chasm that was born when he'd had to sit alone in the carriage bound to Scotland and watch his family and Grandhampton Court grow farther away into the distance.

Only, the wound didn't hurt anymore. His chest tightened with love and gratitude for his younger brother. He knew he must say something, but his throat was a painful knot, so he simply clasped Richard's hand for a moment and squeezed it.

Richard continued, understanding and sparing Preston

from having to reply. "First of all, before you forgive Lord Beckett, you must forgive yourself. Or you'll never be able to get past it."

Preston nodded. Richard was so right. He felt the poison of revenge corroding his own life as well as Penelope's and her father's, twisting his very soul. He also knew what it felt like to be free of it. The light and the ease of breath he'd felt in those happy moments with Penelope.

Spencer wouldn't want Penelope's father to live like this. Spencer was the kind of man who would see past those things. He'd tell Preston happiness and love don't come often in this life. That he should cherish that love. Protect it.

Live it.

Because his brother would never be able to.

Forgiveness swept through him in a hot onrush of energy. The walls around his heart had crumbled down and he could be himself.

And he had to go and get Penelope back.

29

PRESTON WALKED into the Countess of Whitemouth's salon the next evening, his gut twisting. The room was full of guests who sat in rows of chairs facing the very end of the room where Lady Isabella, the daughter of Earl and Lady Whitemouth, played something very pretty, and a short woman in her forties sang so beautifully, something squeezed in his gut.

Footmen stood along the walls of the room at attention. The chandeliers and the candelabras were unlit, with the only light coming from the lamps and candles standing on the pianoforte and on the sideboards behind and on both sides of the singer and the pianist.

He craned his neck, trying to see which of the heads in the three rows belonged to Penelope and Lord Beckett. Penelope was regarded by the ton with intrigue and curiosity thanks to the auction. He had managed to intervene a couple of times to ensure she was still invited to society events, but most importantly, the Duchess of Ashton hadn't excluded her from her circle of acquaintances, which was all that Penelope cared about because of her art.

Even for those who didn't know about the auction, the fact that they had wed so quickly gave rise to another wave of speculation. Perhaps they thought she'd been compromised. Or she may even be with child.

Preston didn't care about those rumors, and he knew she didn't, either, but people such as the Countess of Whitemouth would not want to invite Penelope, unwilling to risk an association with someone of questionable reputation, especially since she had Lady Isabella to marry off.

He had been worried about how Penelope would get on without him interceding on her behalf, but with a powerful patroness such as the Duchess of Ashton, Penelope was managing very nicely. His loyal spy, Calliope, had told him that the Duchess of Ashton had insisted Lady Whitemouth invite Penelope to her musical soirée if she wanted Lady Isabella to continue receiving invitations to soirées at Neverton. Calliope and Richard were in attendance, as well.

Sebastian and Emma were never invited to any of the countess's events as it had been understood that Sebastian would marry Lady Isabella, but he had instead married Emma.

It was so dark, Preston couldn't distinguish where any of them were. A stately female left the chairs and hurried to him.

"Your Grace..." the woman whispered loudly as she came near and then stopped before him, with her eyes blazing. It was the Countess of Whitemouth. "I did not think you would come. The invitation must have gotten lost. I am ever so sorry..."

"I realized it must have," he said, craning his head to see if he could spot a powdered wig or Penelope's lovely dark blond hair. "Is my wife here?"

The countess looked over her shoulder. "Indeed, she is, with Lord Beckett and Lady Calliope and Lord Richard."

"Where are they? I must speak to her immediately."

He made to brush past her, but the woman stopped him by laying her hand on his arm. "Your Grace... She's in the first row, and I beg of you, you cannot mean to interrupt such a lovely performance. My daughter is playing, you see."

"I see that, and she's doing it so well, however—"

"Your Grace, the journalist from *The Society* is here, reporting on the singer, Miss Renata Democrito. Isabella's suitors are here, too. Please do not make a scandal out of a lovely night."

Preston stared at the countess's imploring eyes, at her hand still clutching his elbow. He was determined. He didn't care about a scandal or how people would see him or what they said.

He was ready to lay open his heart before her. To stand with his soul bare and vulnerable and wait for her to give her verdict. He didn't care if he must humiliate himself.

He was ready to take all her anger and go through the seven rings of hell if only she would return to him.

"Only if you promise to include my wife in all your invitations and stop any gossip about her. She's a duchess and her reputation is flawless. She has done nothing wrong and should not be punished for something she has no fault in."

The countess's face fell and her hand dropped. Her large bosom rose and fell quickly. "Gossip? How dare you imply it is I who spreads gossip."

That was ridiculous. Everyone knew the countess held regular tea parties and picnics with the most talkative women in the ton, mulling over the events and the gossip. She and several others were the patronesses of Almack's balls and decided who was worthy of inclusion and who was not.

And yet, her daughter, Lady Isabella, had not received any marriage offers. He glanced at the lovely young woman who played the pianoforte so passionately, so skillfully, she could as well have accompanied the singer on her tour.

"Please, Lady Whitemouth," he said. "Do not offend my intelligence by denying something everyone knows. I will not interrupt your soirée for the sake of your daughter. And if you promise to stop excluding my wife and to stop spreading nasty rumors about her."

Lady Whitemouth's lips curved downward in a contemptuous expression.

"No one else may hear us," he insisted. "We can be honest with each other. Just give me your word and I'll wait until the concert is over. *The Society* won't write about your failed soirée. Your daughter will finish it as masterfully as she has started, and perhaps she will finally charm one of the unmarried gentlemen in attendance."

Lady Whitemouth nodded. "Very well. Your wife will be invited from now on."

"Thank you," he said as he pushed his hand through a pocket in his waistcoat and stood still, watching the heads of the spectators and listening to the beautiful concert.

Lady Whitemouth nodded and walked away from him, taking her seat at the back of the rows and throwing an angry glance at him.

Twenty torturous minutes Preston waited, rehearsing every possible word he could say and imagining ways for Penelope to forgive him. His life without her didn't make sense. But he had made so many mistakes with her, he was afraid he was too late and that he had broken her beautiful, soft heart with no hope to heal it.

Finally, the music and the singing ended, and the room burst into applause. To distract the guests from the footmen lighting the candles, other footmen walked through the room offering trays with champagne and canapés. The room slowly became lit in a warm golden glow and filled with the chatter of voices and the shuffling of feet as people stood from their seats.

Then he finally spotted them—Penelope stood from her chair and, together with Calliope and Richard, approached Miss Democrito while Lord Beckett moved through the aisle towards the footman holding the tray with champagne, who stood two feet away from Preston.

Lord Beckett still wore a powdered wig, but he looked better. Somehow, his back was straighter, and he wasn't as puffy and red in the face as before. He looked more like a lord and less like a common drunkard. His clothes were still in the fashion of the last century—with a bright ochre waistcoat and a white cravat—but they looked new and recently laundered.

Preston's gut wrenched as he looked at him. He'd hated the man for months, ever since he'd learned of his wrongdoings in October of last year. Too long, Lord Beckett had been his enemy, the object of his hatred and anger. A furious voice in his head kept saying if it weren't for this man, Spencer would be alive.

His fists clenched. It had been one thing to decide he was ready to let it all go, to choose love. It was quite another to see the man in flesh walking towards him. Now he was truly being tested.

Would he really be able to make peace with this man and declare that he was no longer the enemy?

His gaze fell on Penelope's back as she talked to the singer. He could see the delicate outline of her shoulder blades, the curve of her slim neck he had loved to kiss. He knew exactly how her skin smelled, so delicious and soft at that spot under her ear.

Oh, how he'd missed her. Just four days without her and he

felt like part of his soul was lost forever. And seeing her now... nothing else mattered.

Just her.

His entire being filled with love, warmth spreading through his chest, and the hatred and anger melted away from his heart like snow in the sun. He was such a fool. There had never been a choice between love and revenge when it came to Penelope.

It had always been her. Every breath, every step he took, everything he did would be for her.

Whether she would choose him today or not, he'd be there for her for the rest of his life. And even if there was no love left in her heart for him, he'd watch over her and those she loved like a loyal dog, protecting her and ensuring her happiness.

But first, he had to try.

As her papa took a glass of champagne from a footman, Preston walked up to him. "Lord Beckett."

The baron looked up from his glass and froze. His eyes widened in terror, and he took a step back.

"No," said Preston, stretching out his hands in a placating gesture. "Please, do not be alarmed. I have come to make peace."

Lord Beckett looked around like a trapped animal. Guests threw puzzled glances at them.

"She doesn't want you," Beckett said. "She told you, you ruined everything."

Preston came to stop before him and nodded. "I know. You're right. She doesn't want me, and I did ruin everything. But I'd like a chance to redeem myself."

Lord Beckett frowned. "Oh?"

"Is everything all right?" demanded Lady Whitemouth as she approached them with an alarmed expression.

"The Duke of Grandhampton," said a tall, thin man next to her. "Is that right?"

"Yes, Mr. Springer," Lady Whitemouth hissed. "He is. But he was just leaving. Weren't you, Duke? Remember our earlier conversation? You told me you had another engagement. What a pity that Mr. Springer of *The Society* can't interview you."

Ah. The journalist. Well, Preston didn't care. More people turned around to watch, no doubt wondering why they heard raised voices and why Lady Whitemouth had such a panicked look on her face.

In the farther corner of the room, Penelope's worried gaze met his as she made her way towards him, Calliope and Richard following behind her.

Good. Let the whole ton see this. Let the whole ton witness how much he loved this woman, and how he was ready to do anything for her.

"Lord Beckett," he said. "Your debt is hereby pardoned."

Lord Beckett gulped audibly, and the glass in his hand shook dangerously. "The whole debt? Ten thousand pounds?"

"Ten thousand?" asked Mr. Springer with a curious glint in his eyes. "Was that a gaming debt?"

"That doesn't concern you, sir," said Preston. "It was a family matter and now it's resolved."

Something like a circle formed around them, and Penelope, Calliope, and Richard took their places in it. But his eyes were only for his wife. She looked a little paler, with dark circles under her eyes, which gleamed as she stared at him. Her chest rose and fell quickly. How pretty she was in her creamy dress with delicate, intricate crystals woven into the thin material. All ethereal and unearthly, like an angel that had come into his life and made everything better. Brought him happiness he didn't deserve.

"And I'd like to ask for your forgiveness, Lord Beckett," Preston said. "Due to my pride, I dragged you through things I shouldn't have." Lord Beckett's eyes widened, blinking rapidly.

"What things?" asked Mr. Springer.

"I'll give you an income-earning estate of your own, Lord Beckett. It won't be much, but it will be comfortable. I will support you because otherwise you won't be able to survive, but you need to be held accountable for what you did. There is one condition." He glanced at the journalist. "We will speak of it in private."

The condition was, of course, that he had to retreat from all gentlemen's clubs and promise that he would never gamble again.

"Whatever your condition is, I accept," Lord Beckett hurried to respond, his face hopeful.

"I accept," repeated Lord Beckett, his eyes watering. "And thank you. It must have been hard to do this after...after what I did."

"What did you do?" demanded Mr. Springer.

But without paying any attention to him, Preston met the eyes of the only person whose good opinion mattered. "I regret my harsh actions. I regret my foolish choices. And I choose love. I choose you."

Penelope gasped in a shaky inhale, her eyes wet and glistening. He came close to her and dropped to one knee in front of her. People gasped and murmured around them. With his side vision, he saw Mr. Springer take out a notebook and write something very hastily.

"And I ask for your forgiveness, Penelope. I love you. You're everything I ever wanted."

He took her hand in his and kissed it, inhaling her sweet scent. "Preston... Everyone's watching..."

"That is exactly the point. What do you say, Penelope? Will you continue to be my wife and let me love you for the rest of eternity?"

30

Penelope watched him, breathing hard. Her cheeks were hot, and she couldn't get any air. She couldn't say anything, seeing Preston on his knees in front of her, breaking every social rule of high society.

One didn't proclaim their feelings openly in front of everyone, and especially not a journalist. One didn't humiliate oneself, didn't pour one's heart out like a commoner. Things like that were barely said in a bedroom.

Shock had her frozen in place, overcome. This prideful, stubborn duke was down on one knee in front of her.

The sight was enough to make her wonder if she was dreaming.

It was so quiet in the room, it seemed as if everyone held their breath. Only the scribbling of the journalist's pencil against paper interrupted the silence.

And the loud beat of her heart because Preston, who had spent months trying to destroy her papa, had asked publicly for his forgiveness.

But there wasn't a doubt in her mind that she loved him. Her heart sang like that opera singer and soared and did reels.

He accepted his fault.

He chose love.

He chose her.

There was just one thing to say.

"I will."

Preston grinned, releasing a loud, shaky exhale. The sight of his smile was enough to make her head spin. He was so gorgeous when he smiled, he became the man she always saw hiding deep inside, under the layers of pride, stubbornness, and cold indifference.

As Penelope pulled him up to stand in front of her, gazing into his eyes, the room erupted in happy gasps and exclamations. She craved to kiss Preston, to have him take her into his arms, to hide her face against his chest and inhale his scent, which she'd missed for the past four days.

But they couldn't do it so publicly. They couldn't give the gossip mill even more fodder. They both knew it. His eyes engulfed her, so dark and deep and open. There were no more barriers between them, no more hesitations, resentments, or secrets.

There was just love. He was hers and she was completely and irrevocably his.

He took her hands in his and kissed them, never breaking their gaze.

"I love you," he said quietly, just to her.

"And I love you," she said just as quietly, sinking in his onyx eyes.

She felt like she was so light she could float and soar, as weightless as a feather.

"May I take you home now?" he asked. "I'd like very much

to undress you and make love to you. I missed you. Everything was wrong in my life without you."

"Which home, Preston?" she asked.

"Newdale Place. Not all the rooms are ready as I wanted you to decorate them as you wish. But I assure you, the most important room is ready. The bedroom."

Newdale Place...that warm, wonderful house she could make her own. Their own. Without the shadow of the past or resentment or anger or secrets. With a space for her studio and plenty of room for children and one bedroom for Preston and her.

Her smile grew broader. "Let us leave, please, or we'll give *The Society* another scandal to talk about."

He offered her his elbow, and as she hooked her hand through it, jolts of pleasant warmth spread through her as their bodies touched. She was ready. So ready for their future. For a lifetime of happiness with the man she loved and who loved her.

As they walked together, she was still unable to break away from his gaze, unable to stop smiling.

But a cough sounded next to them, and they stopped.

It was Papa.

Lord Beckett stood with his hands behind his back, watching Preston with a strange, intent expression. "Before you leave, a word, Duke, please? In private, Penelope dearest, if you don't mind. I think we have had quiet enough of public declarations." He threw a frown at Mr. Springer. "I'm afraid you've given the newspaper enough material to write for a year."

Mr. Springer kept scribbling, throwing quick glances at

Penelope and Preston. Preston thought Lord Beckett was right. The rest of the guests dissipated around the room, talking excitedly, casting curious looks at Preston and Penelope and Lord Beckett.

The last thing Preston wanted was to delay his reunion with his wife. She loved him. She accepted him. He felt like fireworks kept bursting right in the middle of his chest. He was the happiest man alive.

He looked at her, but there was no sadness in her eyes, just love and joy shining through. "Go, Preston. I'm only glad you and Papa can talk like family now. We have all the time in the world."

Preston nodded and squeezed her hand. "We do, darling."

Then she left him and joined Richard and Calliope, both of whom looked ready to burst with excitement.

"Of course," said Preston, but before he could move, Lady Whitemouth stepped up to him.

"Your Grace," she said, her face alight with joy. "You did give *The Society* a scandal, only a good one. A duke declaring his love and asking forgiveness of his wife is quite different from the usual gossip of ill reputations and fallen maidens and husbands and wives being unfaithful to each other. And I like that such a happy event is associated with my name and my house. Well done. Our agreement stays."

Preston nodded and so did she.

"Pardon me," he said to her as Lord Beckett and he walked away to the corner of the room where no one could hear them.

Lord Beckett gave a long sigh and looked at Preston without malice. "I wanted to thank you, sir. It was a kind thing that you did for me. I did not deserve it. And I understand your rage with me. And your desire to destroy me. I do. I did a terrible thing that ended in an even worse outcome."

Preston nodded, his throat tightening.

"Penelope told me to make amends. And they are long overdue. I should have asked for your forgiveness long ago. For your family's forgiveness. I am so sorry for the grief my actions caused you."

Something warmed in Preston's heart. He'd thought the man was evil. Cold. Heartless. But that wasn't the man he was seeing in front of him.

"Recently, I came across some information that you need to know. You all thought your brother was dead..."

Preston frowned. "Wait just a moment... We *thought* our brother was dead...?"

Lord Beckett took in a deep breath and exhaled slowly. "That is what I said. You *thought*."

Shock rippled through Preston like a stone thrown into deep waters. Forgetting himself, he grabbed Lord Beckett by the lapels of his tailcoat. "What are you saying, man?" he growled low.

"Let me go and I will tell you," said Lord Beckett. "Do not do this to Penelope. Do not undo the good you did for her today."

With his heart slamming so hard he couldn't hear his own thoughts, Preston let him go and looked over his shoulder. Luckily, no one seemed to notice, and the rest of the guests kept chatting, drinking, and enjoying the canapés.

Lord Beckett straightened his waistcoat. "When I hired Thorne Blackmore and his men to do the deed, it was not to kill your brother. It was only to give him a black eye...a cut lip...a few scratches. So that he couldn't show his face at the ton's events. So that he couldn't seduce Penelope. And I could arrange that marriage for her..."

"Right." Preston's jaws worked so hard he thought his bones would snap. "And it went wrong and he died."

“Well, that’s the thing, my boy,” said Lord Beckett sadly. “When you forced me out of my house, I went to Thorne Blackmore, hoping he might help me. He didn’t, of course. But he did tell me the man that his men beat up wore your brother’s clothes and had his ring, but they later discovered that it wasn’t him.”

EPILOGUE

Two weeks later, the sitting room at Newdale Place was glowing with light and love. Dozens of candles illuminated the warm pastel blue walls boasting paintings of sunlit, blooming gardens and spring landscapes. The windows were open, and warm air wafted in, stirring the curtains. The room was full of guests. Calliope and Richard spoke with Miss Alexandria, Penelope's cousin, and Penelope sat on the sofa next to his grandmama... Well, they weren't guests, Preston supposed as he looked at the dearest faces in the whole world.

They were all family.

He sipped port from a small crystal glass as he looked around at their relaxed faces. It was Penelope and his first dinner party since they bought Newdale. The first of many, he was sure.

The house had become lovely and homey after Penelope and he had decided on the decor together. He loved that it wasn't as dark and imposing as Chalworth Place yet different from Sumhall and Grandhampton, where he had grown up. This home held something of the Grandhampton dukes, such as the ancestral vases and other art pieces and paintings his footmen had managed to save from Chalworth.

But it was also hers. So hers, with its light colors, modern, comfortable, and yet beautiful furniture, and soft, light-colored rugs with intricate designs.

As he met his wife's gaze across the room, she beamed at him, and he grinned back, unable to resist as his heart melted from sheer happiness. Every day he had to pinch himself. Could he really be so lucky as to have this woman in his life? So strong, so kind, so incredibly talented. He was very proud of her for standing up for herself and making her own path in life, doing what she loved.

Lord Beckett had left London a few days ago to settle into the estate that Preston had promised him. He said he looked forward to a country life away from gambling hells and temptations. He'd been good at managing his estate before he'd let things fall and crumble. He was eager to get acquainted with his new tenants, see if things could be improved, and go deer stalking, hunting, and fishing.

Miss Alexandria had come to London by Penelope's invitation. His wife missed her, and now that they were established and happy, she wanted Alexandria to stay for a visit and see a bit of the Season.

As he held Penelope's gaze, a question arose in her eyes. He knew what she meant to ask him. Was it finally time? Preston's stomach quivered as he thought about the announcement he had to make in front of his family. He gave her a slight nod, and she excused herself from Grandmama and came to stand by his side next to the fireplace with the warm, shining grate.

He removed a paper from the inner pocket of his coat. His hands shook as he loudly cleared his throat.

"May I have your attention, please?" he asked.

It came out a bit stiff and formal, but what he had to say was not a matter of jests and laughs.

As Calliope, Richard, and Miss Alexandria came closer, Grandmama shifted in her seat. "What is it, Preston?"

He took Penelope's hand in his. Only she knew. She, Preston, and the coroner.

"I have something important to tell you," he said and held up the paper. "This is the coroner's report of Spencer's body."

"Why do you have it now?" asked Calliope, her voice shaking. "We already read it in September."

"Because this one is different," Preston said. "It's from yesterday."

"Why did the coroner need to make another report?" asked Richard, alarmed. "And how? Spencer is buried."

"We had to exhume the body, Richard," said Preston. "Because information came to me recently that it may not have been Spencer that we buried."

Complete silence fell over the room. Only the coals crackled softly in the grate, and a horse's hooves clacked against the road in the distance through the open window.

"This is nonsense!" cried Calliope.

"How can this be?" asked Grandmama at the same time.

Only Richard stepped forward, his blue eyes burning. "And?"

Preston's throat clenched. He knew he was about to turn their worlds upside down just as this report had turned his. "And it is *not* Spencer."

Gasps and cries rang through the room. Shock was written on their faces. Calliope clutched her dress. Richard, the perfect gentleman, stood frozen, but Preston saw the storm thundering behind his eyes. Grandmama was breathing hard as she opened her reticule with shaking hands and removed her vinaigrette. She opened the lavishly decorated silver box and inhaled the strong, sharp scent of smelling salts, then let out a gasp and shook her head. Miss Alexandria stared at him with wide eyes.

"Is that for certain?" asked Richard. "How could this have happened?"

"It is certain," said Preston. "I went in and identified the body myself."

It hadn't been a pretty experience, and certainly not something he would speak of in front of the ladies. The man's body was nothing but skeleton, but that allowed the coroner to study the bones and teeth.

"The body," he said, "whomever it was, had unhealthy, cracked yellow teeth, and he was missing exactly two of them."

"Spencer always took good care of his teeth," said Richard. "He had fine teeth and wasn't missing any."

"Precisely," said Preston. "Besides, this body had a broken ankle that had healed poorly, and the coroner wrote that the person likely had a limp."

"Spencer didn't limp," said Calliope.

"Whoever it was, he had been dressed in Spencer's clothes," said Preston. "The coroner had never met Spencer or seen his likeness, and the face had been so bruised and swollen it would have been hard to recognize him anyway. That is why the coroner didn't give it another thought in September."

Calliope held on to Richard's arm. "Wait, Preston, if it's not Spencer who's buried there...could our brother be still alive?"

Penelope's hand squeezed his tighter. That was what they had talked about since last night when he'd told her this news. It was exactly the thought he kept turning over in his mind.

"It is one possibility, yes," said Preston.

"It is the only possibility!" cried Calliope.

"No, sister," said Preston. "I am sorry, but another possibility is that he could be dead and mistaken as *this* man...or just as some pauper who was killed in a brawl."

"Well, I refuse to believe in that possibility," announced Richard.

"So do I," said Grandmama.

That was what Preston was afraid of. To give them all false hope only to have them grieve Spencer all over again. And who knew if they would ever find out what had happened, let alone find him?

"How do we find him?" asked Richard, echoing his thoughts.

"Yes, we simply must do everything in our power to find him!" Grandmama exclaimed.

"We will," said Preston. "The man to talk to is Thorne Blackmore, the owner of Elysium. He was hired by Lord Beckett to rough Spencer up. Not to kill him. But it seems they took more than one misstep, first targeting the wrong man and then beating him to death. Blackmore or his men may know more about what happened that night."

"What is Elysium?" asked Calliope.

Preston and Richard exchanged a glance. "That need not concern you, sister," said Richard. "It's a club gentlemen shouldn't know about, let alone ladies."

Calliope exchanged a cheeky look with Miss Alexandria. Preston didn't like it one bit. When Calliope was determined to do something, she did it without regard for any rules.

"I'll take care of it," said Richard. "You're a married man now. And it's out of the question that Calliope gets involved or even shows her face in Whitechapel. I'll go and talk to Blackmore."

Preston nodded. "This is a good idea, Richard. But you must inform me of whatever he tells you."

"Of course, brother," said Richard. "We will find Spencer. Whatever it takes."

They had to find him. Of course they did.

But even though hope filled Preston's entire body like hot air, there was a dark worm of worry in the pit of his stomach. Because if they found Spencer alive, he'd discover the woman he loved married to his brother...

And that was yet another pain Preston would have to inflict on Spencer.

When their guests left, Penelope pulled Preston to her studio. She hadn't wanted to tell him her own world-changing news before he'd had a chance to share what he'd learned about Spencer with the rest of the family.

But now that everyone knew about Spencer, she couldn't wait to tell him. They went down the hall from the sitting room and entered the studio. She'd asked the footmen to keep it well lit, and, as it did every time she walked in here, her heart soared and lightness and happiness spilled through her. Seeing her paints, the easels, and canvases with her work still in progress, it was like someone plucked the string of her very soul and it rang and reverberated in every part of her.

"Why are we here?" asked Preston. "I'd like very much to take your clothes off and to wash you and then make love to you."

She chuckled. "You can do just that in a moment. I want to show you something."

His eyes dropped to a recently started portrait of himself. "This?" he asked.

It looked almost like the one she had done of him when

Miss de Luca came to teach her, only it was even better. She was pleased to see that Penelope had improved.

"No," she said and walked past where the landscapes of Grandhampton stood propped against the wall, along with watercolors and sketches she'd done.

In the corner of the studio, she leaned down and picked up a smaller painting, still unframed, and showed it to him. He studied the brown-dotted spaniel puppy sitting among flowers. If its big, cute, shiny eyes with long eyelashes didn't give him the message...

"It's pretty, Penelope," he said and leaned down and gave her a short, soft kiss on the lips. "You're so talented. I have never noticed your interest in painting dogs before. Where would it even go? Are you intending to sell it?"

"No, silly." She giggled. "It's not for sale. And the only room where it belongs is the nursery."

"The nursery," he said and nodded. "Yes, that'll do fi—" His eyes widened and darted to her, then dropped to her still-flat belly. "Wait, the nursery?"

She couldn't contain her smile, the tears of joy blurring her vision. She nodded. "Yes, Preston, it's very early, but the physician confirmed it."

"Heavens!" He propped the painting against the wall and scooped her into his arms, squeezing her in a bear hug. "Penelope! Darling! A baby!"

He pulled away and looked her over, his eyes shining. "How are you feeling?"

"I'm fine." She chuckled. His fussing over her was endearing. "Everything is all right."

"Just tell me if you're tired...need to lie down...or whatever ladies feel like when they're expecting."

"Of course I will."

"Can we even... Can I have you without injuring the baby?"

"Yes, of course..."

He sighed and laughed. "I suppose it all sounds funny to you. A grown man like me, with no idea what to do."

"No," she said and took him by his hands. "It's not funny. It's all new to me, too. I love you and we'll learn all this together."

He wrapped his arms around her, and she hugged his torso, their eyes locked. "And I love you," he said slowly, giving her that charming grin of his that was just for her and no one else. The grin that meant his walls were down and he was bare and open and vulnerable for her.

As she was for him.

"Whatever life has thrown at me, I'm glad for it. No matter what turmoil I went through, it brought you to me. You're the biggest gift I could ever have wished for, because you taught me to be kind and forgiving and when it's time to set my pride aside."

He blurred before her as she teared up. And when he kissed her, and desire and love washed over her, she knew this was just the beginning of a happy future.

And Preston and she would be by each other's side every step of the way.

Thank you for reading ALL DUKE AND BOTHERED. If you loved Preston and Penelope's story get your free bonus epilogue now:

https://mariahstone.com/all-duke-bonus/

Find out what happens next when Lord Richard Seaton agrees to a fake marriage with Miss Jane Grant in his quest to find his missing brother in book 2 of the DUKES AND SECRETS SERIES, HER RAKE FIANCÉ.

Powerful lord. Infamous rake. Forced into a fake engagement with a wall-flower...that sparks true love.

Read HER RAKE FIANCÉ now >

Fancy a Highlander?

If you like historical romances and haven't read Craig and Amy's story yet, be sure to pick up **HIGHLANDER'S CAPTIVE.**

Breathtaking, passionate, romantic -- for all fans of Outlander! In her arms he finds strength. In his arms she finds hope. Can their love outlast the ages?

"One of the MOST ROMANTIC AND HEART-WRENCHING TALES I've read in a long while! Absolutely loved it!"

• • •

Read HIGHLANDER'S CAPTIVE now >

Or stay in Regency London, and keep reading for an excerpt of HER RAKE FIANCÉ.

London, 1813

"You oughta go back to Mayfair, where you come from!"

The words, expertly dropped by one of the seven children before her, cut through Miss Jane Grant like a headman's ax. All of them were dressed in what looked like rags, their dirty skin showing through the rips and holes. They fidgeted behind their school desks, ripping the precious paper she'd carefully chosen and ordered months ago in preparation for the opening of her school. Chairs and desks scraped against freshly laid wooden floor as the four boys and three girls threw pens and paper balls, pushed each other, yelled, and cackled.

Her dog, Hercules, an English foxhound with large brown and gray spots on his white body, sat at attention next to the door, his ears perked, giving cautious barks. Reuben, a tall and large man in his forties with a shaggy beard, stood in the opposite corner of the room with his massive arms crossed over his chest, watching the scene with a concerned frown. He was one of her brother Thorne's most trusted men and often accompanied Jane around Whitechapel as her bodyguard and chaperone.

"Back to Mayfair," red-haired Alfie echoed, his steely blue eyes locked on her, before spitting out, "princess..."

How did the boy know exactly what would hurt her? She

supposed it was as clear as the light of the day she didn't belong here. Jane blinked against the burn of tears building behind her eyes. She was their teacher; she couldn't give up in the first few minutes of her little school's fragile existence.

She drew in a quick breath and plastered a brave smile on her face.

"Children!" Jane cried, trying to yell above the cacophony. "Please, be quiet! If you let me speak for a minute..."

As the noise in the classroom swelled, she caught Reuben's eye. He slowly shook his head, a deep frown of uneasiness mixed with empathy etched onto his features. Jane knew he wanted to help.

He made his way through the row of simple oak desks and chairs she had ordered a year ago from the local Whitechapel carpenter. The man had salvaged the wood from broken furniture and was so grateful for the large order, he'd had tears in his eyes.

A quill pen crunched under Reuben's feet as he walked. Sunlight streamed through three small windows, illuminating the blackboard hanging at the front of the room. Fresh maps she had managed to buy at a cartographer in Cheapside, and educational posters with the alphabet, numbers, and the arithmetic table she'd painted herself adorned white-paneled walls.

The building used to be the abandoned kitchens at the back of her brother's exclusive gentleman's club, Elysium. Over a year ago, Thorne had hired unemployed local men to renovate it for Jane's school, and the room still smelled of fresh wood, paint, and faintly of chalk.

As Reuben stood next to her, his eyebrows like two small storm clouds over his eyes, Jane felt a flutter of gratitude. She knew his presence was not just out of duty to Thorne but out of a bond they'd formed during storytelling and shared meals.

Reuben glowered at the children and boomed, “Shut up, you rascals!”

The silence that fell over the classroom was absolute. Hercules gave a final, approving bark, and settled into his dog bed, his head still high as he threw warning glances at the boys and girls. The children stilled and turned to face Jane and Reuben, their eyes wide, eyebrows knit, shallow faces somber. Jane let out a small breath of relief. She would have liked to get the children to behave by herself, but she had to admit, Reuben’s tactic was more effective. Reuben turned to her and gave her a small, conspiratorial wink, then scowled at the children once again.

“Yer a bunch of ungrateful brats,” grumbled Reuben. “Miss Grant, she’s been toilin’ over a year to make this school for you. Got all these books, pens, and paper on her own. And now look...”

He walked to the first of the desks, picked up a turned-over inkwell, and returned it to its place, then wiped his black-smeared fingers against his brown coat. The pool of ink dripped down from the desk and onto the fresh floor. Would Ruby, her maid and housekeeper, even be able to get rid of the stain?

“Ink spilled,” Reuben continued, “quills broken, paper wasted...”

Jane chuckled nervously. “It’s all right, children. I have more supplies. All that matters is you’re here.”

“Why are we here?” questioned Lily, a girl of eight. “Should be at the mill, earnin’ me keep.”

“You wanna get yer hands mangled by the machine, workin’ for a measly penny?” demanded Reuben.

“Sometimes that penny means a crumb or two for me little sis.”

Jane’s skin crawled. She had walked door to door in the

neighborhood for weeks, talking to the parents, inviting them to send their children to her school.

"And I should be helpin' me uncle," stated Alfie.

"Out on the streets, Alfie?" Reuben barked. "Lifting wallets, that's yer best talent, eh?"

Alfie threw a scowl at him. "We were gonna do my first big job. Ma is six months late with rent."

"The lady's just eatin' up our time," grumbled nine-year-old Peter, a lad with a mop of black hair.

She knew how she must seem to them. During the five years since she'd moved to Whitechapel from her father's house in Mayfair, she'd seemed so strange to the inhabitants. Her clothes were simple but clean and tidy. Her hair was always meticulously done by Ruby, not a hair out of place. Her hands and face were clean. Her spectacles must have told them volumes about who she was—someone educated. She didn't talk like them, didn't dress like them, and didn't look like them. She didn't have to worry where her next meal came from. Thorne made sure of that. And despite living in the criminal district of London, she felt quite safe with Thorne's men guarding her like their princess.

Besides, all of Whitechapel knew that Thorne Blackmore's sister, a legitimately born baron's child—unlike him—was untouchable. If a hair on her head fell out of place because of someone's actions, their own head may soon be missing.

But if Jane wanted to help these children, she needed to find a way to relate to them and make them want to be here.

"Education is not a waste of time," she said. "Peter, if you learn to read and write, you won't have to work in dangerous mills, or pickpocket, or beg on the streets. You could find work in service or as someone's apprentice, learning a skill such as carpentry, cooking, or shoe-making..."

And not on the gallows, she wanted to add. But the mere

thought of that made a chill run down her spine. A mental image slapped her internal vision: a ten-year-old boy hanging by the neck, swinging, black against the dark storm clouds. Two years ago, she'd witnessed a public execution when the coachman took the wrong turn, and they were stuck in a crowd of onlookers.

Thorne had told her not to look, but she couldn't turn away. When she asked him what the boy had done, Thorne had said somberly, "He did what many Whitechapel children do every single day. The difference is, he got caught."

She prayed she could help these children escape that fate. And, if her school was a success, not just these seven, but many more.

"Young'uns, don't you worry your heads about work or stealin'," said Reuben. "Mr. Blackmore, that's Miss Grant's brother, he's gone and paid your folks for the work you're missin' today."

While the children murmured among themselves with satisfied smiles, shock hit Jane like a slap.

It was all false. It wasn't her doing that these children sat here.

It was all Thorne. Always Thorne, protecting her, shielding her, making sure her every wish and whim came true.

And yet, she had thought, finally, it was all her. She had assumed she'd succeeded in convincing the children's parents to send them here after weeks of going door to door. She'd thought that she had managed to make a difference, that she'd taken one small step to feeling like she belonged here, like she mattered.

She'd believed that she wasn't just a criminal lord's over-protected, lonely, aristocratic sister who didn't know what to do with herself among thieves, sex workers, and thugs.

"Time for me to head off," Reuben announced, lifting a

finger. "Now, you lot better listen to Janie—er, I mean, Miss Grant. If you don't, I'll tan yer hides so hard you won't be able to sit right for a week."

Jane stared at Reuben with horror. "No, no, Reuben," she said. "There will not be corporal punishment, not in this school. The children struggle enough already."

Reuben chuckled but threw a warning scowl at the children, who glared back at him. He pointed his index finger again without a word.

"I'm not jokin', Janie," he said quietly as he leaned to her. "If these little devils cause you trouble, they'll have to deal with me."

With that, Reuben left under the watchful eyes of Hercules. With the sound of the door closing, seven pairs of rebellious, challenging eyes landed on Jane. She smiled, stepping from foot to foot.

Never had she felt more out of place. What could she know about their lives? What did she know about needing to survive day to day with a growling stomach and only rags on her shoulders? What significance could reading and writing have for them when they didn't know if they would eat tomorrow?

Nevertheless, she had to go on. Perhaps it would be difficult today, but later on, it might mean the difference for them between the gallows and a safe home. She took a deep breath and walked up to the blackboard.

"Let's start with the alphabet," she said. "A is for apple, B is for ball..."

She went through the entire alphabet, writing the letters out. The children repeated after her, but their voices were dull and uninterested. Until, when she reached W, they started giggling and yelling again.

She turned around. Alfie had drawn a surprisingly skillful sketch of a lady in spectacles and with a perfectly tied knot at the back of her head, her skirts flapping in the wind and her petticoats quite scandalously exposed. As she gasped, a satisfied roar of laughter sounded from the children.

"Alfie," she said, "that is quite enough. This is inappropriate."

"What are you going to do, Miss Grant?" demanded Peter. "Send us home?"

An approving, joyful howl rolled through the room.

Jane's cheeks blazed with heat. Whatever Thorne's good intentions were, he couldn't help here. It was between her and the children. But it was as though she simply couldn't find the right words to make them see why they should want to be here.

"No, of course not, but you have to understand—"

But they weren't listening. Alfie jumped on the chair and started some sort of a wild dance. Peter started to shake Alfie's chair, threatening to drop him on the floor, and Jane yelped. While Lily giggled, the rest of the children crumpled the remains of their paper into balls and started a fight. Hercules jumped to his feet and barked in earnest, adding to the mayhem.

"Please!" cried Jane, desperation clawing at her chest. Who was she jesting? She was not a governess, not a teacher or a mother. She was simply a lady, a lady who had been raised to understand etiquette and act with grace, not to control a room full of children. Her upbringing as the daughter of a baron was meant to prepare her to be the wife of a noble lord, spending her time in a drawing room, not the schoolroom. Yet here she was, with no intention to ever marry, chasing a dream that felt as distant as the stars. "Please, everyone, calm down!"

In the midst of the chaos, Hercules ran to the door, barking madly.

The door was flung open, and the most handsome man she'd ever seen stood in the doorframe.

He was tall and muscular under his rich, dark waistcoat, which sat somewhat askew. His high cravat was undone, and his breeches were crumpled. He was the embodiment of her every romantic fantasy. He had thick auburn hair, the fashionable windswept hairstyle disheveled. His features were perfectly correct and chiseled—high cheekbones, straight nose—like those of a Greek god. Dark auburn eyebrows knitted above his intense blue eyes as he looked over the children and her. Then his broad mouth quirked in a crooked grin.

Though the children quieted, staring at the stranger, Hercules did not. With a ferocious growl and spate of fierce barking, the dog jumped at the man.

Shocked, the man backed through the open doorway, stomping on the filthy, muddy backyard behind Elysium, mud slurping under his shiny boots. Hercules jumped through the puddles and the mud and kept advancing on the man as he backed away.

Jane ran after Hercules. "Stop! Sit, Hercules!"

But Hercules was much too riled up to listen to her.

Instead, he backed the beautiful man against the back wall of Elysium, his muddy paws leaving black smudges all over the man's white shirt and light breeches.

Hercules growled and barked right into the man's face. To his credit, the man threw his arms up, calmly saying something soothing to the dog, however futile. Jane ran to Hercules and pulled him by his collar.

"Sit, Hercules!" she cried. "Sit!"

Hercules, the little protector that he was, finally listened. He sat down, whimpering, growling, but his tail still wriggled as he ached to keep tormenting the stranger who may have come to threaten his mistress.

Jane stared at the man. She breathed hard, inhaling his intoxicating, masculine scent—expensive cologne and brandy—mixed with the whiff of the stables, the alehouse, and the chicken pen that always hung over Elysium's backyard.

"Well, it seems that dog doesn't like me much," the stranger said, his voice deep and smooth.

She suddenly became very aware of his proximity. His warm blue eyes were on her, and she was sinking in their beautiful—if slightly bloodshot—depths. No doubt he was a lord, not just a solicitor or a bank clerk from somewhere in Cheapside. In a ballroom, a man like him would never notice someone like her. She belonged with books, hiding behind the rims of her spectacles. She would never gain the attention of a gorgeous, charming, and no doubt rich man like him.

But she would notice him anywhere.

She wished she wore better clothes than the mousy gray frock Ruby had made for her three years ago, and she wished she had a more fashionable hairstyle than the simple bun. He was all saturated, bright colors, while she was gray and washed-out. For the first time in five years, she felt a longing to match him and an acute awareness that she did not.

He looked somewhere behind her. "Forgive me," he said, "aren't those your children?"

She turned around and groaned as she watched her pupils scatter out of the school, run across the backyard, and disappear through the door in the carriage gates.

Anger roared in her. What was she thinking? This man, clearly one of Elysium's frequent members—dressed like he hadn't been home all night, reeking like a distillery—had barged into her school and disrupted her lesson, and now, because of him, everyone had left!

"Sir, I beg you to refrain from entering the backyard of

Elysium!" she said, her voice stronger than she felt. "Was it not clear that only the front door is for visitors?"

He chuckled, eyeing her softly. She did not like that amused glint in his eyes at all. Nor the warmth in her whole body as she found herself the object of his unwavering gaze. She reminded herself to not let his charm sway her. "I find myself wishing to become a bad boy as long as I have a governess such as you to teach me manners."

She felt heat rush to her cheeks at his words. She was not used to such forwardness. But she had to stay focused. "What, heavens help me, did you want with me, then?"

"As much as I begin to regret this, I did not come for you, miss. I was looking for Thorne Blackmore. No one is answering the front door of Elysium."

"And so, being a frequent visitor, you felt entitled to find your own way in," she declared.

His eyes narrowed into a smoldering glare. "Not all is as it seems," he spat out, a tempest brewing in his voice. "But surely, someone as sanctimonious as yourself has the wisdom to discern right from wrong, isn't that so?"

She stood tall, the pulsing beat in her ears echoing the heightened tension in her whole body. "As a matter of fact, I do. Clearly, your modus operandi is to disrupt, rebel, and incite chaos. Someone like me is left to pick up the pieces in your wake."

His expression twisted into a snarl. "So, you've got it all figured out, have you?" he spat, his voice rough with anger. "You stand there, on your high ground, casting judgments. How bland and boring your perfect life must be then. Remember, miss, those that sit on high horses do so alone."

The blow was like a punch to her gut. The tears she'd fought down earlier prickled again at the backs of her eyes. She had no words to contradict his. They rang too true.

"If you wish to see Thorne Blackmore," she said, her voice low and trembling, "the servants' entrance is behind you. Please, do not come near me or my school again."

She watched his large, broad-shouldered back as he walked away, her heart still racing.

She turned and walked into her school. She had a purpose, a goal. And she would see it through, no matter what. Regardless of unkind, handsome strangers or painful memories.

Keep reading HER RAKE FIANCÉ now.

GET A FREE MARIAH STONE BOOK!

Join Mariah's mailing list to be the first to know of new releases, free books, special prices, and other author giveaways.

freehistoricalromancebooks.com

ALSO BY MARIAH STONE

MARIAH'S TIME TRAVEL ROMANCE SERIES

- Called by a Highlander
- Called by a Viking
- Called by a Pirate
- Fated

MARIAH'S REGENCY ROMANCE SERIES

- Dukes and Secrets
- Seven Dukes of Sin

VIEW ALL OF MARIAH'S BOOKS IN READING ORDER

Scan the QR code for all ebooks, paperbacks, and audiobooks.

ENJOY THE BOOK? YOU CAN MAKE A DIFFERENCE!

Please, leave your honest review for the book.
As much as I'd love to, I don't have financial capacity like New York publishers to run ads in the newspaper or put posters in subway.

But I have something much, much more powerful!

Committed and loyal readers

If you enjoyed the book, I'd be so grateful if you could spend five minutes leaving a review on the book's sales page.

Thank you very much!

ABOUT MARIAH STONE

Mariah Stone is a bestselling author of historical romance novels, including her popular Regency series Dukes and Secrets, her historical romance series Called by a Highlander and her hot Viking, Pirate, and Regency novels. With nearly one million books sold, Mariah writes about strong women falling in love with their soulmates across time. Her books are available worldwide in multiple languages in e-book, print, and audio.

Subscribe to Mariah's newsletter for a free historical romance book today at mariahstone.com/signup!

- facebook.com/mariahstoneauthor
- instagram.com/mariahstoneauthor
- bookbub.com/authors/mariah-stone
- pinterest.com/mariahstoneauthor
- amazon.com/Mariah-Stone/e/B07JVW28PJ

Printed in Great Britain
by Amazon

53986245R00158